LOVE THY NEIGHBOR

JACQUELINE ASHLEY

Harlequin Books

TORONTO • NEW YORK • LONDON
AMSTERDAM • PARIS • SYDNEY • HAMBURG
STOCKHOLM • ATHENS • TOKYO • MILAN

God often sends His blessings to us
in care of our friends.
In gratitude for my own blessings,
I dedicate this book
to those many precious friends of
mine—including the ones who also
happen to be related to me by blood or
marriage—who are friends indeed and have been
there
for me whenever I've been in need.

Published October 1989

First printing August 1989

ISBN 0-373-16316-9

Chapter One

Emma Springer, her eyes barely open, her brain not yet functioning, opened her apartment door to fetch her morning paper from the hallway. Behind her, Oscar silently slithered around the doorjamb and scampered madly toward his favorite home away from home, the apartment next door.

Oscar was in luck. The door to the Spencer apartment stood open because Emma's neighbors, Nancy and Brad, were outside loading their car with luggage. He dashed across the threshold and disappeared under the couch in the living room.

Oblivious to Oscar's unauthorized excursion, Emma reentered her apartment and shut the door.

VICE DETECTIVE JACK SPENCER had his eyes closed, his head propped against one of his hands and his feet up on his desk. He was half listening, half dozing as his sister-in-law, Nancy, chattered instructions at him over the telephone. Jack was going to apartment sit for Nancy and his brother, Brad, while they were away in Florida for six months, and at the moment she was explaining the building rules for trash disposal.

Jack was too tired to care what the trash disposal rules were at the Oakwood Apartment complex. The department was shorthanded because of a flu epidemic that was rampaging through Kansas City, so he'd not only had to work the night before, but still had a full day's work ahead of him. Therefore, he was paying just enough attention to Nancy to be able to tell when she was about to wind down.

Finally his bloodshot brown eyes blinked open. His sister-in-law seemed to be finished. "Don't worry about anything, Nancy," he said on a yawn. "You and Brad enjoy the sunshine in Florida. Drop me a postcard once in a while."

"Sure," she said. And then, before Jack could hang up, she thought of one more thing. "Oh, I almost forgot."

Jack stifled a sigh and closed his eyes again.

"Oscar, the hamster from next door, often gets out of his cage and when he does he likes to come over here for some reason," Nancy said. "So if you see a brown ball of fur dashing across the floor sometime, don't panic. Emma will be over looking for him eventually."

"Emma?" This time, Jack's sigh was audible.

"Emma Springer. She lives next door. Even if Oscar doesn't get out of his cage, you'll be meeting her because when I told her about the lousy way you cops normally eat, she offered to invite you over for dinner occasionally while you're staying here."

"Fine, Nancy," Jack said. "Uh...I gotta go now. The lieutenant wants to see me about something." That was a lie, but Jack knew he was going to fall asleep if he didn't get up on his feet for a while.

He said goodbye to his sister-in-law and, thinking wearily that he was getting too old to work double shifts anymore, got up from his chair and headed toward the coffeepot. It was going to take a lot of caffeine to get him through the day.

TODAY WAS GOING TO BE one of those days. Emma was running late for work because one of her nursery school students had a birthday and she had to wear her clown outfit and put on all the makeup that went with it. Hurrying out the door she forgot to check on her pet hamsters, Oscar and Wilhemina.

An hour later she was standing in front of a rapt audience composed of three- and four-year-old boys and girls. "And now," she said brightly, "Chuckles needs an assistant for her last trick. Who wants to help me?"

Immediately a thicket of hands shot up among the crowd of wide-eyed children clustered on the floor in front of her. Typically, however, four-year-old Johnny Brubaker, whom Emma fully expected to be ensconced in a profitable life of crime before he got through kindergarten, didn't bother with any such polite nonsense as raising his hand. Instead he shot to his feet and made a beeline for Emma, obviously expecting audacity to triumph over fairness.

When he arrived expectantly at her side, Emma whispered to him out of the side of her mouth. "Not so fast, Johnny. It's Eric's birthday, and that means I'm going to pick him to help. Go back and sit down."

Johnny scowled at her, but he turned on his heel to obey. She should have known he wouldn't depart without having the last word, however. And true to form, before taking a step, Johnny looked back over his shoulder at her. "You gonna do the same old hanky trick?" he asked.

Now it was Emma's turn to scowl, although she doubted if all the clown makeup she was wearing permitted the expression much effectiveness.

"That's what I thought." Johnny smirked. "In that case, I don't wanna help ya anyway." And having won the battle of wills to his own satisfaction, he returned to his place and sat down, still with a pleased smile on his preternaturally adult four-year-old face.

"Eric?" Emma then said, smiling at the shy three-year-old. "Why don't you come help me?"

Embarrassed at being singled out, Eric ducked his head for a moment, but Emma had seen the sweet, delighted smile appear on his face—the one that always made her heart turn over.

"Come on now," she coaxed teasingly. "It's your birthday, so you should be the one to help with the next trick." He then obligingly stood and shuffled his way toward Emma, his head still down.

"It ain't no big deal!" Johnny growled loudly enough for Eric and all the other children to hear. "I done it twice already."

Emma ignored Johnny, but noticing that Eric was sporting a new watch, she sighed inwardly. Johnny would be after that watch, and if she didn't keep a sharp eye out, he would have it by the end of the day.

Eric's part of the trick was to try to pull a colored handkerchief out of one of the huge pockets in Emma's clown outfit. But, of course, the handkerchief would lengthen and change color as he pulled. Eric marched around the room to the hilarious delight of himself and all the other children.

After the clown act was over, Emma and her assistant, Megan, started the children fingerpainting. She kept her eye on Johnny as the kids smeared their paints on sheets of white paper, and as she'd expected, he finished his painting in record time, then got up and headed toward Eric.

Emma waited a moment before stepping in to foil his plot. She always found it fascinating to observe Johnny's skill at conning the other children. He never actually took anything from his peers—there was always a trade. It was just that he always came out ahead in the deal.

She saw him drag a wrinkled, dirty baseball card out of his jeans pocket and whisper something to Eric.

Eric shook his head and covered the Mickey Mouse watch on his wrist with one paint spattered hand. That didn't stop Johnny. He merely drew out a marble from his pocket and added it to the pot. But Eric was proving to be a tough sell today.

Johnny scowled and leaned over and whispered in Eric's ear, whereupon Eric looked as though he was about to cry. Obviously Johnny had resorted to some kind of a threat. It was time to interfere.

Emma walked over to the two boys. "Go back to your chair, Johnny," she said firmly, pointing to his seat in the next row. "Now."

Johnny gave Emma a dirty look. He never liked to be thwarted in his work. But Eric's Mickey Mouse watch was obviously a birthday present, and she wasn't about to send him home without it the very day he'd received it.

When Johnny had gone to his chair and slumped down in it, Emma turned to Eric, who was looking pathetically grateful for her intervention.

"That's a great watch, Eric," she said warmly. "Is it a birthday present?"

He nodded and smiled his sweet smile. "My mom give it to me at breakfast," he informed Emma.

"Was it what you wanted?" she asked.

Eric nodded again. "Uh-huh."

"Well, that's fantastic." Emma beamed and then squatted down beside him. "But Eric," she added, so softly that no one else could hear, "you're getting fingerpaint all over it. So why don't you give it to me to keep for you until the end of the day?"

He looked stricken at the idea of taking off his new watch. Emma figured half the fun of wearing it was having the other kids envy him. "I don't wanna," he said with doleful stubbornness, and he again covered the watch with his free hand as though to protect it. "I wanna wear it."

Emma sighed then patted Eric's shoulder. "Just give it to me while you're painting then," she suggested. "You can have it back later."

Throughout most of the day, Emma managed to distract Eric from remembering to get his watch back, and she returned it to him only a few minutes before the parents started showing up to collect their children.

Emma caught Eric's mom when she arrived, explained the situation and suggested she somehow try to keep her son from wearing his watch the next day.

Mrs. Jenkins sighed. "He'll have a fit if I try to make him leave that watch at home," she predicted. "But I'll be darned if I want to see it turn up on Johnny's arm. He's already conned Eric out of too many things this year. You'd think the kind of money his dad makes, the child would have enough toys at home to satisfy him without having to get hold of every other kid's.''

"I suspect it's the thrill of making the deal that interests Johnny more than anything else," Emma said smiling. "I don't think he really cares all that much about the things he gets in his trades."

"I see what you mean," Mrs. Jenkins said, shaking her head. Then she added, wistfully, "I suppose you couldn't expel Johnny or something?"

Emma grinned. "No. I suspect there's gold somewhere behind that con act of his. And one day I'm going to find it. Besides, Johnny is one of my teaching tools. He's taught more of my kids to beware of smooth talk and the value of standing up against intimidation than any lectures I could ever give them."

Mrs. Jenkins smiled ruefully. "He's just like his father, isn't he?" she said. "Once Jim and I made the mistake of browsing at Mr. Brubaker's car showroom, and I thought the man was never going to leave us alone, even when we told him we'd bought a car somewhere else."

"Yes—" Emma nodded "—I think you can safely say that Johnny is a chip off his father's block. But I have hopes," she added firmly, "of teaching Johnny a different way of behaving before he graduates from nursery school."

"You'd better hurry then," Mrs. Jenkins said dryly. "He'll only be with you another few months."

"I know time is running out," Emma agreed. "But I've promised myself that somehow I'll convince Johnny Brubaker that the other kids don't exist solely so he can con them."

"Good luck," Mrs. Jenkins replied in a skeptical tone. "I'm just happy this is his last year." Then she called Eric and left.

After the children and Megan were gone, Emma locked up her nursery school, climbed into her Ford Pinto and headed home. It was only as she pulled into her parking space and saw that the one beside hers had a strange car parked in it that she remembered her neighbors had left for Florida that day. Brad Spencer was taking a six-month sabbatical from his position as a university law professor. The car probably belonged to Brad's police detective brother, who was going to apartment sit for them while they were gone.

Emma wondered if she should invite Brad's brother to dinner that evening since this would be his first night here, but then she remembered that all she had in the kitchen was spaghetti and half a pound of hamburger. She decided to wait until Saturday night after she'd done her weekly grocery shopping.

After arriving in her apartment, Emma automatically checked the hamster cage she kept by the back window. She grimaced when she saw that the door of the cage was open. It looked as if she was going to meet her new neighbor sooner than expected. Once again Oscar had managed to manipulate the faulty catch and was missing. Wilhemina was crouching innocently in one corner of the cage.

"Why can't Oscar be happy staying at home where he belongs?" Emma complained to the hamster, then headed for the apartment next door.

JACK LOOKED LONGINGLY at the couch, debating whether he should give in to his exhaustion and take a nap first, or fix himself something to eat.

And then he saw something that banished both propositions from his mind: a small ball of fur raced across the room and disappeared under the couch he'd been thinking about stretching out on.

Jack sighed and shook his head. "Ah, hell," he muttered, "maybe if I don't bother it, it won't bother me."

At that moment, someone knocked and he answered the door only to find himself looking at a woman dressed in a clown outfit wearing enough makeup on her face to stock a cosmetic counter.

Jack didn't blink an eye. He was accustomed to dealing with bizarrely dressed people. Nothing surprised him anymore.

"Yes?" he said wearily.

"Mr. Spencer?"

"Yes," Jack repeated, and now there was a tinge of impatience added to the weariness in his tone.

Emma thought the man looked terrible. His large brown irises were drowned in a sea of red-streaked white, his thick brown hair was tousled as though he never combed it, and his face, which Emma suspected would normally be attractive, was carved with lines of fatigue. He didn't sound very friendly, either.

"I'm Emma Springer," she said, holding out her hand. "Your neighbor," she added for clarification.

Jack shook Emma's hand without enthusiasm. Her appearance on his doorstep meant he couldn't just ignore the little fur ball under the couch . . . he was going to have to help her capture the trespasser.

"You the one with the hamsters?" he asked as he let go of her hand.

Wonderful, Emma thought fatalistically. *He's obviously already met Oscar and didn't enjoy the experience.*

"I'm afraid so," she said, nodding. "In fact—"

"He's under the couch...or she is," Jack interrupted.

Emma brightened. "Oh, good. It's easy to catch him when he hides there."

Jack merely sighed and stepped back, holding the door open for her to come in. He obviously didn't have a sense of humor about hamster invasions and wasn't polite enough to hide his annoyance.

"His name is Oscar, by the way," she said, as she headed for the sofa and fell to her knees. "And as soon as I get the chance," she added, her voice muffled because she was lifting the skirt of the couch to look underneath, "I'm going to buy a new cage with a better lock. Oscar's the adventuresome type, but luckily Wilhemina isn't. Otherwise we'd be hunting two hamsters and..."

She stopped speaking. Oscar wasn't under the couch. Raising her head, she saw that Jack had a decidedly long-suffering look on his face. "He isn't here," she said in an apologetic voice.

Jack sighed...again. "Where do you think he might be?"

"I'll try the closet," Emma said, hastily getting to her feet.

He followed her to the closet and stood behind her staring gloomily at her baggy rear end as she got down on her knees and began looking.

The search began to take a long time. His eyelids drooping and stomach growling, Jack became more and more impatient.

"Why don't you call him?" he suggested.

Emma heard the growling of Jack's stomach, and she immediately decided to ask him to dinner to make up for Oscar's intrusion.

"It wouldn't do any good," she said. "Oscar doesn't come on call."

About that time the hamster sprang from his hiding place behind a pair of boots and headed for less perilous territory. Emma missed him, but Jack swooped on the creature and caught him before he could disappear somewhere else.

"Here," he said with obvious relief as he handed over the wriggling animal.

"Thanks." Emma quickly took Oscar and dropped him into one of the large, deep pockets of her clown outfit. Then she noticed that Jack was staring with muted curiosity at the way she was dressed.

"I guess you're wondering why I'm dressed like this," she said with a smile as she turned to head toward the door of the apartment. "It's because I run a nursery school and whenever one of the children has a birthday, I dress up like a clown to entertain them."

"Lucky kids," Jack said with a shrug as he trailed tiredly at Emma's heels. He was glad the hamster search was over and she was leaving.

As he opened the door for her, Emma said, "Listen, I don't imagine you've had time to get settled in yet, so if you'd like to join me for supper, I'm having spaghetti in about an hour."

Spaghetti was Jack's favorite meal, he was hungry, and an hour would give him time for a short nap. But he wasn't in the mood to be a polite guest.

He took so long considering the invitation that Emma began to grow irritated enough to wish she hadn't extended it.

"I guess I will," he finally said. "I don't know whether there's anything in the kitchen here to eat or not."

Emma's temper rose further over the lack of graciousness in Jack's acceptance. "Fine . . . see you in an hour, then," she said, her tone cool.

"Okay," Jack replied unenthusiastically.

When Emma was sure the door behind her was closed, she turned, stuck out her tongue, then grimaced and walked away.

JACK WAS PLEASANTLY SURPRISED when he arrived at Emma's apartment. Without her clown makeup and outfit, she was an attractive woman about his own age. She had short, curly brown hair, warm hazel eyes and beautiful skin. Her figure wasn't bad, either. But he wasn't about to let himself become attracted to another woman so soon after his disastrous affair with Janice.

"Come in," Emma said.

"Thanks," Jack said, forcing a smile to his lips.

"Dinner's not quite ready yet," she explained as she led the way to the living room. "But I'll have it on the table in a few minutes. Would you like a glass of wine?"

"No, thanks." And without waiting for an invitation, Jack collapsed into a chair.

"Well, just make yourself comfortable," she added wryly, certain that he intended to do just that. "I have to go finish up in the kitchen."

"Mmm-hmm," Jack responded sleepily, and when Emma departed the room, he promptly closed his eyes and began to doze.

As Emma prepared dinner and set the table, she was feeling annoyed. It would have been polite of her new neighbor to offer to set the table . . . or at least to come into the kitchen to chat a little while she finished up.

"Dinner's ready," she announced a few minutes later, and was further upset when her guest blinked his eyes open in a disoriented fashion. He'd obviously been asleep! Unaware of Emma's rising temper, Jack reluctantly hauled himself out of the comfortable chair and followed her to the table.

A while later, Emma raised another forkful of spaghetti to her mouth, and as she chewed, she eyed Jack with muted disfavor. He wasn't bad looking. Nice thick brown hair, heavily lashed big brown eyes, firm jaw, fit physique. But was he a bore! Trying to talk to him was like trying to converse with a zombie. Surely his police work had to provide some interesting fodder for discussion. But he just sat there, shoveled food in his mouth, and answered her questions in monosyllables.

"Is it six months that Nancy and Brad plan to be gone?" she asked, wishing it wasn't going to be that long.

"Yes," Jack answered as he picked up his glass to take a sip of wine. He told himself he should have asked for water. The wine, coupled with his already exhausted state, was making him more tired. But it happened to be a vintage he favored, so he hadn't been able to resist.

"Isn't it lucky you were able to apartment sit for them?" Emma commented idly, just for something to say.

Lucky? Jack thought wryly. Obviously Brad and Nancy hadn't told her why he had been available to move in.

"Yes, well," he said dryly, "my ex-fiancée didn't give me much warning before she kicked me out, so this arrangement is great for me."

Startled by the bluntness of his reply, Emma said, "I beg your pardon?"

Jack shrugged. "My fiancée thought she could handle being married to a policeman," he explained, "but I thought it might be a good idea to allow her to experience what it was really going to be like, so we lived together for a while. It turned out she couldn't take it, and broke off the engagement."

Emma was intrigued. Finally the man was talking, and furthermore, he was saying something interesting.

Curious, she asked, "What's so hard about being married to a policeman?"

Jack sighed and wished he'd kept his mouth shut. He wasn't in the mood to talk. He just wanted about twelve hours of uninterrupted slumber.

"Cops work long, erratic hours, have a generally paranoid personality and are always at considerable risk of getting killed," he said with a shrug. "A lot of their marriages end up in divorce."

"Oh," Emma said. She could tell he didn't want to talk anymore, so she let the matter drop, thinking Jack Spencer certainly had a lot of negatives going against him. Not only was he a bore, but he was also a man on the rebound...which wasn't surprising if cops were such poor prospects for marriage.

Jack finished his meal, apologized wearily for eating and running, then stood to leave. Emma stared at him in disbelief. The man's manners were atrocious!

Not that she wanted any more of his company, but a polite guest would stay after dinner for a while, or at least offer to help her clear the table!

"Fine," she said, her tone stiffly disapproving. "I didn't intend to take over your whole evening. I just wanted to welcome you with a meal."

Jack hesitated, belatedly aware that he wasn't behaving in a gentlemanly fashion. At least, he decided, he could explain why he was behaving the way he was.

"I'm sorry to be so rude," he apologized, "but I was on duty for sixteen hours straight before I came over here today, so I haven't slept in over twenty-four hours. I'm dead on my feet. But I appreciate the meal—it was delicious, by the way—and your neighborliness. The next time we meet, I will be more sociable, but right now all I want is a bed."

Emma was slightly mollified by the explanation, but she still thought his manners left a lot to be desired. She also didn't care whether they met in the future at all.

"I understand," she said in a civil tone. "By all means go back to your apartment and get some sleep." She got up from her chair and walked him to the door.

"It was nice to meet you," Jack said, attempting a smile as he paused in the doorway. "And thanks again for dinner."

"Good night," Emma said aloud. Silently she was vowing she would make sure Oscar didn't go visiting again, until Brad and Nancy returned home.

Chapter Two

"Come on, Willy," Jack said to the prisoner sitting across the table from him. "Use your brain, man. Either you help me out on this, or I bring you up on charges for lifting that money out of Jan Wilson's purse."

"Ya can't prove I took anything," Willy protested sullenly. "She coulda lost it out of her purse while we was dancin'."

Jack sighed long-sufferingly. He had no intention of informing Willy that Jan Wilson, an out-of-town businesswoman who'd made the mistake of hiring an escort from Suave for an evening, was refusing to press charges. Now that she was over her initial outrage, the idea of testifying against Willy in court was too humiliating.

"Willy, Jan Wilson *saw* you slip the money out of her purse. You must be losing your touch. You never used to be so sloppy," Jack said.

"Ah . . . she just turned around at the wrong time," Willy unconciously defended himself. "If she had just gone on lookin' in that mirror a few seconds longer..."

Jack's satisfied smile—and the tape recorder spinning on the table—informed Willy it would do no good to try to take back his incriminating words. So he whined for mercy instead.

"Tony'll kill me if I do what you want and he finds out you're a cop. Suave is just small potatoes anyway. Why ya wanta go after him for that? So what if a bunch of lonely dames wanta little kiss and tickle when the dinin' and dancin' is over? They get what they pay for, and it ain't no big deal."

"But it *is* a crime, Willy," Jack reminded his prisoner. "And since we haven't been able to get Tony on any of the big stuff, we'll take anything we can get to make his life miserable. Besides, he probably hasn't been able to resist cooking the books on his little escort service, so we may be able to get him on tax evasion as well as on a morals charge."

Jack wasn't going to tell Willy about the other crime he hoped to prove against Tony Caro—that he was blackmailing many of the women who made use of his escort service into investing in a phony stock scam he was running.

"All you have to do," Jack said patiently, "is vouch for me so I can get hired on as an escort. That's not so hard, is it?"

Willy's gloomy expression didn't lighten. "And when you lower the boom on Tony, he's gonna remember who did the vouchin' for ya," he predicted sourly.

"So?" Jack shrugged. "I'll let you off the hook. All you have to do is act outraged that I fooled you."

Willy shook his head. "Tony don't like nobody workin' for him to make that kind of mistake. He's got a suspicious mind."

Jack decided to turn the screws a little harder. "Okay," he said. "I guess I'll just have to make sure

Tony knows you've been arrested and that you've been singing like a bird about Suave ever since you were brought in. You think he's going to appreciate you getting him into trouble over a lousy hundred bucks?''

Jack started to get up from his chair, but Willy lunged across the table and grabbed his arm.

"Okay...okay!" he conceded. "I'll get you in at Suave. But if you get me killed, my pore old ma is gonna starve, and it's all gonna be your fault!"

Jack grinned. "Willy, your 'pore old ma' is going to get herself arrested any day now for selling those homemade cosmetics she concocts in her kitchen. The State will be buying her meals soon. And anyway—" he shrugged "—she's a better crook than you ever were. She'll end up on her feet eventually, you can count on it."

Willy scowled. "While I'll probably end up with my feet in a block of concrete on the bottom of the Missouri River," he predicted direly. "And all 'cause o' you!"

"Into each life some rain must fall," Jack said with a smile.

"You gonna let me outta here tonight?" Willy asked hopefully.

Jack shook his head. "Not unless you can set up a meeting with Tony for me this evening," he said dryly. "I still remember the last time I let you out on good faith, and the next morning you were in St. Louis instead of coming in to the station to file a statement like you were supposed to."

"I shoulda stayed in St. Louis," Willy groused. "Tony's outta town till tomorra. I ain't gonna be able to fix a meet for you till then."

"So be it," Jack said as he got up and called a policeman to come get Willy and stash him in a cell until the next day.

As Jack drove home that evening, he thought about the assignment he was about to undertake. He hated dressing up fancy. And he had absolutely no rhythm in his soul, so he wasn't a great dancer, either. But some women seemed to find his ineptitude on the dance floor funny. He just hoped it was going to be that kind of woman who turned out to be his first assignment. He also hoped she didn't have any "kissing and tickling" on her mind when the evening was over.

UPON ARRIVING HOME from work, Emma checked to see that Oscar hadn't gnawed off the rubber band she'd used to augment the faulty latch on his cage. She smiled when she saw that, though he had clearly been working on the problem, he hadn't succeeded in disposing of the impediment. She substituted a new rubber band for the now half-chewed one, and just as she was finishing, the telephone rang.

"Hi, Emma," her neighbor and friend, Joe Truman, said when she answered the phone. "I'm cooking up some barbecued ribs. Wanta join me for dinner?"

"Sure!" Emma agreed. "I'll be there in fifteen minutes."

After she hung up, Emma spent a futile moment wishing she had something more exciting to anticipate than an evening with Joe. No doubt he wished the same thing. Joe was ready to marry, settle down and have children. Emma sometimes thought along those lines herself these days. But she and Joe were just good friends who liked and understood each other and spent time together when neither was dating anyone in particular.

As Emma left her apartment to walk down the hall to Joe's, she saw Jack Spencer standing outside his apartment fumbling with a key ring. Emma had to pass him, but she didn't intend to stop and chat. A polite greeting was all she felt he deserved...or probably wanted considering his behavior the previous evening.

At seeing Emma coming toward him with a politely reserved look on her face, Jack remembered how rude he'd been the previous evening and decided it would be a good idea to ask her out to dinner to make up for his behavior. It was Friday night, and he wasn't in the mood to spend the evening alone anyway.

"Hi," he said in a pleasant tone, giving her his best smile.

"Good evening," Emma responded politely, noting that he looked a good deal better now than he had the night before. His eyes weren't bloodshot and his hair was combed. Also, he was actually smiling, and his smile was startlingly charming.

"Say," Jack said, still using his friendly tone. "Thanks again for dinner last night. You're a great cook."

Emma gave him a less conservative smile than she had before. "Thank you," she said, "but it was nothing. I had to cook for myself anyway, and there's always too much spaghetti for one person."

Jack shrugged, still smiling. "Well, it was nice of you anyway." Then he added, "And if you're free this evening, I'd like to return the favor. There's a good restaurant in Fairway that serves homestyle food. I go there a lot. Would you like to join me?"

Emma was disconcerted by the invitation. It was the last thing she'd expected, even if Jack did seem to be in a more sociable mood this evening. She had eaten at the small restaurant on the Kansas side of the state line he was talking about and enjoyed their food. But even if she hadn't already had other plans, she was still wary about spending much time in Jack's company. Who knew when he would revert to his unmannerly, uncommunicative state?

"Thank you," she said, "but I was just going down the hall to have dinner with Joe Truman. I don't know if you've met him yet, but he's your neighbor on the other side."

"No, I haven't met him," Jack said shaking his head, feeling unaccountably disappointed that she had turned down his dinner invitation. "Sorry you can't make it tonight," he added, "but maybe another time."

"Sure," Emma said with perfunctory politeness. "Another time." *Unless I see you coming in time to avoid you,* she added silently. "Good night," she said, as she started moving in the direction of Joe's apartment.

"Good night." Jack nodded. "Have a nice evening."

In a couple of seconds, she knocked on Joe's door.

"Hey, gorgeous, you look terrific!" Joe stepped outside his door. "How about a hello kiss?" He then planted a loud, smacking kiss on Emma's lips.

When he let her go, Emma was laughing. "Cut it out, Romeo," she teased. "You haven't been out of town long enough to miss me that much."

Placing a hand over his heart, Joe responded in his most exaggerated romantic tone. "I always miss you, my darling! Every day, every hour, every minute, every second without you is—''

"Oh, for heaven's sake." Emma cut off his nonsense. "Shut up and let me in. I'm hungry."

Laughing, Joe turned to draw Emma into his apartment and saw Jack, who was still fumbling with his key ring. Being a neighborly, curious fellow, he raised a hand and said, "Hi. You're Brad's brother, aren't you?"

Jack looked up, nodded and smiled. "I'm Jack Spencer," he said.

Joe, encouraged by Jack's friendly tone and smile, dragged Emma down the hall toward the new neighbor. "I'm Joe Truman," he introduced himself. "Welcome to the building."

"Thanks," Jack said as he took Joe's hand and shook it. And then he glanced at Emma, thinking these two must be having an affair, judging from the way Joe had greeted Emma.

"Do you know Emma?" Joe asked.

"We've met." Jack nodded.

Emma didn't explain that she'd had Jack over for dinner the evening before. She was afraid if she brought it up, her voice would disclose how unpleasant she'd found the experience. She merely nodded

Jack wondered why Emma didn't explain about the dinner they'd had. Was Joe the jealous type?

"Good," Joe said easily, then added, "Well, if you ever need anything, feel free to knock on my door. I travel a lot with my job, but when I'm home, I'll be glad to help out any way I can."

"Thanks," Jack said. "What is your job?"

"I'm a financial planner for one of the local utilities," he explained. "And you're a police detective, aren't you?"

"Yes, I am," Jack nodded.

"Must be exciting work," Joe said smiling.

Emma was beginning to wish the men would stop talking. She was starved. And then Joe surprised her.

"Say," he said to Jack, "Emma and I are about to have barbecued ribs for dinner. There's plenty for three if you don't have plans for the evening and would like to join us."

Emma unconsciously frowned. She considered one dinner with Jack Spencer enough to last her for a long time.

Jack saw Emma's frown and almost refused the invitation, thinking that she wanted to be alone with Joe. Or maybe she was afraid Jack would be as poor a guest as he'd been the night before? An imp of perverseness seized him. If that was why she was frowning, she was in for a surprise, he vowed.

"Sure, I'd be glad to join you," he said. "Just give me a minute to dump my coat and wash my hands."

"Great," Joe responded. "I'll leave the door to the apartment open. Just come in when you're ready."

Emma was put out with Joe, but tried not to show it. He knew her so well, however, that once they were in his apartment, he looked at her in a curious manner and said, "Don't you like the guy?"

Emma shrugged as she went to Joe's kitchen cabinet to get out another place setting for the table. "I had him over for dinner last night," she explained. "It was in penance because Oscar got out again and invaded his apartment."

"And the two of you didn't hit it off?" Joe asked, surprised.

"Well, he was pretty rude and uncommunicative." Emma grimaced. "And though he apologized before he left and said he hadn't been a good guest because he'd been up for twenty-four hours and was exhausted, I have the feeling he's just the moody type."

"Ah, Emma," Joe chided. "It's not like you not to give a person the benefit of the doubt."

She merely shrugged.

"Well, let's see what he's like tonight," Joe suggested. "If he's not our type, we'll cross him off both our lists."

"Fine with me," Emma agreed, "but don't expect him to liven up the evening by talking about his work. When he had dinner with me, he hardly opened his mouth except to shovel food into it."

"SO THIS GUY WAS STANDING THERE in his underwear swearing at the top of his lungs that little Mary had gotten him up to her room by telling him her poor old mother needed help, and then had overpowered him and robbed him," Jack said, finishing the latest in a hilarious series of stories about his work, "while Mary, who stands about four foot eleven in high heels, stood across the room in her black bloomers filing her fingernails."

"What did she have to say about her client's story?" Joe asked between gasps of laughter.

"She picked up the guy's money, walked over and stuffed it in his underwear and drawled, 'Here, junior...you need the help more than I do.'"

Emma was also laughing hard. She'd been laughing practically from the moment Jack had come into Joe's apartment, and had completely forgotten her prediction to Joe that Jack would turn out to be a boring guest.

When the latest spate of laughter had died down, Jack got to his feet and picked up his plate and glass. "Let me do the dishes," he insisted.

"Oh, that's not necessary," Joe protested, getting to his feet as well. "It's Emma's turn. We always trade off."

Jack smiled and looked at Emma. He'd put special effort into being entertaining tonight to make up for his behavior the previous evening. And Emma's response had been gratifying. She was no longer looking at him in a polite way, but instead seemed to have accepted him as wholeheartedly as Joe had. During the past hour and a half, he'd found himself liking her a great deal. It really was too bad she was Joe's girl.

"Yes, it's my turn, Jack," Emma insisted as she stood. "Go on into the living room with Joe and relax."

But she couldn't talk him out of helping. Not only did he help clear the dinner table, but he helped load the dishwasher as well.

As they worked in the kitchen together, Emma became even more aware of how attractive Jack was. Standing side by side at the sink, she realized he was just the right height she liked a man to be. And he was so reassuringly solid. His after-shave smelled good, too. But despite how entertaining he'd been this evening, she still thought he was probably a moody sort. And maybe his ex-fiancée had been right that being involved with a police detective was hard to put up with?

Jack stayed for another half hour before he decided it was time to give the lovers some time alone.

At the door, he said, "If I could cook I'd ask the two of you over for dinner sometime. But since I can't, I'll have to take you out one night instead."

"Great," Joe replied sincerely. "We've enjoyed your company enormously, haven't we, Emma?" He put his arm around her shoulders and looked down at her with a teasing, devilish look in his blue eyes.

She knew Joe was thinking about her prediction concerning Jack's behavior. "Yes, we did," she said amiably, smiling.

Jack almost didn't hear her. He was wondering why he didn't particularly like seeing Joe's arm draped so possessively around Emma's shoulders.

"Uh...thanks," he said, coming out of his thoughts with enough presence of mind to answer appropriately. "It's always nice to know you haven't bored the socks off new acquaintances."

"You certainly didn't do that," Joe assured him. "Emma and I have dinner together quite often, and I'm sure I speak for both of us in saying we'd like to include you in from here on out. Right, Emma?"

That remark puzzled Jack. Why would a guy want a third party at his romantic dinners with his girlfriend?

"Of course," she chimed in agreeably. But inwardly she wondered if it might be a mistake on her part to see too much of Jack. Although he was very attractive and appealing tonight, she still wasn't sure about his overall character.

After goodbyes were exchanged, Jack went back to his apartment, picturing Joe and Emma necking now that he was out of their hair. And even though he couldn't think of a single reason why he should care what his new neighbors did with each other, the pictures in his mind chased his former good mood away and replaced it with a feeling of lonely disgruntlement.

JOE LOOKED AT EMMA in a teasing manner. "Admit it," he prodded. "You had a great time tonight. Jack wasn't boring at all."

Emma shrugged and headed for the bar to pour herself a glass of wine. "Yes," she said lightly, "he was good company."

"Better than good," Joe snorted. And then he looked more closely at the expression on Emma's face and smiled.

She looked at him over the edge of her wineglass as she took a sip, then lowered the glass and hesitantly smiled back. "What are you smiling about?" she asked.

"I'm smiling because I think you're more than a little attracted to our new neighbor," Joe responded.

Emma was annoyed. Joe saw entirely too much at times. "Don't be silly," she scoffed. "I barely know him. And besides, I don't have any desire to be attracted to a vice detective. He told me his fiancée couldn't take his weird hours and all the things that go with being involved with someone in his line of work, and I imagine she had the right idea."

Joe looked skeptical. "But you do like his looks?" he persisted.

Emma shrugged. "He's reasonably attractive, I suppose."

"Uh-huh. And do you like his personality?"

Emma pretended interest in her wine. "He's reasonably amusing, I suppose," she responded in an offhand manner.

"And he's sexy," Joe provided helpfully.

This time, Emma couldn't think of a reply. And before she knew it, her mind had drifted off and she remembered staring at Jack's mouth as he'd talked that night, wondering how well he kissed.

"I think that about clinches it," Joe said, and his grin was obnoxiously knowing.

Emma came out of her thoughts and grimaced at her friend. "Clinches what?" she asked irritably.

"What were you thinking about just now?" Joe countered.

"Nothing," she lied firmly. "Nothing at all."

Joe laughed and shook his head. "Okay, Emma," he said. "So you're not interested in Jack Spencer as a man. And therefore, when he joins us for dinner in the future, I can be sure you'll be thinking of him in just about the same friendly way you think of me."

Emma shrugged non-committally and quickly changed the subject.

JACK COLLECTED WILLY from jail and drove him to the seedy offices of the Suave Escort Service. As they got out of the car, Willy looked so nervous that Jack was afraid he was going to blow the whole thing.

"Buck up," he said lightly. "This won't hurt a bit. And when it's all over, you'll be in the clear."

Willy merely scowled. But when they stepped into Tony Caro's dingy private office, he rose to the occasion.

"Hi ya, Tony," he said in his normal breezy style. "What's cookin'?"

Tony Caro, a large, overbearing lout of a man with no sense of humor, looked up through his bushy black eyebrows at Willy and scowled.

"Nuthin's cookin' till you tell me who this is you got with ya," he growled. "You know I don't like no strangers around here."

"This ain't no stranger," Willy whined. "This is my buddy, Jackie. Jackie needs a job, Tony, and he ain't half bad lookin'... you can see that. So I brought him around to see if you could use him as an escort. You been sayin' you need more guys, ain't ya?"

Tony had been hunched over some papers on his desk. Now he reared back in his chair and fixed a black, stony gaze on Jack.

Jack tried to look dumb and happy. He knew from Tony's file that the man didn't like anybody around him who had any brains.

"You ever done this sorta thing before?" Tony growled.

"No." Jack shrugged and then gave him a cocky grin. "But it shouldn't be too hard. Women like me. I've never had any problem getting what I want from them."

Tony nodded. "You look like the type women fall for, all right," he grunted. It was clear from his tone that he didn't think much of women and their tastes. "And you talk kinda fancy. That's good. The kind of women I want to attract to the service like men who talk right. You got good manners, too?"

Jack shrugged again. "I know which fork to use and how to dab with a napkin," he acknowledged.

Tony stared hard at Jack a few minutes longer, and Jack, knowing what was expected of him, faked being intimidated by the long stare. After he started shifting uneasily in his seat, Tony nodded with satisfaction.

"I'll think about it and letcha know," he grunted. "Get outta here now. I wanta talk to Willy."

Jack didn't like leaving Willy alone with Tony. The man had no backbone whatsoever, and if Tony put him through a third degree, Jack was afraid he would crack. Fortunately, Willy wasn't with Tony long.

Back in the car, Jack gave Willy a hard look. "What did he say?"

Willy shrugged. "He wanted to know how my date with the Wilson dame turned out."

"Did you tell him the truth?" Jack smiled.

"Nah . . . you think I'm crazy?" Willy snorted. "I told him the date went peachy dandy and the dame would probably wanta see me again next time she's in town."

Jack's smile turned to a grin. Then he changed the subject. "How will Tony let me know if he decides to hire me?"

Willy's expression turned gloomy. "He'll call me after he makes a decision," he replied.

"Which means you're going to have to stick around to be called," Jack said firmly. He was sure Willy planned to head for St. Louis at the first opportunity . . . or parts farther east.

"Yeah." Willy agreed too easily.

Jack gave him a look to impress upon him the dire consequences of carrying out any plan of escape. "Willy," he said softly, "if you try skipping out on me, I'll put your picture out on the wire to every police department in the country."

Willy's expression turned to one of unhappy entrapment.

"But," Jack went on, "if you stick around long enough for Tony to hire me, you're free and clear. After I'm on the payroll, I don't care where you go."

Willy brightened a little. "Then I'll stick," he agreed.

EMMA STOOD IN FRONT of Jack's apartment door Monday evening and for the third time, lifted her hand to knock. But once again, she lowered her hand.

Now, let's get this straight, she addressed herself firmly. *You're here strictly to get Jack's advice. There's nothing personal about this visit at all, right?*

She was annoyed when her mind didn't immediately affirm the statement. She was also annoyed because the fact that she'd even had to ask herself the question meant more was going on here than she wanted to admit.

Shaking her head, Emma finally stepped back a pace, intending to forget the whole thing and go back to her own apartment. But at that moment, Jack opened his door. He looked startled at finding her right across the threshold.

Emma seized upon the fact that Jack had his coat over his arm and was obviously on his way somewhere. "Oh," she said. "You're about to leave. Well, I won't keep you. I was just going to ask your advice about something, but it can wait."

"I've got a few minutes," Jack said, trying not to frown. Whenever anyone asked his advice, it was usually about something unsavory. And Emma seemed slightly nervous.

"Are you sure?" Emma said hesitantly.

Jack's curiosity was on the alert. "I'm sure, Emma."

Emma hesitated a second, then decided to delay telling Jack the real reason for her visit until she could determine if he was the type who might think she was an idiot to be so concerned over such a seemingly minor matter, considering the type of problems he normally dealt with.

"Well, it was just that I was wondering if you ever do any public-service work?" she said. "I mean, do you ever do anything like visit nursery schools to tell the children about police work?"

Jack smiled. He felt relieved that it wasn't anything more serious. "I'm a vice cop, remember?" he said. "You don't really want me telling your kids about prostitutes, dope dealers and gambling, do you?"

"Oh, that's right," Emma said. "No, I guess that wouldn't be appropriate, would it?"

But then Jack frowned. Emma had said she wanted his *advice* on something, not to *ask* him something. And her manner was slightly odd. He had a good idea her question about his doing public-service work was just a delaying tactic.

"Are you sure that's all you wanted to ask me?" he said, using the gentle, encouraging tone that sometimes made prisoners who weren't too hardened want to confide in him.

Emma warmed to his tone and manner. Suddenly, he seemed exceptionally easy to talk to. Maybe he wouldn't think her coming to him for advice about such a small matter was so strange, after all. "Well, there was one more thing," she said. "Have you had much experience with conmen, Jack?"

Jack felt a sinking sensation in his stomach. Had Emma gotten herself mixed up in some flimflam scheme? Was she in real trouble? He was amazed at how protective he suddenly felt toward her.

"Yes, I have," he said quietly. "Why? Do you know about some con scheme that's going on?"

"You might say that," she hedged. "May I come in?"

Jack, the sensation in his stomach growing stronger, nodded and stepped back. "Sure. Come on in."

As Emma passed him on her way into his apartment, Jack looked at her back, thinking absently that her figure was just right.

He motioned for her to sit down.

"Now tell me about it," he said gently. "Who's working the con and what's it about?"

Emma sighed. "It's Johnny Brubaker."

"Johnny." Jack nodded, and that heavy feeling inside him escalated. She said this person's name as though she knew him intimately. "What has Johnny done?"

Emma shook her head, her expression exasperated. "He finally conned Eric's Mickey Mouse watch away from him today," she informed him in a tone of utter seriousness, "just like I knew he would eventually. And he won't give it back no matter what I say!"

Chapter Three

His voice sounding strangled because he was trying so hard to keep from laughing, Jack finally managed a reply to Emma's statement. "Did you say this Johnny conned a Mickey Mouse watch from somebody?" he asked.

Emma nodded. "From Eric," she explained. "And it was a birthday present, too!" she added indignantly.

Jack simply couldn't believe she was serious. He was positive this was all a joke she was playing on him, and he decided to do his part and go along with it. Composing his face into a serious expression, he intoned a question in the best imitation of Jack Webb's voice he could manage.

"I'll need some facts, ma'am," he said in the sober *Dragnet* tradition. "How old is this Johnny?"

Emma was startled by his manner, and blinked at him in a puzzled fashion, but she answered him seriously. "He's four," she said. And then she frowned. "Chronologically, that is. Otherwise he's as old as time and the trickiest little devil I've ever come across."

Jack tried to keep going along with Emma's joke. He really did. But this was one of the funniest things anybody had pulled on him for a long time, and he finally couldn't help it. He started howling with laughter.

Emma was startled by Jack's laughter. And then she understood that he thought she'd been playing a joke on him. For a moment she wished she'd kept her mouth shut. She felt foolish. But then Jack's laughter became so infectious that she couldn't help joining in. And as she laughed with him, she thought about what his reaction was going to be when he learned she hadn't been joking.

"That was great!" Jack gasped as his laughter died down. "You sucked me in good at first!"

Emma shook her head, laughing so hard there were tears in her eyes. "You don't know the half of it," she gasped out. "I was serious!"

At that, Jack stopped laughing and looked at Emma incredulously. "You mean you really do want my advice about this four-year-old kid?"

Still chuckling, Emma wiped her eyes as she nodded. "Four-year-old or not, he *is* a con man," she said.

Jack shook his head, beginning to grin again. "This is the first time I've been consulted about a crook that young. Sorry I laughed but . . ."

"You don't need to apologize," Emma said grinning back. "It was pretty funny." And then something else occurred to her, and she gazed at him in astonishment. "Jack, at first when I said I needed your advice, you thought I was in trouble myself, didn't you?"

He nodded. "I'm working a case right now where a guy is preying on women with a phony stock scheme and for a minute I thought . . ." But then Jack realized Emma would probably be pretty offended if he thought she had to get her dates by contacting a place like

Suave. "Well, never mind," he said. "Go on with your story about this kid."

Emma got back on track. "If you knew Johnny," she said dryly, "you'd realize why I'm so concerned about him . . . and his victims."

"What, exactly, is it about him that worries you so much?" Jack asked. He was still amused, but at the same time, he admired Emma for having the ability to laugh at herself.

"Have you had experience with children?" Emma asked. As she looked at Jack inquiringly, she was trying not to focus on his sexy brown eyes or his charming smile . . . trying to ignore the warm feeling that had coursed through her when she'd realized how concerned for her he'd been at thinking she was in trouble.

"No," Jack said, "I haven't."

"Well, I have a theory," Emma went on. "I think children are born with certain . . . well, for lack of a better word, inclinations. Their character is inclined in certain directions from the day they're born. Now, if their environment is such that those inclinations, if they should be unsavory, are reinforced—and I believe that's the case in Johnny's family—they just get worse. I believe it takes some pretty strong outside influence to make the child change direction."

"In other words, if a kid's born inclined to be a crook and his family doesn't try to teach him differently, he's headed for jail," Jack put Emma's theory into his own words.

She nodded.

"So what's going on in Johnny's family that makes you think his criminal tendencies are being reinforced?" Jack asked.

Emma sighed. "I'm not really comfortable putting it that strongly," she hedged. "Mr. Brubaker probably doesn't do anything that's actually criminal. It's just that his idea of business is to intimidate his customers and then take them for all he can get."

"Sounds like a lot of businessmen," Jack said. As he watched Emma, he realized how much he liked the warmth in her eyes and the sweet curve of her mouth. And he liked the way her rich, silky brown curls looked slightly tousled.

"I suppose so," Emma agreed. "But there's a chance Johnny's inclinations might grow from taking an unusually hard businessman's approach to people into a complete disregard for their feelings. I wouldn't feel right if I didn't at least try to make him change his attitude. The only problem is, I haven't been able to think of a way to make him respect his peers. He just likes to outsmart them."

Jack nodded. He suspected that Emma was entirely too softhearted to deal with the type of kid this Johnny Brubaker sounded like.

Then the clock sounded the half hour, and Jack realized that if he didn't get a move on, he was going to be late picking up the remainder of his personal things from Janice's apartment. And his being late was one of the things she hadn't been able to tolerate when they'd been living together. Of course, it didn't make any difference any longer if he made her mad. It was just that if he could avoid a rancorous scene, he would prefer to.

"I'll tell you what," he said, leaning forward with his elbows on his knees and smiling at Emma. "I'm willing to help, but it might take a little time for me to come up with the right idea to make an impression on Johnny. Why don't I give the matter some thought, and when I get an idea, I'll check it out with you and see what you think.''

Emma surmised that Jack was in a hurry. She quickly got to her feet.

"Thank you," she said. "I don't want to impose on your time, and if you can't come up with anything, don't worry about it at all. I just thought it was worth a try to get a fresh viewpoint."

Jack stood as well and reached for his coat. He carried it on his arm as he accompanied Emma to the door, smiling down at her as they walked.

Jack's smile was so charming that she could hardly believe this was the same discourteous cretin she'd had over for dinner only a few nights ago. She stared up into his face, wondering if Jack Spencer had missed his calling, and instead of being a vice detective, he should be bottling that smile and selling it for a hefty fee.

"I hope I can help," he said. "Policemen have to be as devious—or more so—as the crooks they go after. Otherwise they'd never catch anybody."

Emma grimaced. "But children are in a class by themselves," she said. "You don't know the meaning of 'devious' until you've tangled with a few four-year-olds like Johnny. He's exceptionally gifted in that direction."

Jack grinned. He was beginning to look forward to meeting Johnny. He sounded like a boy after his own heart.

"We'll think of something," he said confidently. "There's an answer to most problems given enough time to think of a solution."

"Yes, well, this is February," Emma said. "In May, Johnny leaves my domain for good. Do you think three months is enough time to turn him around?"

"Sure," Jack said. "It's two against one now, isn't it?"

Emma considered that and nodded. Jack's confidence was having the effect of bolstering her own.

"You're right," she agreed, and smiled. "What chance does a four-year-old have against an old hand with children and a vice cop?"

Jack pulled his door open, still grinning. Emma tried not to look too closely at that grin. It was as charming as his smile.

"That's the spirit," he said. "I'll do some hard thinking and get back to you."

"Thanks," she said, and automatically held out her hand. As Jack shook it, she found herself reacting to the hard warmth of his fingers... and was it her imagination or did he prolong the handshake just a little longer than was necessary?

"Good night," Emma said, and she was unaware that she was looking up into Jack's smiling face with a rather bemused expression on her own.

"See you soon," he said softly.

Emma watched him go, liking the way he moved. He walked with such male confidence and surety. Then she turned and headed for her apartment, thinking, *Johnny Brubaker... you may be about to meet your match.*

"I MIGHT HAVE KNOWN you'd be late," were Janice's first words to Jack when she opened the door to him.

Inwardly Jack sighed. "I was helping out a neighbor," he said, though he knew even before opening his mouth that his explanation would be disregarded.

"Ha!" she scoffed. "A neighbor with a black miniskirt, a fake fur around her neck and four-inch heels on her feet, no doubt!"

Jack didn't say anything. He wasn't going to argue with her if he could help it.

"Your stuff is on the dining-room table," Janice said stiffly. "It's amazing how little of it there is, considering we lived together three months."

"I'm not much of a collector," Jack said mildly as he headed for the table. "Besides, I already took almost everything of mine when I first moved out."

When he turned from picking up the box on the dining-room table, he was surprised to see that Janice was no longer looking hostile. In fact, she was biting her bottom lip and appeared to be on the verge of tears.

"Hey," he said gently. "It's all right. We don't have to be mad at each other, just because things didn't work out."

At that, Janice's wide blue eyes clouded even more, and she raised a manicured hand to tug at a long strand of blond hair.

"No," she admitted soulfully. "I just . . . oh, Jack, I know it's crazy . . . I know it can't work between us. But I miss you and . . ."

She would begin crying in a moment, and Jack hated to see her cry. So he put down the box, went to her and folded her into his arms. To his surprise, Janice immediately wrapped her arms around his neck and pulled his head down for a kiss. And it was during the kiss that he realized the affair was truly over. He felt affection, sadness and concern for Janice. But he didn't feel sexually drawn to her anymore. He didn't feel about her the way a man feels about a woman he intends to marry.

Jack wondered how all the emotion that once had consumed him could have disappeared so quickly. Could it be that it had been infatuation rather than real love he'd felt for Janice all along? Was that the real reason why he'd insisted they live together for a while?

He knew he'd made less of an effort than he could have made to appease her when his job had begun to get in their way. But her predictability, which had once been the very thing that had drawn him to her, comforting him after a day spent dealing with the unpredictability of his work, had begun to bore him very quickly. And now that he was able to admit it to himself, he knew that when she'd broken their engagement, he had felt more relieved than heartbroken.

Such thoughts troubled Jack and made his response to Janice's kiss even less enthusiastic than it might have been. And when Janice drew back, her tears had dried. Hostility was back in her eyes.

"You've already found someone else, haven't you?" she demanded, her tone jealous and accusing.

Jack sighed. "Janice, it's only been a week. How could I have found someone else in that short a time?"

Janice's prettiness dissipated when she sneered, and she was sneering heavily at the moment.

"You could find someone in five minutes, much less seven days!"

Jack shook his head. "I haven't found anyone else," he said firmly, counting on the truth of his statement to come through in his voice. He was disconcerted, however, when an image of Emma suddenly appeared in his mind, robbing his statement of some of its veracity.

Janice's mouth trembled. "But you don't want me back, do you?"

Jack tried to think of something to say that wouldn't hurt her, but his hesitation was the same as an affirmative answer.

Janice's temper erupted. "Take your things and get out!" she ordered. "I was right to break things off with you, Jack Spencer! You can't love anybody! You're just a philandering, self-indulgent little boy, and that's why you love your work so much, because it's like a game instead of a real job. I pity the woman who finally does make the mistake of marrying you—if it's even possible to get you to the altar, that is!"

Jack shook his head and bit his tongue. If he started answering back, they would be in a full-blown fight, and he'd had enough arguments with her to last him a lifetime.

A few minutes later, after the door to Janice's apartment had slammed behind him and he was driving to a restaurant to have some dinner, Janice's words made him frown, however. He wondered if there was any truth to her evaluation of his character.

Sure, he loved his work. But he wouldn't call it a game. If it was a game, it was too often a boring one, and when it got exciting, it usually meant that his life was in danger. Some game!

But it was more the part about his inability to really love a woman that troubled Jack. When he'd met Janice, it had been love at first sight for him, or so he'd thought. A tall, classic blonde, Janice had the look that he always went for. And she'd seemed to have a calm, even temperament. Jack got enough volatility in his work. He didn't want to come home to a woman who was likely to blow up over nothing. But after he'd moved in and his work was a reality, her calm temperament had frayed considerably.

Still, if ever there had been a woman Jack would have said was perfect for him, it would seem to be Janice. So where had all his feelings for her gone? And why, he wondered thoughtfully, had an image of Emma appeared in his mind when he was denying he'd found another woman to replace Janice?

Jack shook his head as he parked in front of the restaurant where he intended to have supper. He didn't understand why he'd thought of Emma at just the wrong time, but he was positive it didn't mean anything he should take seriously. She was cute, and had a terrific sense of humor. But she was dating someone else, and anyway, he shouldn't get involved with a woman for the time being. He had other things to deal with right now...such as the Suave Escort Service.

As Emma was decorating the nursery school for Valentine's Day, she decided it was time she had a party of her own. She was going to have scads of decorations left over, so why not?

She bought the invitations on the way home from work.

"I need ya to come down to the office this afternoon," Tony Caro growled over the phone into Jack's ear.

Jack's face lit with a smile of satisfaction. "Does that mean you're hiring me?" he asked.

"Nah, it means I want ya to come down to the office so we can talk about it," Tony grunted sarcastically. "Be here at three o'clock...sharp!" And he slammed down the receiver.

The guys Jack worked with teased him unmercifully as he got ready to leave for the interview with Tony.

"Ooh-la-la, Jackie's gonna escort the ladies," Freddie May, who resembled a wrestling pro who'd lost a lot of matches, trilled in a feminine voice. "You gonna give 'em the *full* treatment, Jackie boy?"

"No way," Jack replied amiably.

"Ooh, Jackie's particular," Freddie simpered. "He don't wanna go to bed with just anybody!"

"I'm a law-abiding cop," Jack said grinning. "And it wouldn't be strictly legit to take the ladies to bed before they show up on the witness stand, now would it, Freddie?"

"You gonna let a little thing like that stop ya?" Charlie Browne yelled from across the room. "Whatcha gonna do if one of the ladies *insists*, Jack? You gonna arm wrestle her like ya done Goldie?"

Goldie was an aging prostitute whom Jack had arrested many times, but who never resented it because she was unduly fond of him. He had lost track of the number of times Goldie had offered to take him home with her for a little free service, and he'd gotten so tired of it that once he'd offered to arm wrestle her. If he won, she didn't proposition him anymore. If she won, he'd go home with her.

That was one of the few times his job had almost cost him more than he was willing to pay. Goldie had turned out to be exceptionally strong. Or maybe she was just so enamored with him that her desire infused strength in her arm. In any case, he had won by a margin that had been much too close for comfort. But it had been worth it. She had kept her word, and now when he arrested her, she merely gave him a soulful look that accused him, silently, of breaking her heart.

"No, I learned my lesson the last time I arm wrestled a woman," Jack said ruefully.

"So how're you gonna say no, Jackie boy?" Eddie asked with a huge white grin. "You had much practice at sayin' no?"

"I'll think of something," Jack said grinning back. "Believe me, I'll think of something."

He just hoped he would.

"THERE'S A FEW THINGS I wanna get straight with you before I hire ya on," Tony grated around the huge black cigar in his mouth.

"Like what?" Jack asked innocently.

"Like, are you gonna quibble if a customer wants more than just dinner and dancin'?" Tony snorted.

Jack hesitated, hoping the wire he was wearing was picking up this conversation clearly. "You mean, if a customer wants to pay me to go to bed with her, will I do it?" he asked for the benefit of the recording being made.

Tony scowled. "Whaddya think I mean?" he growled. "I ain't talkin' about playin' tiddledywinks with 'em."

"What if I don't like her looks?" Jack asked.

Tony shook his head as though he couldn't believe any guy could be this dumb. "You ain't in it for the kicks, kid," he said disgustedly. "You're in it for the money. And the customer is always right, no matter what she wants . . . as long as she's willin' to pay for it. Now do you want the job or don't ya?"

Jack nodded. "When do you want me to start?" he asked.

"We're always busy Valentine's Day," Tony said, his heavy face betraying no satisfaction over Jack's acceptance of the job. "I got enough guys to handle things till then, but I'm gonna need extra that night. If you do all right then maybe things will pick up for you."

The implied "maybe they won't" was in Tony's voice. He was clearly not an employer who favored pampering or encouraging his employees.

"What's the pay?" Jack asked.

"Your share's half the total fee for four hours if it's a regular escort. If it goes overtime, you get half of the overcharge. And you don't take nuthin' less than a hundred an hour for the fun and games in bed, understand, and you give me back fifty bucks an hour of that."

"Do I have to spend all night with her, or can I leave after she's got what she's paying for?" Jack asked.

"It's a hundred bucks an hour however long you stay." Tony shrugged. "You and the dame make your own schedule. If you need money, you gotta figure out how to make her keep you longer. You ain't got no overhead, 'cause these women are usually from outta town and got a hotel room, see? If she ain't from outta town, you make her spring for the room."

Jack nodded. "Sounds simple enough," he agreed. And he added silently, *and illegal enough to haul you in right now, Tony. But we'll wait awhile and see what else we can hang on you . . . hopefully something that will put you away for a good deal longer than a simple morals charge.*

"So that's it," Tony said heavily. "You're hired. Leave me a number where I can reach you twenty-four hours a day."

"Twenty-four hours a day?" Jack said, raising his eyebrows.

"What . . . you got somethin' better to do with your time?" Tony responded in a sarcastic tone. "Some of these dames got screwy schedules."

Jack was thinking of the arrangements that would have to be made to patch the special number at the station into his home phone. But it could be done.

"Sure...I'll be on call," Jack nodded. He wrote out a number, tossed it on Tony's desk, then got to his feet.

Back at the station, Jack endured the catcalls and salacious inquiries from his cohorts as to whether he'd gotten the job. He affected the pose of a sophisticated, urbane actor and pretended he was performing a TV ad for the Suave Escort Service.

"Need an escort, ladies?" he drawled in a sexy voice as he flashed a white-toothed smile. He picked up his stained, cracked coffee mug and mimicked taking a delicate sip of champagne from it. Then he pretended there was a flower in his buttonhole and sniffed it before lifting his head and bestowing another dazzling smile upon his grinning coworkers. "If you need someone to escort you on a night around town, call 666-6666. For a reasonable fee, your every sinful wish will be some lucky Suave man's command."

That last sentence earned him some ribald comments, and there was a great deal of good-natured laughter over his performance before he could settle down to make the arrangements necessary to fulfill his role as a "Suave" man.

As EMMA ADDRESSED the party invitations, she paused before writing Jack's name on one of them, wondering doubtfully if he was the type to enjoy a Valentine gathering. But she couldn't exclude him, of course.

And if he didn't want to come, he could always make up an excuse.

Therefore, she scrawled his name across an envelope and addressed one to Joe also. They were the last two. Stamping the other ones, she went downstairs to put them in the mailbox, then headed upstairs to Joe's apartment.

"Hey, this is a great idea," Joe said as he read the invitation Emma had handed him. "Too bad I can't come, but I'll be in New York that day."

"Oh, Joe," she said, grimacing. "I should have checked with you first...then I could have set the date for when you would be in town."

Joe looked surprised. "Hey, it's no big deal," he said, eyeing her curiously. "I've missed some of your parties before and I'll no doubt miss some of them in the future. You don't have to have me there—you know that."

"Oh, I know, but I like you to be there," Emma said. "You're always a barrel of laughs. I can always count on you to liven things up if people start to sit around looking bored."

Joe smiled. "Emma, nobody's ever bored at one of your parties. So cut the blarney. Why is it so important—" He stopped speaking and looked at her as though a thought had hit him.

Emma hastily headed for the door. "I've got to get home," she said. "I'm expecting a call from Mother, and you know how she is if I'm not standing right by the phone, waiting to pick it up on the first ring...."

"Hold it," Joe said, blocking her way to the door. "It couldn't be that you wanted me there as camouflage, could it?"

Emma affected a puzzled look. "What in the world are you talking about?"

"Ah, come off it," Joe scoffed. "This is me, remember? The guy who knows you like a book."

"Don't be silly," Emma sniffed. "No one can ever know anyone else all that well. And I don't have the foggiest idea what you—"

"That's it, isn't it?" Joe interrupted. "You wanted me there so you could pretend you and I are involved with each other if the situation called for it. You know, the way we did when Mary Mandiver was after me."

"Joe," Emma said, her voice reproving, "you are out of your tiny little mind. In the first place, I don't care what Jack Spencer thinks, and in the second place—"

"Who said anything about Jack Spencer?" Joe drawled triumphantly, grinning. He was clearly delighted by her slip of the tongue.

Emma flushed and bit her lip.

Joe laughed and then shook his head in a puzzled manner. "I've never seen you react this way to a man," he said. "When you're interested in a guy, you usually don't have any trouble flirting with him. Instead of using me as a safety net, I'd have thought you'd want me to make it clear to Jack that you and I aren't involved, in case he got the wrong idea when we had him over here to dinner that night. How come you're so ambivalent about the guy? I know he appeals to you."

"Well, I don't know any such thing," Emma said grumpily. "And even if I did find him as attractive as you seem to think, I wouldn't do anything about it. As I said before, there are some serious disadvantages in getting involved with a police detective."

Joe snorted. "Talk about ambivalence. Emma, is it really possible that for once I know more about what's going on with you than you do? I'm beginning to wonder if you really don't realize how attracted you are to Jack."

Emma was well aware of how attractive she found Jack. But she didn't want to discuss the matter with Joe. She wanted to avoid the subject of Jack Spencer entirely because she didn't understand herself why she felt so ambivalent where he was concerned.

Instead of giving Joe more food for thought by continuing to protest, she teased him instead. "If you say another word," she threatened cheerfully, "I will make my special cheese cake tonight, invite Jack Spencer instead of you to eat it, and never have a qualm of conscience about depriving you of your favorite dessert. So hush. *Hush!*" she added more fervently when Joe opened his mouth to say something else.

Joe closed his mouth. His eyes were alive with words, but he remained silent until Emma stood on the other side of his threshold.

"I'm very sorry you can't come to my party, Joe," Emma said with an unusual amount of polite dignity in her voice. "But that's the breaks. Good night. Have a nice trip to New York." And she began to walk away.

Joe waited until she'd taken three steps before the words burst out of him. "Can I watch while you give Jack *his* invitation?" he asked, and when Emma turned her head to look at him, he nodded his head toward the pink envelope Emma carried in her hand. "I'd like to see a vice cop's reaction when he gets handed a pink invitation to a Valentine's Day Party."

Emma saw his point. And immediately wondered if it was such a good idea after all to invite Jack Spencer to her party.

"What makes you think I even intend to invite him?" she asked coolly. "I never said I was going to, did I?"

"Isn't that his name on that card?" Joe drawled. He knew it was. He'd glimpsed the card earlier.

Emma turned the card where Joe couldn't see the name on it. "Not necessarily," she said lightly. "Maybe this is just a card I had left over."

Joe would have argued the point, but he didn't have to because at that moment, Jack Spencer stepped into the hallway and headed straight for them, smiling a greeting.

Joe grinned. "Hey, Jack!" he called delightedly. "You're just in time. Emma has an invitation to a party to give you."

"Great," Jack said. "I'm always up for a party."

Emma wondered if that were true, considering that it was a Valentine's party. She watched his face carefully after she handed him the pink invitation and while he was reading it. She could have killed Joe when it became apparent that Jack was going to make an excuse not to attend the party.

"I'm sorry," he said regretfully. "I have to work an assignment that night."

Emma shrugged offhandedly. "That's too bad," she said simply. "Joe can't come, either."

She glanced at her friend then, and was grimly amused by the look of chagrin on his face. She knew he was genuinely sorry to have put her in the position of being embarrassed.

"Well, I've got to get home," Emma said lightly. "See you two later." And she quickly walked away and entered her apartment.

Jack stared after her. The fact that Joe wasn't going to be at her party made him wish even more that he could have gone himself. But then he glanced at Joe and felt guilty over his thought. Damn it, he was a nice guy.

"I hate to disappoint her," Joe said.

"Me, too," Jack agreed. "But it can't be helped."

"You're sure?" Joe persisted. "Isn't there any way you could arrange to be at Emma's party?"

Jack frowned. He was surprised by the note of insistence in Joe's voice. He began to wonder about something.

"Say, Joe," he said slowly. "Maybe I'm talking out of turn...but I sort of had the idea you and Emma were involved."

"Involved? You mean as in lovers?" Joe responded, managing to sound surprised.

Jack nodded.

Joe shook his head, smiling. "Hell no, Jack—Emma and I are just really good friends."

Jack immediately felt a strong wave of relief. But hadn't he just recently decided it would be best if he steered clear of women for a while? So why was he reacting this way to the news that Emma was apparently as free as he was?

"Well..." he said. He couldn't think of anything else to say.

Joe's smile broadened. "I guess you're even sorrier now that you can't go to Emma's party, right?"

He was right, but Jack wasn't ready to admit it. "I'd have liked to have gone," he said in a casual way.

Joe nodded. ''I think she would very much have liked for you to be there, too,'' he said in a neutral tone.

Jack got the message loud and clear. And as he looked at his new friend, he began wondering if it really was too soon to get involved with another woman. But the next moment his thoughts turned around and he found himself unexpectedly feeling a little gun-shy. Janice wasn't the first woman who'd broken up with him because of his job.

After Joe left, Jack stood in the hallway, feeling undecided. *I owe Emma a dinner anyway. One dinner can't hurt,* he thought, as he stared at Emma's closed door.

Conveniently ignoring the fact that he owed Joe a dinner as well, Jack abruptly swung away from the door of his own apartment and headed for Emma's instead.

Chapter Four

"Hi," Jack greeted Emma cheerfully, when he saw the expression on her face after she opened her door.

"Oh...hi," Emma responded. She had been so sure it was Joe at the door coming to apologize to her for what he'd done in the hallway that she was having a little trouble adjusting her expression from one of stern chastisement into something more friendly.

"Have you had dinner?" Jack asked.

"Not yet." To Emma's surprise, her heart rate began to speed up a bit in anticipation of the invitation she was sure Jack was about to extend.

"Do you like Chinese food?"

Emma nodded.

"Then why not come out with me to eat?" he suggested. "There's a good Chinese restaurant on the Plaza."

"Well . . . sure. Let me get my coat."

When she came back to the door, Emma almost asked Jack if he was inviting Joe along as well. But as they walked down the hall past Joe's apartment, she got her answer. And again, her heart rate picked up. Emma unconsciously grimaced over her reaction. It was silly to be this excited over a simple dinner date.

Jack saw the look on her face and decided Emma must be upset with him for turning down her party invitation. So as they headed for his car, he poured on the charm. He did such a good job that by the time they reached the restaurant, he was gratified to see that her mood had changed.

They ordered their food and after the waiter left the table, Jack looked over at Emma and smiled.

"I really am sorry I can't come to your party," he said, projecting honest sincerity into his voice. "But my job's not always an eight-hour-a-day proposition."

Emma shook her head. "Don't worry about it," she said lightly. "What sort of assignment do you have that you can't come?" she asked, her curiosity stirring.

Jack hesitated.

At seeing his reaction, Emma quickly backed off. "Never mind," she said. "I didn't realize it might be something you can't talk about."

Ordinarily he didn't take the chance of discussing with a civilian a case that was in progress, but he liked Emma's refusal to pry. Janice had always wanted to know every little detail of his day's work, and he'd gotten tired of having to give her blow-by-blow descriptions.

"If you'll keep it to yourself, I'll tell you," he offered.

"I wouldn't tell anybody something you told me in confidence," she said, "but if you feel uncomfortable about discussing your work with me, don't do it."

"I don't feel uncomfortable," he answered, and was surprised to note that he was telling the truth. He told her about the Suave Escort Service and what he hoped to prove against Tony Caro.

"Of course, it would be better if I were working with a female operative on this," he finished. "Then we'd have her testimony if Tony tried to blackmail her with the stock scheme he's running. But there's no one available to work with me on this. So after I'm able to get a look at the list of Tony's clients, I'll just have to contact each of them and hope one of them might be willing to testify in court. And that isn't going to be easy. If they're being blackmailed, chances are they're not going to be willing to testify in open court."

Emma had listened intently to every word Jack spoke. Now she shook her head. "I can't imagine women contacting a service like that. Why do they do it?"

Jack looked at Emma's pretty face and smiled. "I don't imagine you have any trouble finding dates," he said softly, "but some women aren't so lucky. Consequently they're lonely enough to do just about anything. Or maybe some of them are looking for the same kind of illicit excitement that makes men patronize prostitutes. Or it could be that some of them have husbands who are having some difficulties in the bedroom. Maybe the women love their husbands and don't want an affair, but they are also sexually frustrated. They may think the escort service is a way to take care of their needs without any unpleasant complications." He shrugged. "There are probably lots of different reasons they do it."

Emma blinked. "Well," she finally said hesitantly, "I guess men have done that for centuries. I just never thought women's liberation would go quite that far." And then she frowned and added indignantly, "But since it has, I suppose it's inevitable that some unscrupulous male would find a way to take advantage of the situation."

Jack shrugged. "It's been my experience that both sexes are capable of unscrupulous behavior," he commented mildly. He had nothing against women's liberation, but his experience as a cop had taught him that some women could victimize others just as readily as some men could.

Emma glanced sharply at him for a second, then relaxed. She considered herself a feminist, but she wasn't such a fanatic that she couldn't recognize the truth of Jack's statement.

The waiter brought their dinner, and as they were eating, Emma was thinking. She couldn't see how Jack was going to get any of the women who had used the Suave Escort Service to testify, especially if they were married women. And even single women wouldn't welcome the sort of unpleasant publicity that might arise from their being involved in such a case. There could be unwelcome repercussions in their business or personal lives. Men who patronized prostitutes were seldom anxious to have that fact become public, though the humiliation they suffered as a result of exposure, even in these so-called liberated days, probably wasn't as harsh as it would be for a woman who did the same and was exposed.

Emma couldn't imagine doing what Suave's female clients had obviously done. But even so, she despised the idea that someone like Tony Caro was blackmailing and harassing women simply because, out of loneliness or unhappy personal circumstances, they'd used poor judgment.

Sure, part of the purpose of women's liberation was to give women the opportunity to exercise their own judgment, whether it turned out to be poor or not, just as men always had. But though women's liberation had made great strides, it seemed to Emma that it was still far too common for women to come out on the short end of the stick. They'd always been victimized as prostitutes, and that was still happening, regardless of women's lib. And even now that they had the dubious freedom of turning the tables, at least in the case of the Suave Escort Service, they were being victimized again. It made Emma plain mad.

"Jack," she finally said thoughtfully, "if you found someone to help you who wouldn't mind testifying, would it get the case thrown out of court if the woman admitted she'd set out to help you?"

Jack frowned, and an uneasy suspicion took hold of him. "You mean, would it be considered entrapment?" he asked.

Emma nodded.

Jack's frown deepened. "I doubt it," he said. "The FBI has used private citizens for this kind of thing, and the cases stood up in court." He paused, then added, "And I presume it was a private citizen you were thinking of having help me?"

"Actually," she said slowly, making up her mind as she went along, "I was thinking of volunteering myself."

Jack immediately shook his head. "No way," he said firmly.

Emma frowned at how emphatic he sounded. "Why not?" she asked.

"For one thing," he said, "you've got a reputation to protect. How many parents would want to send their kids to a nursery school where the owner patronizes a place like the Suave Escort Service?"

"That's why I asked if it could be brought out in court that I was working with the police and wasn't a real customer of Suave's," Emma pointed out. "I'm as anxious to protect my reputation as you are."

"And for another thing," Jack went on, "Tony Caro's too dangerous for someone like you to push. Who knows what he might do to keep you from testifying?"

Emma paused with her fork halfway to her mouth. "Well, there is that to be considered," she said in an alarmed tone. She hadn't thought about such a possibility.

Jack nodded firmly.

Emma slowly took the bite and chewed it without tasting it. She didn't like the idea of having someone like Tony Caro mad at her. On the other hand, the idea of such intimidation being used against people to keep them from testifying made her even angrier than she'd been before.

"What if," she asked a second later, "I gave a false name and address to the escort service. You could set up a phony telephone number for me, couldn't you? That way Tony wouldn't know who I was until I had my day in court, and then it would be too late for him to try to stop me from testifying."

Jack was astonished by her proposal...and alarmed. "Emma, what is this?" he asked, frowning. "This kind of thing is nothing to play around with. It may seem exciting on the surface, but it's too dangerous for the glamour to last very long."

Emma stared at Jack. "Exciting?" she repeated. "You think I'm offering to do this because I want some excitement in my life?"

Jack recognized from the tone in her voice that he was on dangerous ground.

"No...no..." he protested. "I didn't mean that. I just meant that to a civilian, police work may seem more...ah..."

"Exciting," Emma provided the only appropriate word.

"Just forget it, Emma," he said, shaking his head. "I'm sorry I mentioned the whole thing."

"Jack, I'm not anxious to put my life in danger. But I was brought up to be public spirited. My father was the mayor for years of the little town where I grew up, my mother volunteered for organizations that were in the community's interest, and I have a brother who went to West Point and is a captain in the Army. My family believes in civic duty."

For a minute Jack actually found himself considering her offer. Then he shook his head, annoyed with himself for even thinking of putting his job above her welfare.

"No way," he said firmly.

"But if we handled this properly, I wouldn't have to be in any danger," Emma persisted. She hesitated, then added, "And actually it isn't only that I consider it everyone's civic duty to cooperate with the police in putting someone like Tony Caro out of business. There's more to my desire to help you than that."

"Oh?" Jack raised his eyebrows.

Emma shrugged. "It particularly makes me mad that he's victimizing women."

Half afraid that she was one of those fanatical women's libbers who wore blinders where her own sex was concerned, Jack answered cautiously.

"The women who patronize Suave for the express purpose of paying for sex have to be aware that what they're doing is illegal, Emma. I don't see that it's any worse for them to have to pay for their mistakes than it is for men in the same situation."

Emma got a stubborn look on her face. "I'm aware that what those women have done is as illegal as it is for men to do it," she said shortly.

"But?" Jack knew there was more.

"But it seems to me that women are more vulnerable than men are," Emma went on, frowning at Jack. "I live alone, and I know some of the difficulties women face being on their own."

"Such as?" Jack kept his voice neutral.

Emma glared at him. "Well, for one thing, when there's something wrong with the car and you take it in to a shop, do the mechanics try to snow you into believing it needs everything done short of constructing a new chassis for it?"

At that, Jack smiled. "Hey," he said, his voice softly teasing. "I never worked as a mechanic in my life. In fact, I barely know the difference between a spark plug and a battery. So don't blame me for the shortcomings of the mechanics of the world."

Emma's tone softened, and then she smiled. "Okay. But though I think the women who've used Suave ought to have their heads examined, I guess I still feel a certain sense of responsibility toward them. They may have done a dumb thing, but they're still part of the sisterhood. There but for the grace of God go I and all that sort of thing. And that's really why I offered to help."

Jack was relieved by Emma's change of mood, but he still didn't feel comfortable with the idea of letting her help him on the case, which made him wonder what was really going on inside himself where Emma was concerned. He had a pretty good idea that if another woman had offered him this golden opportunity, he might have been naturally concerned for her welfare, but he would have accepted her proposal in an instant. But his protective feeling toward Emma seemed to be out of the ordinary.

"Well, thanks, Emma. It was great of you to offer, but I can't do it," he said, shaking his head. "So let's just forget it, okay?"

There was something in his tone of voice that made her look at him thoughtfully. "You can't or you won't?" she asked, her voice quiet.

"I won't," he admitted softly, holding Emma's gaze with his own, "not where *your* safety is concerned."

The look in Jack's brown eyes, and the meaning of his words, made Emma's heart rate speed up again. She didn't say anything immediately, but she didn't look away, either . . . at least not for a long, rather meaningful moment.

"Would you if I were someone else?" she finally couldn't resist asking.

Jack didn't answer. He'd gone as far as he was willing to go for the time being. But his look answered for him.

Jack's expression made Emma feel ambivalent. On one level, his protective attitude warmed and excited her. But on another level, it annoyed her.

"That's rather a paternalistic attitude, isn't it?" she asked, careful to keep her tone controlled.

"Am I about to receive a more detailed women's liberationist lecture than I've already gotten?" he asked forlornly.

"That depends on whether you're a male chauvinist," she said.

"I'm not," Jack said. "I've worked with a lot of policewomen, and I respect them." He paused, then added, "But you're not a trained policewoman. That's the point."

He was right. Therefore, Emma didn't pursue the subject any longer. But now she was unsure whether Jack was refusing her help because he viewed her as a member of the weaker sex and felt protective of her, or whether it was because she was an untrained civilian.

Jack thought it was time they changed the topic. "How's Johnny doing?" he asked. "Still active with his con schemes?"

"Yes," Emma said with a smile. "Have you thought of any way to head him toward the straight and narrow road yet?"

"Not yet, but I will." He then asked Emma to tell him more about her nursery school.

She couldn't imagine that Jack was really all that interested in a nursery school, but she chatted amiably about her own work for a while, then asked him to tell her more about his.

He talked about a stint he'd done as an undercover narcotics agent. "It's hard to do that kind of work for very long, though," he said with a dismissive shrug. "You can start losing touch with reality and begin to think the whole world is a cesspool. So I wasn't sorry when I was offered something else."

As they talked, both became more and more aware that something was happening between them. Jack found Emma increasingly attractive the longer they were around each other. Later, when he pulled his car into the apartment parking lot, though neither of them was yet ready to openly admit what was happening between them, neither of them made an immediate move to get out of the car either.

"I thought you were involved with Joe Truman," Jack finally said.

Emma looked at him and debated about giving up what she considered her ace in the hole. But then she decided she was being silly. She might have ambivalent feelings about Jack, but she was an adult, not an adolescent who needed someone to protect her from herself.

"Joe?" she said. "You thought I was dating him?"

Jack nodded.

"We're just friends," she said.

"I know. Joe told me that tonight."

At hearing that, Emma was relieved she hadn't lied about her relationship with Joe. But following on the heels of her relief came a sort of nervous wariness. Her heart was misbehaving again. "How did the subject come up?" she asked.

Jack turned in his seat to face her. "I wanted to know," he said softly. "So I asked." He then reached over and ran his finger lightly down Emma's cheek.

She would never have believed so light a touch could have such a startling effect on her equilibrium. But suddenly she couldn't catch her breath and she was afraid to speak. If she said anything, she was sure her voice would reveal how disturbed Jack's touch had made her feel.

But then he leaned forward and turned her face toward his. When she was looking into his eyes, he closed the distance between them and kissed her as lightly as he had touched her cheek.

As far as Emma was concerned, Jack stopped kissing her all too soon. When he drew back, she opened her eyes and stared at him for a long moment, her expression enchanted.

"It's getting cold out here," Jack said softly. He was pleased by the effect he seemed to be having on Emma. But at the same time, he wasn't sure if he was happy about the effect she was having on him. He wasn't feeling as confident with Emma as he normally did with a woman. His breakup with Janice was making him wonder whether he was ever going to find a woman who could accept his job. "Let's go in," he suggested.

Though she didn't feel in the least cold, Emma nodded and climbed out of the car, wondering if Jack was going to want to come in when they reached her apartment. She didn't know whether she wanted to extend the evening with him or not. Wouldn't it be better to give herself a chance to think things over before encouraging him?

After opening her door, she turned to him, not quite sure what to say. And then her mouth opened, seemingly on its own, and she heard herself ask, "Would you like to come in for coffee?"

Jack was pleased by the invitation, and he smiled. "I would like to, yes," he answered. "But we both have to get up early in the morning. Maybe we can do this again this weekend, though?"

Emma was both relieved and disappointed. "Yes," she said. "Maybe we can."

"Good night, Emma," Jack said very softly.

"Good night, Jack."

He told himself he should leave well enough alone. But the next thing he knew, he had leaned forward and fastened his mouth on Emma's. He did manage to keep from putting his arms around her, but the kiss still turned out to be more ardent than he'd intended.

Emma kissed him back. And again she was disappointed when the kiss seemed to end too soon. But the look in his eyes before he turned away to walk down the hall made up for the brevity of his kiss.

EMMA WAS AT HER DESK thinking about Jack and staring into space when her assistant Megan interrupted her thoughts.

"What?" Emma came abruptly back to the present.

"I just thought you might like to know that Molly and Susan are having a knock-down-and-drag-out fight over whose turn it is to ride in the wagon and whose it is to pull it," Megan said mildly.

Emma then became aware of the fight going on between the two little girls who had been putting on their coats to go outside and play. It was more a screaming fight than a physical one, and Emma wondered how she could have been deaf to the goings-on. She sighed and looked at her young assistant in a long-suffering manner.

"You don't remember whose turn it is?" she asked. But she knew the answer before Megan shrugged goodnaturedly and smiled. She was not the most organized assistant, but she was exceptionally patient with children and had a loving heart.

"Okay," Emma said as she got up from her chair. "I'll settle it."

When she couldn't get a straight answer from either Molly or Susan to decide whose turn it actually was, Emma resorted to the short-or-long straw method of decision making, then accompanied Megan and all the children out to the play yard.

It was cold, but the sun was shining, and as Emma walked around monitoring the children's play, she couldn't help thinking about Jack and the way she'd reacted to his kisses. She wished he hadn't kissed her at all until they'd gotten to know each other better... or at least until she'd figured out why she felt so uncertain about him. Part of her wanted to run toward him and the other half wanted to back away fast—before it was too late.

Emma frowned at that thought. Too late for what? She'd had relationships with men before that hadn't worked out. But she wasn't afraid of falling in love again. That was just part of life. So what made Jack different? His job?

Despite what she'd said to Joe about it being unwise to get involved with a police detective, she didn't think Jack's job was the real problem. Though she was reluctant to admit it, Emma had the feeling the real dilemma was that she sensed she could come to care about Jack more than she ever had about any of the men in her past. Therefore, there might be more at stake here than another simple plunge into romance.

Emma also worried about Jack's seemingly chauvinist attitude. He said he didn't have any problems working with women, but did he really want a liberated one in his personal life?

The matter played on Emma's mind throughout the day, and by the time she got home she knew what she was going to do and was sure she was doing it for the right reasons. She had made up her mind the night before to help nail Tony Caro. But when Jack had refused her help, hadn't she been just a little too relieved not to have to get involved after all? Hadn't she used Jack's refusal as a convenient excuse not to have to back up her convictions with courage and action?

It wasn't up to Jack to decide whether or not she did the right thing. It was up to her own conscience. And if while following her conscienc she also found out Jack wasn't the sort of man who could appreciate a woman with strong convictions and the courage to act on them in spite of his disapproval, that was all right, too. Things hadn't gone far enough between them yet for his attitude to hurt her.

After closing her apartment door behind her that evening, the second thing Emma checked after making sure Oscar was still in his cage was the telephone book. And after finding the number for Suave Escort Service, she dialed it with a decidedly nervous, yet grimly determined look in her eyes.

"WHAT'S UP?" Jack said when Tony Caro finally called him.

"I gotta date for you," he grunted.

"When?"

"Valentine's. Some dame wants you to be her escort at a party she's givin' that night."

"Great."

"You're supposed to show up at her place at seven sharp," Tony said. "Here's the address."

When Jack heard the address, he had to grit his teeth to keep from voicing a curse of shock. It was Emma's apartment Tony was talking about!

"What's her name?" Jack asked, trying not to sound as grim as he felt.

"Josephine Truman," Tony answered. "You know the name?"

At that Jack's grimness faded slightly to humor. "No...never heard of her," he said. "Why?"

"She described what kinda guy she wanted, and it fit you perfectly," Tony said.

Jack thought he heard a hint of suspicion in Tony's voice, so he made sure he sounded puzzled when he answered.

"What do you mean?" he said. "What'd she say?"

"She was definite about wantin' a brown-haired, brown-eyed, well-built guy 'bout six feet tall who had manners enough to fit in with her crowd."

"Huh," Jack said, projecting bafflement. "Well, I never heard of her. I don't hang around that part of town."

"Didn't figure you did," Tony answered sarcastically. "If you had that kinda money, you wouldn't be workin' for me."

"Hell, no," Jack said agreeably.

"Well, get yourself over there on time," Tony instructed, "and while you're there, look around a little."

"Look around for what?" Jack said in a puzzled tone as he glanced at the tape recorder to make sure the conversation was being recorded.

"See if the dame lives like she's got money to invest, for example," Tony said.

"How come?" Jack asked, though he knew the answer perfectly well.

"Never mind...just do what you're told, and report back to me when you got the lady satisfied," he growled in an intimidating manner, and then slammed the phone down.

Jack sat back in his chair shaking his head. He didn't know whether to be furious with Emma or to admire her gumption. She'd taken a chance, though. What if there had been another male escort working for Suave who fit his description? She might have been in for a real shock when she opened her door Valentine's night.

Jack toyed with the idea of waiting until the last minute, then calling Tony on Valentine's night and saying he was sick. But there was too much of a chance Tony could come up with another escort to send to Emma's.

Still shaking his head, Jack decided he had no choice but to go through with the scenario Emma had set up. But he was damned sure going to give her a piece of his mind before he did!

As EMMA STOOD WATCHING her young students drag their parents around the room to gaze at their artistic ventures tacked on the walls, she was glad her nursery school open house just happened to fall on the night after she had called Suave. She had a pretty good idea Jack was camped on her doorstep at this very moment, and she didn't think he was awaiting her arrival with flowers and candy. It would be better to have their discussion about what she'd done another time—after he cooled down.

It was lucky Joe had left for New York already, too, and wouldn't be back until the sixteenth. She didn't know whether he would appreciate her giving out his address and telephone number as her own to the man who had answered the phone at Suave. But surely he would be a good sport about it when she told him. He would particularly like the fictitious name she'd chosen for herself. Joe had a marvelous sense of humor. But even if he wasn't understanding in this particular situation, he owed her one for pulling that dirty trick about Jack's invitation in the hallway.

"Miss Springer?"

Emma came out of her thoughts and gave her attention to Mrs. Farrow, Susan's mother.

"Yes?" she answered, smiling.

"I don't mean to put you on the spot, but don't you think Susan's clay figures are a cut above the other children's?" Mrs. Farrow was speaking softly so no one else could hear, and her blue eyes gleamed with the light of a parent who thought she had a budding female Michelangelo on her hands.

"Susan always tries hard and does her best," Emma responded tactfully.

Mrs. Farrow nodded with satisfaction as though Emma had concurred wholeheartedly with her own evaluation of her daughter's talent.

"I'm thinking about giving her art lessons," the woman confided. "Don't you think that's a good idea? I mean, if Susan does have unusual artistic abilities, don't you think early training will help her?"

"Has Susan said she'd like to have art lessons?" Emma asked.

Mrs. Farrow looked surprised. "Why, no," she answered reluctantly. "But I thought . . . I mean . . ."

"Isn't Susan already taking tumbling, music lessons and—"

"Are you saying we're pushing Susan too hard?" Mrs. Farrow interrupted, starting to bristle a little.

Emma hesitated, then gently suggested, "Why don't you ask Susan if she'd like art lessons? And if she doesn't feel all that interested right now, there's no real reason to push it for the time being, is there? She does have a rather heavy schedule for a little girl her age,

Mrs. Farrow. And I think she'll get more out of her extra studies and try harder if she's learning something she's really interested in. Don't you?''

Mrs. Farrow grudgingly agreed, then moved off to inspect Susan's clay figures again as though trying to decide if they really showed the talent she had thought they did at first look.

All in all, the evening went well. Almost everyone—except for Johnny Brubaker's father, as usual—had showed up for the open house.

Emma was pleasantly tired when everyone left. Upon arriving at her apartment building, she was relieved not to find Jack waiting outside her door in order to rake her over the coals. Nevertheless, she was careful to make less noise than usual as she let herself in.

Safely inside, she grimaced, feeling both amused and irritated at having to skulk home silently like a criminal. But she was much too tired to endure a scene with an angry policeman this night. In fact she thought she might conveniently remain too tired for such a scene until the night of her Valentine party. By then Jack surely would have cooled off. And even if he hadn't, he wouldn't take her to task in front of all her friends at a social occasion.

But remembering Jack's lack of social grace the first night she'd met him, Emma frowned and had second thoughts. Jack Spencer, she feared, might be capable of almost anything.

IT WASN'T UNTIL JACK GLANCED at Joe's door as he passed it that evening that he realized Emma had not only appropriated Joe's name when she'd called Tony

Caro—she'd appropriated Joe's apartment number as well.

Well, that's something at least, Jack thought irritably. *And I've got what she's doing documented in the file and cleared with the lieutenant, so she ought to come out of this with her reputation intact, anyway. But that's the last time I ever tell Emma Springer about any case I'm working on! Who would have thought the woman would jump in with both feet and thumb her nose at me in the process!*

He dumped his coat in his own apartment, then went next door to Emma's and knocked. There was no answer.

She's probably afraid to face me, Jack thought, and he immediately wavered between wanting to reassure her that he wasn't mad as hell over what she'd done, and wanting to shake her silly.

Back in his apartment, he looked up her number and dialed it. But she didn't answer the phone, either.

Jack hung up and stared into space a moment. Then he slowly began to smile. Most women he knew wouldn't appreciate being woken at six in the morning. But under the circumstances, he thought Emma deserved it.

Chapter Five

Only half awake as usual, Emma opened the door to get her morning paper. She nearly jumped out of her skin when she found Jack standing there, his hand ready to knock. When her heart settled down again, she frowned, peered at him blearily and automatically lifted a hand to smooth her tangled hair.

"Looking for this?" Jack held out the paper he'd picked up from her doorstep. He was feeling very pleased with himself. Emma's awkward, fumbling attempt to smooth her hair confirmed his opinion that she wasn't a woman who enjoyed having a man see how she looked first thing in the morning. Revenge was sweet. So sweet that he wasn't about to tell her she looked sexy enough to eat, even with her hair tousled and eyes bleary.

"Yes, thank you," Emma mumbled. She reached to take the paper from him, hoping he was going to go away. But he held the paper out of her reach.

"Why don't you invite me in for a cup of coffee?" he suggested in a falsely amiable tone.

The idea dismayed Emma. It was bad enough that Jack had seen what a mess she looked first thing in the morning. If she let him in, he was sure to want to talk about what she'd done, and she never felt up to discussing anything with anybody first thing after waking—especially if the discussion was apt to turn acrimonious.

"I don't have any coffee made," she lied. "And I'm not ready for company at this hour of the—"

"I'll make the coffee then," Jack interrupted as he began to move forward, forcing Emma to step back into her apartment. Noting that her frown was wobbling toward a glare, he again felt satisfied. One thing he'd found out in his years of police work was that catching someone he wanted to question first thing in the morning tended to net him more information than after they'd had time to get their wits about them.

"Jack, I don't . . ." Emma's voice died as he passed her and headed for the kitchen. She slammed the door shut, followed him into the kitchen, and was not the least bit embarrassed when he discovered that she'd been lying about the coffee.

"Ah," Jack said, smiling as he reached into the cabinet for two cups. "You must have forgotten you'd already made coffee. Have a little trouble concentrating early in the morning, do we?"

"Not usually," Emma replied sullenly. "It's just that I don't *like* to concentrate first thing in the morning."

Jack was pouring coffee into the two cups. "Well, I won't stay long," he promised in a pleasant tone. He picked up the two full cups, set them down on the kitchen table, then looked at Emma, who wasn't making a move to join him. "Just long enough to find out what the hell you thought you were doing calling Suave behind my back," he added, his tone several degrees less pleasant than it had been.

Emma sighed and shuffled over to one of the kitchen chairs. She sat down and pulled one of the coffee cups toward her. Jack sat down as well, but didn't take his eyes off her. As Emma sipped her coffee, she glanced at Jack over the rim of her cup. He didn't look as friendly now as he had a moment earlier.

"I guess you're mad at me?" she asked, sounding unconcerned.

"I guess I am," Jack said.

Emma propped her cheek on her hand and gazed with sleepy thoughtfulness at Jack's stern expression. "What do you want me to say?" she inquired with mild curiosity.

Jack was taken aback. He had thought Emma might react with angry self-defensiveness or that she might apologize. He hadn't expected her to be so calmly self-contained.

"Why did you do it?" he asked, frowning at her.

Emma shrugged. "I told you my reasons the other night."

"And I told you to forget it," he pointed out. "You seemed to accept my decision at the time, so what happened to make you pull this stunt afterward?"

"Mainly I realized it wasn't up to you to decide," she said simply. Then she looked away from his hard stare and added, "And there were other things that went into my decision that I don't think I want to tell you . . . at least not yet. Maybe not ever."

Now Jack was not only angry, but he was thoroughly puzzled. "You're not making much sense, Emma," he said.

"What do you expect?" she responded amiably. "It's six o'clock in the morning. Maybe you wake up cheerful and alert, but I don't. And that's what you were counting on, wasn't it?''

Jack shook his head. This wasn't turning out at all the way he'd expected. And he was getting distracted by the bodice of Emma's lacy white satin nightgown that showed at the neck of her wooly pink robe. Apparently she opted for slinky luxury in bed and practical warmth out of it.

"Must we argue about this?" Emma asked on a sigh. "Especially at this hour? It's done, Jack, and I'm not going to cancel the date. So whatever you have to say to me is going to be wasted breath."

He was annoyed by her attitude. "I ought to back out on you and have Tony send some other Suave escort to your party," he half threatened.

Emma was alarmed for a moment and then realized Jack wasn't going to do any such thing.

"You won't do that," she predicted.

Of course he wouldn't, but her smugness annoyed him further. "You'd deserve it," he said sourly.

"No more than any other woman would who was trying to help out the local police," Emma responded in a virtuous tone.

Jack sighed. He wasn't going to get the best of Emma and he knew it. But he didn't want to leave the field of their battle totally defeated.

"All right," he said firmly. "I've run it by the lieutenant and he's agreed to accept your help on the condition that you do exactly as I tell you to do."

Emma thought that was a reasonable request. After all, she wasn't a trained policewoman, and even if she were, Jack would probably be calling the shots in that case, too.

"All right," she said. "What are you going to tell me to do?"

Again Jack was surprised. He had expected Emma to protest his authority.

"Well . . . nothing as far as the party is concerned. We'll just handle that as though I'm a guest like any other. But you'll be expected to pay Tony in advance for at least four hours of my time," he added dryly.

"I've already sent him the money," Emma said calmly. "I made it a money order because if I sent him a personal check or used my credit card, he'd obviously see that I gave him a false name."

"Good thinking," he said. "What we'll really be looking for is what Tony does after I tell him you paid me to sleep with you after the party." Jack felt an unworthy sense of satisfaction when his statement obviously made Emma feel uncomfortable. "Of course, you won't have to pay me for sleeping with you out of your own funds," he added with bland magnanimity. "The department will pay for that."

Emma gave Jack a disgruntled look. "That's big of them," she muttered.

He hid a grin. "After I tell Tony about sleeping with you, we're hoping he'll call you and try to blackmail you into investing in his phony stock scheme," he added. Then he frowned. "But he'll be calling Joe's apartment, won't he?" he said.

"That doesn't matter," she said. "I have a key to Joe's apartment. And I've already put my answering machine on Joe's phone to intercept any calls from Tony. I didn't know whether he might call to double-check arrangements or something. Joe's not going to be back until the sixteenth, and if Tony calls before then, I'll get the message off the machine and call him back. If he hasn't called by the time Joe gets home, I'll ask Joe to leave the answering machine on his phone and let me know if Tony calls."

Jack was amazed at how well Emma had thought things out. "How do you think Joe's going to react when he gets home and finds out what you've done?" he asked.

"I hope he'll approve," Emma said. "But even if he doesn't, we're good enough friends that I don't think he'll be too mad at me."

"Then he's a better friend than I'd be," Jack responded dryly.

Emma ignored the dig. "So what do you want me to say if Tony calls me after the party?" she asked.

"Are you a good actress?" Jack inquired.

"I don't know," Emma said. "Why?"

"We'll be taping your telephone conversation with Tony and I want you to act upset and indignant and refuse to go along with his stock scheme at first," Jack explained. "We'll want to see how he handles that. Maybe he's dumb enough to try to blackmail you over the phone, in which case we'll have it on tape and with your testimony, that's all we'll need. But if he's smarter than that, we'll just have to improvise. Under no circumstances, however," he said firmly, holding Emma's eyes with his own, "are you to meet him in person if that's what he wants."

Emma looked away. She didn't want to make such a promise. Though she didn't want to meet Tony in person any more than Jack wanted her to, if that's what it took to nail him, she was willing. After going to this much trouble she didn't want it all to be for nothing.

"Emma?" Alarmed by her hesitancy, Jack prodded her. "Promise me."

She sighed and gave Jack a disgruntled look. "No, I'm not going to promise you that," she said just as firmly as Jack had spoken. But before his temper exploded, she added, "But I will promise not to meet with Tony Caro alone. If it comes to a meeting, I will definitely want you somewhere on the scene."

Jack controlled his anger. Maybe it wouldn't come to a personal meeting. He hoped to hell it didn't.

"All right," he said grudgingly, then glanced at his watch. "I'd better go," he added. He finished his coffee and got up.

Emma walked him to the door. But when she reached for the knob, Jack reached down and closed his fingers lightly around her wrist to stop her. She glanced at him somewhat warily. She hoped he didn't want to kiss her. She wasn't feeling prepared.

Jack hadn't meant to put his arms around Emma, but after touching her he couldn't stop himself.

She resisted slightly. "Jack, I haven't combed my hair or brushed my teeth or anything," she said, trying to object. But her voice faltered when she felt his body against hers. And when she looked up at him, he placed his hand along her cheek so that she couldn't look away again. The look in his eyes squelched her protest for good.

"Did I tell you how great you look in the morning?" Jack murmured. He wasn't in the mood for revenge anymore.

Emma felt skeptical and her expression showed it.

Jack smiled. "You look good enough to eat," he added in a whisper, and then lowered his head and lightly, gently, nibbled her lips.

His breath smelled like coffee, and Emma realized her own probably did as well. That made her more willing to submit when Jack turned the nibbling into a kiss. But she wasn't prepared for her own reaction when his tongue slipped between her teeth and the kiss turned intimate enough to cause a delicious sinking sensation in her stomach.

Jack told himself he should never have started this; now he didn't want to stop. He was becoming too aroused to want to do anything but make love to her. And he didn't have time for that.

Finally he forced himself to lift his head. But when Emma opened her eyes and he saw the dazed sensuality in her gaze, he wanted to kiss her again. He knew better, though, than to act on what he wanted. He didn't want to hurry when they did make love. And he was going to make love to her soon, he decided.

"I have to get to work," he said huskily. "Otherwise..." He didn't say anything more. He didn't have to.

Emma swallowed and told herself to stop behaving like a high-school girl.

"Of course you do," she said shakily. "So do I."

"May I come over this evening?" Jack asked softly.

She almost said yes. But then she remembered that she was supposed to be getting to know Jack better before she got in over her head with him. After the effect of the kiss they'd shared, she was afraid to be alone with him, however.

"Ah...why don't I call you later on today?" she said vaguely. "I think I have something to do, but I can't think what it is for the moment. I'll have to check my appointment book at school."

Jack hid a smile. He had a pretty good idea why Emma was stalling. And maybe she was right to want to slow things down a little. But hesitation wasn't going to do either of them any good, and he was in favor of getting on with things himself. However, he didn't tell her that. There wasn't time for such a discussion at the moment.

"I'll call *you*," he promised.

"Okay," Emma replied.

A couple of minutes after he left, Emma shakily decided she definitely faced a dilemma. How was she going to get to know Jack better if she didn't spend time alone with him? But if she spent too much time alone with him, they were going to end up in bed before her head had decided that was the wise thing to do.

Maybe the answer was to spend time with Jack in *safe* places, which meant any location where they couldn't be alone together for too long.

"TENNIS? You want to play tonight?" Jack had pictured Emma and himself sharing a romantic dinner for two followed by a cozy evening of lovemaking.

Emma was glad they were speaking on the phone so that Jack couldn't see the wry smile on her face. She had a pretty good idea what he had had in mind for their date that evening.

"What's the matter?" she asked innocently. "Don't you know how to play?"

"Barely," Jack responded unenthusiastically. "Let's put it this way. I don't think Jimmy Connors would consider me a worthy opponent."

"That's all right," she said lightly. "I'm not an expert, either. I just play for exercise and fun."

Jack sighed. He could think of a much better way to obtain exercise that was a lot more fun than tennis. But obviously she wasn't ready for his idea of a good workout yet.

"I have a membership at a club on State Line," she said. "Do you know the one I mean?"

"Yes." Jack's tone was even less enthusiastic. The club Emma belonged to was pretty ritzy for his blood—and his salary.

"Can you meet me there at five o'clock?" she proposed. "After we play tennis, we can have dinner."

"Uh-huh... fine," Jack agreed.

"Great. See you then. I've got to go. Megan's losing control of the children."

After hanging up, Jack sat for a few moments thinking about Emma. If the way he had felt this morning while kissing her was any indication, a relationship with her might turn out to be more serious than any he'd had previously with a woman.

What if he really fell in love with Emma—the kind of love he knew he hadn't actually experienced yet—and it turned out she couldn't cope with his job? What was he letting himself in for? Wouldn't it be better if he found out how she was going to react to his work before he got in over his head? Maybe she was right to set up tennis dates rather than let things get out of control between them too quickly.

But then Jack shrugged his cautious attitude away. Sure, he could see the advantages of taking things more slowly with Emma. But he wasn't going to be able to resist taking things faster if she would let him, and he knew it. So he might as well accept that he was going to let nature take its course and be prepared to pay the consequences, if it turned out he had to.

DESPITE THE FEBRUARY CHILL in the air, other men on the courts played in their dainty white shorts. Jack didn't feel embarrassed about playing in a pair of nondescript sweats he kept at the station, however, because Emma, claiming it was too cold for shorts, had on a sweatsuit as well.

It turned out they were well matched. Jack didn't play as well as other men Emma had been matched against, but he played well enough to give her a good game. Jack won the last set, and laughing, Emma came to the net to congratulate him.

"See what I mean about Jimmy Connors?" he said, grinning at her.

"Who cares?" Emma shrugged, panting a little. "I'm no Jimmy Connors, and you're just right for me."

She meant Jack was just right as far as tennis went. But her unfortunate—or fortunate—choice of words brought a look into Jack's brown eyes that did nothing to help Emma get her breath back.

After a long moment, she came back to reality. "Are you ready to eat dinner?" she asked.

"Sure," Jack said, nodding. "But is it okay to go into the dining room in these clothes?"

Emma suddenly realized that Jack might be feeling worried about how much dinner might cost in a place like this. It wasn't all that expensive here, but she didn't want him to feel uncomfortable, so she made another suggestion.

"It's all right, but you know what? Ever since you suggested we eat at that little restaurant in Fairway the other night, I've been hungry for their chicken fried steak. Why don't we go there instead?"

Jack felt relieved. He wanted to concentrate on Emma exclusively, with no distractions, and that was easier to do in a familiar place.

After he agreed with her suggestion, Emma said, "I'll follow you in my car, all right?"

Jack felt a little disgruntled at having to separate. He wanted her with him. But as he pulled out on State Line, then turned left at the intersection to drive the short distance to the Fairway Shopping Center on the Kansas side, he consoled himself with the thought that it wouldn't be too long before he would be sitting across from Emma.

The restaurant was small, the decor plain and the clientele mostly elderly. The food wasn't fancy, either, but it was tasty and filling.

"Do you come here often?" Emma asked after they'd filled out their orders on a pad at the table, as was the custom at this particular restaurant, and set the sheet where the waitress could pick it up.

"It's the closest I can come to home-cooked food these days."

"Are you from this area, Jack?" Emma asked, curious about his background.

Jack shook his head. "Emporia, Kansas. My dad teaches political science at the college there. But I came here for college because I wanted to stretch my wings and Brad was already here going to law school. We shared an apartment for a while until he graduated and married Nancy."

"What made you choose police work?"

"I took some courses just out of curiosity and got hooked," Jack explained. "And I haven't regretted it. There're some bad sides to my work, but on the whole, it suits me." He quickly changed the subject. "How about you? Where did you grow up?"

"Oh, I'm from a small town near Manhattan, Kansas, you probably never heard of," Emma smiled.

"Did you go to Kansas State?"

Emma nodded. "And shortly before I graduated with a bachelor's in child psychology, my grandmother died and left me some money. I already knew I wanted to run a nursery school, and I wanted to stretch my wings, too, so I came to Kansas City to start my business."

"You really like kids, then?"

Emma's hazel eyes softened with such warmth that Jack felt a shaft of desire shoot through him clear down to his toes.

"You have to like kids to spend all day with them, Jack," she said smiling. "How about you? Do you like children?"

"I guess. I never thought much about it."

Emma lowered her eyes, wondering what sort of father he would make. That was something she needed to know before she got in over her head with him. And from the way he was looking at her, if he had his way, she would be in over her head before she knew it.

They chatted amiably, filling in details about their pasts, and when they left the restaurant, Jack walked Emma to her car.

He reached up and slid his fingers around her throat, resting them lightly on the back of her neck under her hair. "I'll follow you home," he said softly as he looked deeply into her eyes. "And then I'll make you some coffee at my place."

Though Jack's touch was light, it made Emma feel dizzy. She wanted to lean against his strong, warm body, lift her face and feel his mouth on hers. She wanted him to kiss her the way he had that morning. Swallowing her desire, she obeyed her head instead.

"Oh, I can't go home yet, Jack," she said, forcing her voice to sound normal. "I have to shop for art materials to take to school tomorrow."

Seeing his plans for the rest of the evening begin to fade, Jack frowned. "How long will that take?" he asked.

"Quite a while," Emma assured him. "And then when I get home, I have some preparations to make for tomorrow as well."

Jack stared hard at her innocent expression. He had a good idea what she was doing, but there didn't seem much he could do to change her mind about playing it slow and safe with him. Romantic games were not Jack's style, however. He was inclined toward quick action and blunt confrontation.

"How about tomorrow night?" he asked. "Are you busy?"

Emma looked away. Jack was obviously a man who believed in going ahead full steam. That wouldn't have mattered so much if she were positive that she could stop him. But she wasn't at all sure she could once he put his arms around her and started kissing her.

Then she remembered something. "I have to decorate the apartment, Jack," she said. "For the party. It's set for the night after tomorrow, remember?"

"I'll help you," he promptly offered.

Emma hesitated, wishing fervently that Joe wasn't out of town. If he had been home, she would have invited him to help her decorate as well—and begged him beforehand not to leave her alone with Jack.

"Emma?" Jack prodded.

She sighed. It seemed nothing would work with Jack but to lay her cards on the table. Looking up into his eyes, trying to block out the exquisite sensations his stroking fingers on her neck were causing inside her, she opted for honesty.

"Jack," she said soberly, "if you'll promise decorating my apartment is all you have in mind, I'll be glad to have you come over. But I want to get to know you a lot better before…" Despite her determination to be blunt, she couldn't think of a delicate way to say what she meant.

"Before we end up in bed together?" he said.

Now that the subject was out in the open between them, Emma felt relieved. "Yes," she said matter-of-factly. "That's exactly what I mean."

Jack smiled. "You can always say no if I start to get out of hand," he reminded her softly. "I would never force the issue, Emma."

"That's why I want to take things slowly," she confessed. "I'm not sure I *can* say no to you. So I'd like it if you didn't put me in the position of saying yes before I'm ready to. It would be much better if we got to know each other first, don't you agree?"

Jack was enormously pleased by Emma's admission. He even agreed with her. But that didn't mean he wanted to be bound by such an agreement. However, she was putting him on the spot by appealing to his better nature, and he felt uncomfortably compelled to go along with her wishes…as far as he could.

"Emma," he said. "I don't like to make promises when there's any chance I might break them, so all I'll promise is that I'll try to do what you ask. That's the best I can do."

"Thank you, Jack," she said simply. "In that case come by about six-thirty. I'll make dinner before we decorate."

He was somewhat astonished by Emma's straightforward attitude. Apparently she didn't like game playing any more than he did. And that fact made him feel even more excited and optimistic about where they were headed together in their relationship than he'd felt before.

"I'll be there," he said. "Can I pick up anything for you at the store for dinner?"

"No, I'll stop by the grocer's on my way home from work," she said.

It was time to part, and though the street where they were standing was public, there was no one around at the moment. And Emma, now that she and Jack had discussed what was happening between them, felt less inhibited about following her normal inclinations.

She moved closer to Jack and lifted her mouth a breath away from his, looking searchingly into his eyes.

"Good night," she whispered.

Jack didn't answer. Instead he abruptly pulled her closer and bent his head. Forgetting where they were for the moment, he closed his mouth over Emma's and kissed her as hungrily as he would have had they been in the privacy of one of their apartments.

The desire for him that immediately rose inside Emma convinced her she had been right to get things clear between them. But even so, she was still afraid their previous discussion would count for nothing if Jack couldn't keep his word about doing things her way.

Some people came out of the restaurant behind them, talking and laughing, and Jack reluctantly lifted his head. He held Emma's eyes for a moment, savoring the dazed look of desire shining in the hazel depths.

"You sure you have to go shopping?" he murmured huskily.

All Emma could manage was a nod.

Jack sighed and shook his head. "Emma," he said softly. "As I said...I'll do my best. But waiting seems the stupidest idea anybody ever had considering how we both feel right now."

"Maybe," she allowed. "But five minutes from now, I'm sure I'm going to think it was very wise of me to insist on it."

Jack smiled ruefully. "Well, if a delay will make you feel better, I guess I can handle it." He shrugged fatalistically. "But you do know the time will come—"

"When we're more ready," Emma quickly interrupted.

"I'm already ready."

"Are you really?" Emma gazed at him thoughtfully. "You don't have *any* doubts?"

That silenced Jack for a moment. And then he said, "Not about wanting you."

It was Emma's turn to smile ruefully. "That's not what I meant. Wanting someone is the easy part. I want you, too."

Those last four words sent a shaft of renewed desire through Jack. "Emma..." he said her name, his voice ragged.

"I think I'd better go." She quickly stepped out of his arms. The timbre of desire in Jack's voice had affected her too much for her to feel safe anymore. "Good night," she said as she walked to the driver's side of her car and inserted her key in the lock.

"Good night, Emma," Jack said with dry acceptance in his voice. But inwardly he didn't feel accepting. He felt more frustrated than he could ever recall feeling before. "I'll see you tomorrow night," he added to reassure himself more than to remind Emma of their coming date.

She smiled and nodded, then got behind the wheel and drove away.

THE MOMENT EMMA OPENED HER DOOR to him the next evening, Jack wanted to kiss her. But before he could reach for her, she turned away.

"The steaks are about to burn," she explained over her shoulder as she headed for the kitchen. "Come on in and shut the door behind you."

Jack shrugged and did as he was told. Following her into the kitchen, he stood admiring her flushed cheeks and tousled hair for a second as she rescued the steaks from the broiler. Then he turned his attention to the rest of her. She was wearing charcoal-gray slacks and a white silk blouse, and her clothes emphasized her slim, seductive figure in a way that made him take a deep breath.

"The salad and dressing are ready," she said, nodding in the direction of the refrigerator. "Why don't you get them out and put them on the table. Oh, and get the wine out as well and fill the glasses, I'll have the steaks and baked potatoes there in a moment."

Again Jack did as he was told. But after all the food was on the table, and before Emma could tell him to sit down, he reached for her.

"Jack," she said warningly, trying to step out of his reach. "Remember, you promised—"

"To try," Jack said, taking the extra step that allowed him to pull Emma into his arms. "And I will try. But not right now." And before she could utter another protest, he leaned down and kissed her thoroughly enough that when he finally raised his head, she was in no mood to protest any longer.

Pleased by the look in her eyes and by the lack of resistance in her body as she leaned against his, Jack smiled. "You said you wanted to get to know me," he reminded her softly. "So I thought I'd show you how I like to be greeted when I come home after a hard day's work."

Emma thought that over, then nodded. "You have a point," she said. "It's not a bad way to end the workday and start the evening. I think I'll follow your example." And with that, she reached up and slipped her hands through Jack's thick brown hair, then pulled his head down to hers.

The fervency with which Emma followed his example had Jack feeling a little stunned by the time she stopped kissing him. But when he looked into her eyes and realized she was feeling as stunned as he was, he reached for her again.

"Uh-uh." Emma shook her head and stepped back. Her voice was decidedly unsteady. "Dinner's ready," she reminded him as she moved toward her chair at the table. "We need to eat, and then we decorate the apartment."

Jack sighed heavily. For a moment there, he'd thought he had her willing to forget the promise she'd wrung from him. But she was made of sterner stuff than he'd realized. So he reluctantly sat down. Then he looked across the table and saw Emma smiling at him. There was such warmth in her expression, he was glad he had capitulated as easily as he had.

After they'd filled their plates and begun eating, Emma asked, "Jack, is it true that gambling ensnares people more when they don't lose or win all the time than it does if they did?''

Surprised by the question, he nodded. "Yes, it would lose its fascination for most people if the result was predictable. It works the same way for rats in a maze. If you never reward them for finding the way out, or if you reward them every single time they do, they lose interest in playing the game. Why do you ask?"

"I was thinking of Johnny," Emma explained. "I'm convinced it's the thrill of the deal that fascinates him rather than the reward of actually getting another child's possessions. So I was wondering how I could rig it so that he didn't get any excitement out of his cons anymore."

Jack shrugged. "You mean either have the other kids give in without a struggle every time he wants to make a trade, or completely refuse to trade with him at all?"

Emma nodded. "The only problem is, it's hard to get three-and four-year-old kids to cooperate in a venture like that. I'm not sure they would even understand if I explained to them what I was trying to do, and I'm certain they wouldn't be willing to risk their beloved possessions in the interest of reforming Johnny. They think in terms of the moment, not the long-term."

Jack nodded and smiled. "Yeah, it would have to be something they didn't mind giving up before they'd be willing to cooperate, probably."

"Well, it's a possibility anyway," Emma said. "And if we can't think of anything better, and I start to run out of time, I may try it even if there aren't any guarantees it will work."

"I'm still thinking," Jack agreed, "but I haven't come up with anything so far, either. I haven't given up, though."

"Good," Emma smiled. "So how was your day?"

As Jack was in the process of discussing his day's work, he was surprised when Emma expressed sympathy for the prostitutes he dealt with regularly.

"You feel sorry for them?" he asked, staring at her curiously.

She nodded. "I can't imagine any woman becoming a prostitute because she wants to live that sort of life," she said. "And from what I've heard and read, most of the women are seduced into it by a pimp, aren't they?"

"A lot of them are, yes," Jack agreed. "And you're right. Though there are a few women who do it because they want to—some high-priced call girls, for instance—the type I normally deal with are more trapped than willing. Even if they could get away from their pimps, they don't have many qualifications to make a living any other way."

He paused a moment, shaking his head, his expression grim. "It's the really young ones who bother me the most, both boys and girls," he added. "Maybe they run away from an abusive home or are kicked out by their parents, and they don't have any clear idea of what it's like out on the streets. But they soon find out. There's always someone to teach them how to survive, usually an older man who wants to make money off them. And if they stay in that life too long, pretty soon they aren't kids anymore. They have to turn off their feelings to survive."

"That's sad," Emma said, her gaze troubled. "It must be hard to see that sort of thing every day."

Jack nodded. "It is," he said quietly, liking the fact that Emma seemed to understand without being judgmental. There were a lot of things about Emma that Jack liked. And as he stared thoughtfully at her, it suddenly became clear to him that what might develop between them was too important to risk by acting with blind haste. Reluctantly he decided she was right. As hard as it was going to be to wait, it would be wiser to let her decide when the time was right for them to make love.

They finished dinner, loaded the dishwasher, then started decorating the apartment. Jack clowned around with the decorations, making Emma laugh. She liked his sense of humor.

Afterward they stood back and looked at the colored paper and hearts decorating the room, and Jack shook his head. "Don't we get any valentine boxes like in grade school?" he teased. "I'm in the mood to rush out and buy up every valentine in the store."

"And to whom would you address them?" Emma asked. "You don't know anyone who's going to be at the party other than me."

"So?" Jack shrugged. "You wouldn't mind getting ten or twenty valentines at a crack, would you?"

Emma laughed, not taking him seriously. "Just bring yourself to the party," she said as she started gathering up leftover decorations to put away. "That'll be enough to satisfy me."

Her comment put Jack into an amorous mood again, and he decided if he was going to keep his promise to Emma—and to himself—he'd better go home. He said as much to her.

Startled, Emma looked at him, then sobered as she saw the look in his eyes. "Yes," she agreed reluctantly. "Perhaps it would be best if you went home now, Jack."

"One kiss before I leave?" He smiled and took her in his arms.

"Just one," Emma said softly, though she wasn't sure if she could stick to that rule herself.

Three kisses later, when it became clear to him that she wasn't going to be able to suggest he leave, Jack took it upon himself to let go of her and head for the door. But it wasn't easy.

"Just how slowly do you want things to go between us?" he teased Emma softly as she stood in the doorway, looking up at him with the ambivalence she was feeling reflected clearly in her hazel eyes. "A day, a week, a month...not a *year*, I hope?"

"No," she confessed. "I think I can safely say it won't be that long."

Jack smiled as he reached over and ran a finger lightly down Emma's cheek, making her close her eyes with the pleasure she felt from his touch.

"However long it is," he said quietly before dropping his hand, "it will be way too long for me."

And without waiting for her reply, he turned and walked away. He didn't hear Emma whisper, "It will be too long for me as well, I think."

Chapter Six

Kay Garwood, an old friend, pulled Emma aside halfway through the party and whispered her opinion of Jack.

"He's an absolute hunk," she said, rolling her eyes appreciatively. "Where'd you find him?"

"Next door," Emma responded with a grin.

"Honey, believe me," Kay said dryly. "That one is not the 'boy next door' type."

"What type do you think he is?" Emma asked, interested.

Kay shrugged. "Maybe a little bit Harrison Ford, only better looking."

Emma tilted her head and gazed at Jack objectively. He was trapped by Jim Byers in a corner. Jim sold insurance, and Emma spared Jack a second of sympathy before she went back to trying to figure out if he really resembled Harrison Ford.

After a moment, she decided the only way Jack resembled the actor was that the two shared an aura of toughness.

"You're a little right," she said to Kay.

"And you're a lot lucky," Kay shot back with a grin before angling toward the bar for more wine.

Jack had heard all he ever wanted to know about insurance, and he finally managed to extract himself from Jim Byer's clutches and head for the bar. Picking up two glasses of wine, he headed for Emma, whom he'd seen disappearing into the kitchen. He'd barely had a chance to talk to her all night.

Emma was slicing more French bread for sandwiches and looked up as Jack joined her. She smiled mischievously at him and said, "Signed up for any insurance yet?"

Jack set one of the wineglasses on the table in front of Emma, then leaned down and kissed her neck where it joined her shoulder. She was wearing a V-necked bronze silk blouse and she smelled and looked and tasted delicious.

Jack's kiss sent the sinking sensation with which Emma was rapidly becoming familiar shafting through her stomach, and she had to close her eyes for a moment to regain her equilibrium.

"Not yet," Jack said, smiling, as he lifted his head. "But I have to give Jim points for trying."

"What do you think of my friends?" she asked, pausing in her bread slicing to pick up the glass of wine Jack had brought her and take a sip to give her strength. He was standing so close to her, she could smell his after-shave and almost feel the heat of his body.

"They're nice people," Jack said as he moved to lean his hips against the table and face her. "What do they think of me?"

Emma smiled and her hazel eyes gleamed with warmth and humor as she glanced at him. "I don't know about the men," she responded teasingly, "but most of the women are smitten with you."

Jack nodded, but he wasn't really taking Emma's comment seriously. "Uh-huh," he said. "I was afraid you'd notice how they've been taking turns dragging me off to your bedroom."

Emma's smile turned into a grin. "Maybe I told them you work for Suave," she teased, "and offered them your services on my tab."

Jack rolled his eyes. "Then cut it out," he protested. "A man has only so much strength, you know." He gave Emma a look that raised her blood pressure considerably, and added, "And I'm saving mine to satisfy my real customer . . . after the party."

The kitchen suddenly seemed very warm and Emma unconsciously reached for a napkin to fan her face. She stopped when she saw Jack grinning at her knowingly. Making a face at him, she tossed the napkin back down on the table.

"Well, there's at least one woman here," she informed Jack dryly, "who, if she wasn't already happily married, would really be dragging you off to my bedroom. She thinks you're a hunk . . . says you remind her of Harrison Ford."

Jack gave her a skeptical look. "Harrison Ford?" he repeated, then shook his head. "That's not who I see in the mirror every morning when I shave."

Emma smiled. "I don't see the resemblance, either . . . except for a sort of tough, macho-man aura the two of you share."

Jack laughed at that. "Don't let your imagination run away with you. I may be a cop, but I'm not that tough, and I'm not that macho."

"I'll take your word for it," Emma said mildly, but she thought that Jack might not see himself as clearly as others did.

Having finished slicing the bread, Emma picked up the plate. "Time to get back on the job," she said, crooking her finger at him to join her as she headed for the living room. "I'm not paying you a fortune for four hours work just so you can slouch about in the kitchen pestering the hostess."

Jack sighed. "It's a tough life, this escort business," he commented dolefully as he followed Emma out of the room. "I'd rather be a cop and take my chances getting shot at."

"Count your blessings," Emma snorted. "If there was room in my apartment, you'd be dancing for your pay instead of talking and eating the night away."

THE PARTY WAS OVER, and Emma was satisfied that it had been a success. But as she looked around her living room, she sighed. What a mess!

"I'll help you clean up," Jack offered as he began gathering glasses to take to the kitchen.

"Thanks, but I'll tackle it in the morning," Emma said tiredly.

"No problem," Jack shrugged, and continued clearing up.

Emma helped, and soon the dishwasher was loaded and the apartment was straightened.

"I'll vacuum and dust tomorrow," she said as she collapsed into a chair. "Let's quit for now."

Jack went over, and ignoring Emma's protests, hauled her up from her chair, then sat down on the couch with her on his lap. He touched his mouth to hers in a brief kiss.

With her head on his shoulder, Emma looked into his eyes. She was too tired to argue verbally, but her gaze reminded him of his promise.

"Don't get anxious," Jack said smiling. "I'll go home in a few minutes." He paused, then added, "Though strictly speaking, I haven't earned all I could from you yet."

"You've put in your four hours," Emma said sleepily, and in an absent fashion, she reached up and ran a fingertip over the firm curve of Jack's lips.

Emma's action had an erotic effect on Jack, and without thinking about it, he opened his mouth and took the tip of her finger between his lips.

"Oh, dear," she breathed. "I'm sorry. I shouldn't have done that."

Jack moved his hand to take hold of Emma's and gently pull it away from his mouth. He held on to it as he looked down at her, and though he was smiling, his brown eyes were turning liquid with sensuality.

"I only cost one hundred dollars an hour for extra duties," he murmured. "And the department will pick up the tab, remember?"

Emma's smile was wistful. "Don't tempt me," she teased softly.

"Why not? You tempted me."

"That was an accident. I didn't mean to."

"That's the best kind of temptation," Jack whispered as he lowered his head and began to plant light, drawing kisses on her mouth.

Emma's head was swimming. She struggled, against herself mostly, for some way to keep the kisses from becoming more intimate.

"Surely your pride wouldn't let you take money from a woman?" she chided Jack.

"Depends on the woman," Jack said, then resumed his teasing kisses.

Emma tried to fake a glare. "And what category do I fall in to?" she asked in what was meant to be an accusing tone. It turned out a rather breathlessly inviting one instead. "Free or expensive?"

"Definitely expensive," Jack assured her, and he smothered her protest with one of the intimate kisses Emma had been trying to avoid.

She couldn't seem to find the will to even try to stop Jack from invading her mouth with kiss after kiss. And when he moved his hand from her thigh to her breast, she merely moaned softly in her throat and pressed closer to him.

For a while Jack entirely forgot the promise he'd made Emma. He was lost in the delight of touching her intimately and in her eager responses. Without conscious thought, he soon had both of them stretched out on the couch and was lying half over her, kissing her deeply, one hand stroking her breast, his arousal growing by the second.

And then he made the mistake of raising his head to look into her eyes. He was unaware of the heat in his own gaze, but Emma was. And her response was a deep sigh of acceptance, granting him total submission.

Oddly it was the submission in Emma's gaze that stopped him. It wasn't what he wanted, because he understood that it meant she wasn't deciding for herself; she was reacting to his seductive pressure instead.

"Ah, hell," he sighed frustratedly, and sat up.

Emma sat up as well and looked at him, puzzled.

Jack got to his feet. "Emma," he said, his voice tight with the frustration that rode him, "when you're sure it's time, you come after me. I'll be damned if I'll take all the responsibility! There's too much chance I'll screw things up for both of us if I do."

He turned, headed for the door and pulled it open. He started to leave, then paused, reached in his inside jacket pocket and drew out a small envelope. He set it down on the small table, then left.

Emma sat staring at the closed door for a long moment as she mulled over Jack's words and accepted their meaning in her heart. Then she got up, walked over to the table and picked up the envelope.

Inside was a little valentine...the kind small children give their peers. A chubby, smiling little boy was pictured, and the caption said simply, "Be Mine." Jack had written below it, in capital letters, SOON! But when Emma turned the card over, she saw that he'd written in smaller letters, "However, if it can't be soon, I'll wait. I have the feeling that however long it takes, it's going to be worth it."

AS JACK DROVE to Tony Caro's office the next morning to turn over the money he'd supposedly gotten from Emma, he was in a foul mood. He knew it was immature to cringe at the idea of discussing Emma with a man like Tony. It was just part of the job and didn't mean a thing. But he couldn't help how he felt. He just hoped he could keep himself from decking Tony if the man said anything obscene about her.

When Jack entered the office, Tony was chomping on one of his huge, unlit black cigars and totaling figures on an adding machine. Jack sat down in one of the chairs facing Tony's desk and waited for the big man to deign to recognize his existence.

Finally Tony tore off the long strip of adding tape, glanced at the total, then tossed the paper aside and fixed Jack with a stony gaze.

"How'd ya make out?" he growled.

"Great," Jack answered shortly. He reached inside his coat and drew out four crisp $100 bills, then tossed them onto Tony's desk.

Tony raised his eyebrows, and when he looked at Jack again, there was more respect in his eyes than had been there before.

That look of respect made Jack feel like punching Tony out. But he reminded himself that the values of this man bore no relation whatsoever to those of normal people. Gritting his teeth, he prepared himself to bear with Tony's questions without losing his temper.

"She liked ya, huh?" Tony said as he reached for the bills. Taking two of them, he tossed the other two back in Jack's direction, who leaned forward, picked up the money, folded it and put it back in his pocket.

"How come yer in such a foul mood?" Tony grunted.

"It was a tough night," Jack answered truthfully. After leaving Emma, he hadn't been able to get her out of his mind and had slept badly as a consequence.

"Why? Was the dame old and ugly?" Tony asked.

"No, just particular," Jack said. That, too, was the truth, he figured.

"Well, you musta met her standards since she kept ya four hours," he grunted. "What's her place like?"

"Nice."

"She got money, you think?"

"Enough to live comfortably, apparently."

"What does she do for a livin'?"

Jack thought fast. "She owns a business, I think. I don't know what kind . . . she didn't tell me."

"Well, you done okay for your first time," he unexpectedly complimented Jack. "I ain't got nuthin' for you so far today, but if I do, I'll give you a call."

"Thanks," Jack said, and correctly taking Tony's last comment as a dismissal, he got to his feet and left, taking a deep breath of fresh clean air when he came out of the building.

Back at the office, his fellow cops wanted to know what was happening with his Suave case, and they made their inquiries in their usual ribald manner. They weren't aware as yet that Jack was being assisted by Emma now.

Jack wasn't in the mood for their humor.

"Cut it out!" he said shortly, causing the men to look at one another in surprise. Jack noted the looks and sighed with resignation. "It's coming along, guys," he said in a more amiable tone. "But I've got other things on my mind. So let's forget it right now, okay?"

The men shrugged and went back to their own concerns. Jack sat down at his desk and tried to get his mind off Emma and onto his work.

UPON ARRIVING HOME FROM WORK, Emma stopped by Joe's to check the answering machine before going to her own apartment. And she was both relieved and repelled when, sure enough, there was a message from Tony Caro, speaking in an oily, unctuous tone, asking her to call him back.

Then Emma stopped by Jack's apartment, but he wasn't home yet. So she continued to her own place, changed clothes, fed and watered Oscar and Wilhemina, then started putting together a sandwich from leftover party food for her supper.

She was about to sit down and eat when Jack knocked on her door.

"Hi," she said, smiling at him. He still had on his coat, so she assumed he hadn't stopped by his own apartment before coming to hers.

"Hi," he answered as he stepped inside and shut the door behind him. His eyes hadn't left her face since she'd opened the door to him.

Before taking off his coat, he reached for Emma and she came into his arms without protest. But when he pressed her up against him, she flinched. "Your coat is cold," she informed Jack in answer to his inquiring look.

"Sorry," he said, slipping out of the garment and tossing it aside.

Emma moved back into his arms and lifting herself on tiptoe, she pressed her mouth to his before Jack could make the first move. But he made the second one.

The kiss lasted a long time, and when Jack finally raised his head, his eyes had that look that Emma recognized as meaning he was aroused. She was, too, but she leaned back in his arms and smiled at him.

"Thanks for the valentine," she said softly. "It's the best one I ever got."

Jack raised his eyebrows. "Even though it wasn't big or expensive?"

"Even though," Emma said. And then her expression sobered. "Tony Caro called."

Jack's eyes lost their sensual look and turned alert within the blink of an eye. "What did he say?" he asked.

"He asked me to call him," she answered as she stepped out of Jack's arms, took his hand and pulled him toward the kitchen.

"That's all?"

Emma nodded. "Naturally I haven't returned the call yet."

"Good. I want to record the conversation when you do."

"Do you want a sandwich?" Emma asked. When Jack nodded and sat down at the table, she gave him the one she'd fixed for herself, then made another one.

"Are you nervous?" Jack asked before taking a bite.

"Maybe a little. I'm not used to putting on the sort of act I'll have to put on for Tony Caro." She smiled. "It's easier to act when I have on my clown outfit and a ton of makeup and my audience is made up of children instead of a slimy crook."

Jack smiled and nodded. "If it'll make it easier for you," he said, "go ahead and wear your clown outfit. I won't tell anybody."

Emma laughed and shook her head. "That's too much trouble," she said. "It takes me thirty minutes just to smear on the makeup."

"How often do you do it?" Jack asked, curious.

"Well, I have twenty kids, so that means I do it twenty times a year," Emma said. "I'm thinking about changing my act to something else, though. Something that requires less makeup. Maybe I'll try Cinderella or Snow White next."

"That'll suit the girls, but it probably won't do much for the boys," Jack said.

Emma nodded. "Little boys always seem to be more trouble than girls," she said dryly.

"And how about big boys?" Jack asked.

"Now you're talking *real* trouble," Emma said with emphasis.

"But you get rewarded for your trouble, don't you?" Jack asked innocently.

"Depends," Emma answered lightly.

"On what?"

"On the man."

Jack reached for her, but Emma skipped out of danger, laughing.

After they'd eaten, they went into the living room and she sat down on the couch while Jack attached a recorder to the phone on the table. When he was finished, he stood and Emma scooted over to the phone. Suddenly she felt nervous, and looked at Jack for encouragement.

"Try to keep your reactions as normal as possible," he said in the quiet, gentle voice he sometimes used during interrogations. "Think of how you'd feel if this were really happening to you."

"That's hard to imagine," Emma said shaking her head. "I would never have called Suave in the first place."

Jack smiled. "Then just do the best you can to fake it," he suggested. "I'm going to start the tape rolling, then I'll go into your bedroom to listen on the extension."

Emma nodded abstractedly, and as Jack walked away, she closed her eyes and tried to put herself in the place of a woman who had actually done what she was supposed to have done.

Emma's bedroom wasn't overly frilly, Jack was glad to see. The furniture was traditional, there was a pretty, handmade quilt on the bed and the bolsters around the windows matched it. He sat down on the side of the bed and put his hand on the telephone receiver.

"I'm dialing," Emma called out to him.

"Okay," Jack yelled back. "Tell me when it starts ringing."

A couple of seconds later, Emma called out again. "It's ringing!"

Jack picked up the phone.

"Tony here."

"Mr. Caro?" Emma said coolly. "This is Josephine Truman. You called me, I believe? Is there a problem? Didn't you get the money order I sent?"

"Yeah, I got it," Tony responded. "I'm checkin' to see if you were satisfied with our service."

"Ah . . . why, yes," Emma said. "The man you sent was satisfactory."

"That's what I hear," Tony said meaningfully.

Emma paused a second before answering. "Well, thanks for checking, Mr. Caro. Now if that's all you wanted, I'm quite busy, so—"

"That ain't all I wanted," Tony interrupted.

When she spoke next, Emma sounded a little nervous. "What else did you want?" she asked.

"I was wonderin' if you ever buy stock, Ms. Truman?"

"Stock?" She managed to sound puzzled. "Well, yes . . . at times. But—"

"Good. Then I got a surefire deal for you to think about," he interrupted again.

"Oh. Well, that's interesting, Mr. Caro, but I have a stockbroker, and I never buy without his advice, so—"

"I'll be sendin' some information over to you," Tony cut her off. "Look it over. I think you'll want in when you see what a good deal it is."

"I doubt that," Emma said, sounding less nervous and more firm.

"I don't," Tony said bluntly. "I'll call you again when you've had time to look the information over. G'night." And he hung up the phone.

Emma was puzzled. She didn't know whether or not what Tony had said was enough to convict him. She didn't think so. Getting to her feet she joined Jack in her bedroom and found him lying full-length atop the quilt staring at the ceiling with a thoughtful look on his face.

Emma sat down beside him. "It wasn't enough to get him, was it?" she asked, her tone discouraged.

Jack looked at her and shook his head. "Not yet. Tony's playing it pretty cagey."

"He gives me the creeps," she said with a shudder.

Jack reached over and wrapped his fingers around her upper arm, stroking it absently. "We'll want to see that information he sends over, of course."

Emma nodded. She was staring at Jack, noting how distant he could seem when he had his mind on his work. But she could understand that. And she didn't really mind. She merely sat quietly, waiting until he was through thinking about the case and ready to return his attention to her.

At last Jack came out of his thoughts and noticed how quietly Emma was sitting. Her expression was patiently self-contained.

"Sorry," he apologized. "I was thinking."

"I know," she said simply. "It's all right."

Jack immediately remembered how impatient Janice had always gotten when he'd go off into his thoughts the way he just had. She'd make a sarcastic remark about how he should leave his job at the station when he came home.

His expression softening, Jack raised his hand from Emma's arm to her face and began stroking her cheek.

"You're quite a lady, you know that?" he said softly. "You did just fine on the phone with Tony."

Emma smiled, leaned down and kissed Jack's mouth, using no substantial pressure. She was tasting him, rather than kissing him.

Jack's breathing immediately became constricted, and he slid his hand from Emma's cheek to the back of her neck, starting to pull her closer.

When she didn't resist, Jack lightened the pressure he was exerting with his hand, opened his eyes and studied her expression searchingly.

Emma looked back at him. The conventional part of her still thought that it was too soon for this. But as she studied the warm desire in Jack's eyes she wondered if it really did matter when feelings were concerned? And if she was waiting in order to try to protect herself from hurt, she was certain she was fooling herself. Jack had already caught her heart; it was too late to be cautious.

Finally she answered that searching look in his eyes. "My responsibility this time," she whispered, her gaze open and trusting.

Jack's eyes opened wider, and then closed again as Emma bent her head and placed her mouth gently over his for a brief kiss to seal her decision. When she stopped kissing him, Jack was just about destroyed.

"Are you sure?" he asked huskily, holding her eyes again.

Emma nodded.

"Then just half of the responsibility is yours," he murmured, dropping his gaze to her mouth. "The other half's mine."

"Fair enough," she agreed, smiling warmly at him.

Jack drew her down on the bed to lie beside him, and for a long moment, they simply looked into each other's eyes. Then Jack raised himself and gently turned Emma on her back before bending his head to her mouth. The kiss started out as tender and warm and gentle. But it couldn't stay that way, no more than his hands could resist touching her intimately. And soon, her breath quickened, her eyes liquid with accepting heat, she pushed away and got up from the bed.

Keeping her eyes locked with Jack's, Emma began unbuttoning her blouse. He couldn't take his eyes from her. His attention was so concentrated on Emma as she revealed one smooth, silkily feminine portion of herself at a time, that he wasn't even aware that he'd started to undress himself. But he was ready when she finally lay naked in his arms—ready and stunned by the contact of her warm skin against his.

Emma, pleased by the look on Jack's face, kissed him. And then it quickly became clear to her that he'd only intended the *decision* to make love with him to be half hers. He couldn't help taking most of the execution of the loving into his own hands.

His state of mind suited Emma perfectly for the present. It was glorious to have him want her so much and not be able to hide it. She felt cherished as well as desired, and before long, she was deliciously, passionately swept into exactly the sort of reciprocation Jack wanted. But it was the way she felt afterward that convinced Emma her decision had been the right one. She felt loved then, every bit as much as she had felt desired earlier.

Much later, Jack asked sleepily, "Do teenagers still call it 'going steady'?"

"I don't know," Emma responded, just as sleepily.

"Well, whatever they call it, let's do it," Jack proposed.

"Do what?"

"Go steady."

"Does that mean you don't want me to date anybody else?"

"That means I'll kill anybody else you date."

Emma chuckled. "How about the quid pro quo?" she asked.

"Does that mean you don't want me to date anybody else?"

"That means I'll kill *you* if you date anybody else."

"No problem. I've always planned on enjoying a long life, even if I am a cop," Jack mumbled. Then he kissed Emma's forehead and snuggled her closer to him, and they fell asleep.

Chapter Seven

Johnny Brubaker got out of his chair and headed for Eric.

Curious, Emma watched to see what he was up to, and she was delighted when she saw Johnny offer Eric his Mickey Mouse watch back in exchange for a toy car Eric had brought to nursery school that day. Her delight changed to alarm, however, when Eric took one look at his former watch and started howling at the top of his lungs.

Emma understood the crying a moment later as she looked down at the watch she now held in her hands. Somehow Johnny had managed to pry off the plastic dome covering the front of the watch. The dome was missing...and so were the hands.

Eric was still sobbing and Johnny had his arms crossed over his chest, scowling at him. Emma comforted Eric for a minute, then turned him over to Megan while she took Johnny off for a talk.

Johnny's natural instincts in the matter of battle tactics were extremely good, so he started off the confrontation with an attack.

"Eric's a crybaby," he said with disgust.

"I might cry, too, if you broke my watch," Emma said.

"It wasn't his watch when I broke it," Johnny said. "It was mine. He traded it to me."

Emma held on to her patience. "If it had been your Mickey Mouse watch in the beginning," she said, "and Eric forced you to trade it to him, broke it, then tried to trade it back to you for a perfectly good car, wouldn't you be upset?"

"Nah." Johnny shook his head. "I wouldna traded it to him anyway. But if I had, it would be his then, so he could break it if he wanted to."

Johnny's logic was impeccable. Emma gritted her teeth and dug in for the long haul.

"What if Eric were older and bigger than you are and had forced you to trade the watch to him when you didn't want to?" she asked.

Johnny considered that. Then he shrugged. "I'da give it to him."

"Why?"

"So he wouldn't beat me up."

"Did you threaten to beat Eric up? Is that how you got him to trade you the watch?"

The look in Johnny's blue eyes turned cautious. "Did he tell you I did?"

"Never mind what he did or didn't tell me," Emma said sternly. "Did you threaten to beat him up in order to make him trade you the watch?"

"I don't remember."

At that, Emma turned away for a moment so that Johnny wouldn't see the laughter in her eyes. As exasperated as he could make her feel, he could also crack her up at times. But she knew better than to let him know that he could get to her through humor. If he did, that ability would be just one more weapon in Johnny's ever-growing arsenal of tricks to get his own way at the expense of others.

When she had herself under control, she turned back to Johnny, looked at him thoughtfully for a moment, then asked, "Do you like the other kids?"

It wasn't often Johnny got caught off guard, but Emma could tell her question had surprised him.

"Sure," he answered.

"Then why do you trick them and scare them instead of being nice to them?"

"Because they let me," he said simply.

Now it was Emma who was caught off guard. Johnny had a point. She thought again, then asked, "Do you want the other children to like you?"

Johnny hesitated, and Emma saw something in his eyes that surprised and touched her. He nodded. "But they don't," he answered an instant later.

Emma's eyes softened as she asked, "Why do you think they don't like you?"

"'Cause they just don't," Johnny stated, and he looked down at his hands and began scratching at a splotch of fingerpaint on one knuckle.

"There's always a reason for things," Emma said gently. "Do you think the other children might like you better if you didn't always take their toys away from them in trades?"

Johnny frowned and looked up at Emma. She could see he was genuinely puzzled by her suggestion. "I always give 'em somethin' back," he said.

"Yes, but what you give them is never as good as what you get," she pointed out.

Johnny shrugged. "That's what my dad says to do."

Now Emma was on tricky ground. She couldn't say straight out that she disagreed totally with Mr. Brubaker's philosophy concerning trades.

"Do many people like your dad?" she asked quietly.

"I don't know."

Emma sighed inwardly. "Which would you rather have?" she asked. "The kids to like you a lot or would you rather keep getting the best of them in your trades?"

"I want both," Johnny said.

It was clear to Emma that he hadn't yet realized he couldn't have both.

"Hasn't anybody ever told you about the golden rule, Johnny?" she asked gently.

"Nope. But my dad's got a rule."

"What is it?"

"Get the other guy before he gets you first."

Emma sighed again, thinking she should have been able to predict that answer.

"What's the golden rule?" Johnny asked.

"Do unto others the way you would have them do unto you."

"Huh? What's 'unto' mean?"

"It just means that if you want people to be fair to you, then you have to be fair to them," Emma said. "It means you treat other people the way you'd like to be treated yourself."

Johnny frowned. Clearly he was having trouble sorting out the advantages of the golden rule over his father's rule.

"My dad says good guys finish last," he said. "I don't wanna be last. I like to win."

Emma opened her mouth to make a retort uncomplimentary to Johnny's dad, then closed it again.

"Believe it or not," she said dryly, "good guys can win, too."

Johnny looked skeptical.

Emma decided talk just wasn't going to cut it with him. He was a boy who needed concrete examples. Again she wondered if it were possible to organize the rest of the kids into a concerted action, which would teach Johnny something by example.

For the moment, Emma settled for getting up from her chair, circling the table, and pulling Johnny into her arms for a hug.

Her action took him by surprise. But for a moment, before he remembered to be embarrassed and indignant, Emma felt his arms begin to tighten around her as though he meant to return the hug. Then he stiffened. She immediately let him go.

"Go back and play," she said calmly as she stood.

Johnny took off like a shot.

TONY'S STOCK INFORMATION was in Joe's mailbox that evening, and later, after checking the answering machine in his apartment, Emma sat at her kitchen table reading the material. But the most she could figure out was that you had to have five thousand dollars to get in on whatever "good" deal it was.

Shaking her head, she put it aside and began making a hamburger-and-noodle casserole for dinner. She had just put it into the oven when Jack knocked on her door. Smiling, she went to let him in.

This time, he took off his coat before he kissed her, but once he started, it became plain he didn't intend to stop. He began backing Emma toward the bedroom.

"I've got a casserole in the oven," she said, against his lips.

"Let it burn," Jack said, without taking his mouth from hers. He closed the bedroom door firmly behind them, then pulled Emma's sweatshirt over her head.

"Should I be flattered that you're so eager?" she teased.

"I haven't earned my pay all day today for thinking about this," Jack said, his hands now on the top button of her jeans. "Draw your own conclusions."

"Then I'm flattered," Emma said as she stepped out of her jeans.

"You'd be right to be, too," Jack said, and his eyes were liquid with heated warmth as they caressed her visually. Then he worked on getting out of his own clothes.

"I thought about you, too," Emma said, as she moved to help him.

"Should I feel flattered?" Jack murmured.

"Absolutely," she said.

JACK EYED the casserole skeptically.

"Don't knock it until you've tried it," Emma scolded.

"It'll do," he said, after taking his first bite. And then he grinned to show he was teasing.

Emma made a face at him, then said, "Tony Caro's stock information was in Joe's mail today."

"Where is it?"

She got up to get it, then sat down again and continued her meal.

Jack continued to eat as well, but his face's contortions revealed what difficult reading he was finding the material to be.

Finally he looked up and shook his head. "These things always read like a law textbook," he said, "and this one is worse than usual. But as far as I can tell, it looks legitimate."

Emma was surprised. "Could it actually be on the up-and-up?" she asked.

"No way," Jack snorted. "Not with Tony Caro pushing it. There's a kicker here somewhere. I'll take it with me in the morning and give it to someone who's familiar with this sort of thing and find out what the sting is. Let's hope Tony doesn't call you back before we get the real scoop."

"I checked the machine on Joe's phone when I got home, but Tony hadn't called," Emma said.

"We'd better check it again after dinner. How was your day?" Jack intentionally changed the subject.

Emma told him about the talk she'd had with Johnny.

When she'd finished, he was grinning. "The kid's smart, isn't he? Probably his dad is, too."

"It's just too bad Mr. Brubaker's brains are a lot more devoted to padding his wallet than to teaching his son some ethics," she said dryly.

"I see people like that every day," Jack said, "but the ones I deal with usually aren't that astute. The really smart crooks are the ones dealing in white-collar crime. They don't usually get their hands dirty, their take is in the millions, and it's a lot harder to catch them than it is to find a common burglar."

Emma looked at him curiously. "Do you ever get tired of dealing with the seamier side of life all the time?" she asked.

"Sure," Jack said. "But I don't have it as bad as the guys who work homicides. The things they see are enough to—'' He stopped. He didn't figure Emma would appreciate hearing about the specifics.

After pausing a second, he said, "I came to terms with the downside of my work a long time ago. And I don't plan on making any career changes. As long as we live in an imperfect world, there are going to have to be cops. And being a cop is what I'm good at and what I want to do. So if you were thinking about suggesting that I consider doing something else, forget it. It isn't going to happen."

Emma was surprised, and her expression showed it. "I wasn't thinking any such thing," she said. "I didn't mean that at all when I asked the question about your getting tired of what you do."

Jack felt relieved. "You're sure?" he asked, holding her gaze.

"I'm sure," Emma responded levelly. "Those choices are the kind everyone has to make for himself or herself."

"But would you rather I was in some other line of work?" he persisted.

Emma hesitated, thinking it over. "I don't know," she finally said. "I imagine almost every job has some minuses as well as pluses, and I haven't been involved with you long enough to know all of the negatives connected with your job, though I can imagine some of them."

Jack nodded. "They're considerable," he said. "And not just for the cop. His family has to put up with a lot, too."

Emma looked at him for a while, wondering how specific his warning was intended to be. "I imagine that's so," she said calmly before she continued eating.

Jack stared at her for another moment, wondering how encouraged he should feel by how understanding she seemed to be. But it was too soon to know. Janice had seemed similarly understanding at first...until the reality of living with his job became a day-to-day thing.

After cleaning up the dinner dishes, Jack and Emma went to Joe's apartment to listen to the tape machine. But still there was no message from Tony, so they returned to her place.

Jack wandered over to Oscar and Wilhemina's cage and smiled when he saw the rubber band.

"Is your homemade prison working?" he asked Emma.

"So far," she said. "But I still need to buy a new cage. I just never seem to have the time to shop for one, or else when I do have the time, I forget about it."

"Maybe I can fix it," Jack said, bending down to peer more intently at the faulty catch.

Emma came up behind him and slid her arms around his waist. "Maybe you can," she said, kissing him behind his ear. "But you don't have to do it now, do you?"

Jack immediately lost interest in the faulty catch. He turned and pulled Emma into his arms.

"There's something that needs fixing in my bedroom," she murmured softly.

"What?"

"I'll think of something," she assured him.

"GOTTA JOB FOR YOU," Tony said over the phone.

Jack wasn't particularly happy to hear it, but his tone was neutral when he answered. "Where, when and who?"

"A dame name of Sylvia Baskin wants you to come to her hotel room at Crown Center for lunch today," Tony said. "I figure that means she's got keepin' you for the afternoon in mind."

Jack glanced at the tape recorder, wishing that last sentence had been a little more specific. It was suggestive, but not enough.

After getting the details, Jack hung up the phone, then sat back and shook his head. *God,* he sighed inwardly. *Why do these women do it?* Well, he'd just have to talk the woman out of what she had in mind. And if talking didn't work, depending on his judgment of what kind of woman she was and how big a threat to his cover she represented, he could always pull out his badge, threaten to arrest her, then let her go. That ought to give her a good enough scare that she wouldn't think of contacting a service like Suave again anytime soon.

The other cops noticed Jack's gloomy expression and had a good deal of fun at his expense before Jack left to keep the appointment Tony had made for him.

When Sylvia Baskin opened her hotel room door to him, she turned out to be a handsome woman in her mid-forties or early fifties, obviously fairly well-to-do, who was trying very hard not to seem as nervous as she obviously was. Jack figured she'd never done anything like this before, and he hoped, by the time he left her, she wouldn't dream of doing anything like it again. He smiled at her and introduced himself simply as Jack from Suave.

"Come in," she said with a gracious smile. "The waiter just brought our lunch." She indicated a table set before the window, which was laden with silver-domed dishes. "Would you like to wash up before we eat?" she asked, as she shut the door behind Jack.

He turned to look at her, smiled and shook his head.

"Then shall we sit down?"

Jack nodded, and when they were seated across from each other, Sylvia gave him a nervous smile. "I hope you like what I ordered," she said. "It's steak. My hus— Ah, most men like steak, don't they?"

"Steak is fine," Jack said quietly. And after they'd served themselves, he said conversationally, "What does your husband do for a living, Mrs. Baskin?"

Sylvia flushed, and the look in her dark eyes reflected nervous wariness over the question.

"I'd rather talk about you," she said. "How long have you been an escort for Suave?"

"Not long."

Jack had evaluated Sylvia Baskin and he was positive what her reaction was going to be when he told her who he really was. Therefore, he felt no qualms about blowing his cover where she was concerned. He put down his fork and looked steadily into her eyes.

"Actually," he said calmly, "I'm not really an escort. I'm a vice detective working undercover to nail Suave's owner for male prostitution, income tax fraud and a few other things."

Sylvia Baskin's face immediately paled and she looked absolutely stunned for a moment. And then she dropped her fork and raised her hands to cover her face as she burst into tears.

Jack sighed inwardly and gave her a few minutes to recover. He felt like a heel, but wondered why a woman as intelligent and educated as Sylvia was had ever done something so foolish as calling a place like Suave. Finally, his softer instincts won over his harder ones, and he got up from his chair, went around the table, patted Mrs. Baskin on the shoulder and reassured her that he wasn't going to arrest her.

She raised her head, and with tears streaming down her face, gave him a look of such utter gratitude that Jack again felt like a heel.

"Thank you," she whispered as she raised her napkin to her eyes and wiped away her tears. "Thank you so much. I've never done anything like this before, and I have grown children who would be devastated if..." She shook her head, and her expression was one of despair. But she seemed to have regained her dignity as well. She got to her feet. "Would you mind if I went into the bathroom for a moment?" she asked. "I'd like to wash my face."

Jack was of two minds about that. He was afraid she might do something to harm herself.

"Sure," he said. "But come right back. You can help me on this case by answering some questions. And then you can go home and forget any of this ever happened."

She smiled wanly. "Oh, I doubt I'll forget." And then she looked at him with muted curiosity. "Is your name really Jack?"

He nodded. "I'm Jack Spencer," he said as he reached into his pocket, pulled out his identification and showed it to her.

Mrs. Baskin glanced at the identification and smiled wanly again. "I'll be back in a moment," she said. She went into the bathroom and shut the door.

Jack was nervous all the time she was gone. And he was very relieved when she finally came back out. She had repaired her makeup and her expression was composed as she sat down in a chair.

"I suppose your first question is why I would do something like this?" she said quietly.

Jack didn't want to humiliate her. He just wanted to get some facts, but Sylvia didn't wait for his reply. She began speaking.

"I love my husband very much," she said quietly. "He was a businessman, very loving...the best husband and father in the world."

"Was?" Jack asked. He had a feeling she needed to talk, so he spoke in a gentle, encouraging way.

Her lips moved in a caricature of a smile. "He has Alzheimer's now," she said dully. "He's in a nursing home."

Jack took a deep breath. "I see," he said.

She looked into Jack's eyes, her own containing a sad, hopeless expression.

"Do you?" she said quietly. "I doubt it. And I hope you never do understand completely." And then she looked away.

"I hope I don't, either," Jack said gently, then asked, "How did you hear about Suave?"

She hesitated, then said, "I simply looked in the Yellow Pages." She smiled faintly. "And I'm not entirely a fool, Jack. I realized they were probably providing more than a simple escort service."

Jack admired the way she didn't make excuses and didn't try to shield herself from blame. He knew without asking that there was no way Sylvia could afford the publicity testifying would bring her, so he got to his feet.

She looked up at him with a frown on her face. "Is that all?" she asked, sounding surprised.

"That's all," he said. But then he paused and added, "Except, if you'll take my advice, you won't contact an agency like Suave again. I can't say more now, but if I'd been a real escort, this afternoon might not have been the end of it. You may have been contacted by Suave with a proposal you probably wouldn't have been able to say no to."

Mrs. Baskin frowned, and then a look of enlightenment came into her eyes, as well as one of fear. "You mean...blackmail?"

Jack nodded.

Mrs. Baskin stared at him, horrified. "Could they still...I mean, they have my name..."

"Do they have your real address?" Jack asked.

She shook her head with relief. "No, I sent a messenger to their offices with cash to pay for this. And I don't live here."

"Good," Jack said.

She looked at him with gratitude. "You could have arrested me, couldn't you?" she asked.

"Yes."

"Why didn't you?"

"I can't see that it would serve any purpose."

Sylvia Baskin stared at him, then got to her feet and approached him. She put her hands on his shoulders and kissed his cheek gently. When she stepped back, she shook her head. "You're a very kind man, Jack," she said quietly. "And you don't have to worry that I'll ever do this sort of thing again. I was a complete fool to do it this time. And completely lucky that you were the man who was sent to me."

Jack smiled slightly. "I hope things get better for you soon," he said quietly.

"I don't know how they can," she said simply. "I don't want my husband to die, and he can't get well.

But maybe, as time goes by, I'll learn how to handle the loneliness better.''

Jack didn't answer because he couldn't think of anything helpful to say.

On the drive back to the station, Jack wondered how he was going to explain to the lieutenant about being so easy on Sylvia Baskin. He'd been chewed out before for being too soft-hearted. But sometimes the lieutenant could be as human as the next guy.

Before he reported to the lieutenant, he phoned Tony Caro and told him Sylvia had backed out and gone home before Jack ever got to her hotel room.

Tony was his usual gracious self in expressing his disappointment.

"Damned dames never can make up their minds!" he growled. "It's a good thing we got the money for your four hours before she skipped!" he added, before slamming down the phone.

THAT NIGHT, Emma lay beside Jack in bed as he told her about Sylvia Baskin.

When he was finished, she said quietly, "I feel so sorry for her."

"Yeah. Me, too."

Then Emma put her hand on Jack's cheek and gently pulled his head around so that she could look into his eyes.

"She was right about you," she said softly.

Jack frowned. "What do you mean?"

"You're a very kind man."

Jack didn't feel comfortable with such compliments. He merely shook his head and shrugged.

Wisely, Emma then set about showing her approval of his behavior in a way he could handle without a shred of discomfort.

Chapter Eight

"What's this all about?" Joe asked when Emma opened the door to him the next evening. He held up her answering machine to indicate what he meant.

Emma grimaced. "It's a long story," she said. "Come in."

Jack showed up in the middle of Emma's conversation with Joe and helped her out with the explanations.

When they were finished, Joe's expression was incredulous as he looked at Emma. "You've got to be out of your mind," he said.

"I don't think so."

Then Joe looked at Jack accusingly. Jack shrugged. "I tried to discourage her, but she went around me," he defended himself.

"So can we put my answering machine back on your phone?" Emma got back to the question at hand.

Joe sighed. "That's one thing about being friends with you, Emma," he said in a long-suffering tone. "There's never a dull moment."

She smiled. "Well, don't pick now to chop me off your list of friends, or we'll never catch Tony Caro."

"Okay," he agreed. "But this is against my better judgment."

Emma didn't say anything to that comment. And then she had an idea. Turning to Jack, she asked, "Do you have that information Tony sent me, or did you leave it at the station?"

"I have a photocopy of it," he said, reaching into his pocket. "I gave the original to the guy who's supposed to look it over for me. He hasn't gotten back to me on it yet."

"Joe knows about this kind of thing," Emma said to Jack. "Do you mind if he looks it over?"

Jack didn't mind and he and Emma fixed dinner while Joe read the information on the company Tony wanted Emma to invest in.

When they were all seated around the table and had dished up the food, Joe said, "It looks fairly standard on the surface. They haven't written anything illegal. This is supposedly a private venture capital company that looks for promising businesses to invest in. Nothing strange about that. But since it's a private company, it will be a lot more difficult to get any background information on it. And if you're sure this Caro fellow is up to something, it may be that at a certain point, he plans to take his investors' money and run."

Jack frowned. "I don't think Tony has running in mind," he said. "Kansas City has always been his base. He was born here and all of his family is here."

"Then maybe he plans to produce a lot of phony paperwork to indicate what businesses he's supposedly investing in, when he's actually investing in nothing at all. He can eventually tell his investors none of the businesses panned out and everybody loses. If he has his female investors sewed up with blackmail, they're not going to complain to anybody when their investments go down the tubes—that is, as long as he doesn't keep pushing them for more and more money. If he did that and backed one or more of them against the wall, someone might get desperate enough to go to the police and blow the whistle.''

"I think Tony's smarter than that," Jack commented.

Joe frowned absently and nodded. "But I can't imagine that even with blackmail, Tony Caro would get enough money just from his female clients to make it really worth his while. So there's another possibility.''

"What's that?" Emma asked.

"Maybe the company is just a dummy being used to launder money Tony's getting from other illegal sources," Joe suggested.

Jack looked up. "Now there's a possibility," he agreed. "It wouldn't even have to be his own money... he could be doing it for some of his shadier pals for a hefty cut.''

"But why involve his female clients at all then?" Emma asked.

"To give the illusion of respectability if anyone starts asking questions," Joe explained. "Tony could whip out their names as legitimate investors, and if he's doctored the books, chances are their names will be down for heavier investments than they actually made. If the dirty money is really big, Tony could even pay dividends to his female clients and not miss it much. He sucks them in with the blackmail, then actually pays them small dividends so they relax and aren't as angry as they would be if they got nothing at all out of their investment other than Tony's silence. There's even less chance they would complain then."

Jack took a sip of his wine. "That sounds like Tony, all right. The scoop is that he's claustrophobic and has a horror of going to jail. Therefore, he's probably willing to temper his greed enough to be more careful than some of his ilk about getting caught."

Emma thought of the woman Jack had told her about the night before and felt her anger growing. She wondered how many other women were being victimized by Tony Caro, and was fiercely glad she was helping Jack catch the man. When the time came to testify against him, Emma intended to do so with relish.

"Well, we won't know the truth of it until we get a look at Tony's records," Jack said. And then he looked at Emma with a thoughtful frown. "Maybe if the records are conclusive enough, we won't have to put you on the stand to tell how Tony worked his scheme."

Joe looked at Emma, too, and his glance was troubled. "If she does have to testify, how dangerous is it going to be for her?" he asked.

Emma appreciated Joe's concern, but she didn't want him stirring up Jack's protectiveness toward her, either.

"We've got all that worked out, remember?" she said lightly. "It's your address and telephone number Tony's got, not mine. He won't be able to find me if he looks. He'll find you instead."

"Thanks a lot," Joe said, grimacing.

"You just tell him you never heard of any Josephine Truman," Emma said, trying to sound unconcerned. But she was beginning to regret dragging Joe into all of this. Who knew what someone like Tony Caro would do? It would be different if Joe had volunteered to help, but he hadn't, and she'd never be able to forgive herself if anything happened to him because of her.

"If it comes to that," Jack said quietly, "we'll put both of you into protective custody."

Joe was alarmed by that idea. "Hey, I've got a job," he protested. "I can't just disappear off the face of the earth for a while."

"Maybe we can just assign someone to guard you then," Jack amended.

"And I can't leave my nursery school," Emma said anxiously. "Besides, even if Tony contacts Joe, he doesn't know my name and would have no reason to connect me to this. How could he suspect I only live two doors down from Joe?"

Jack decided not to worry Joe or Emma by explaining how far someone like Tony might go to get information if the stakes were high enough. But if it became necessary to protect either of them, he knew he wasn't going to pay heed to their complaints about having to leave their normal lives behind for a while.

After dinner, Joe picked up Emma's answering machine, saying he needed to get home and get some sleep. But at the door, when it became obvious that Jack wasn't going to leave with him, he began to smile.

"How did the Valentine's party go?" he asked innocently.

Emma knew Joe better than Jack did, so she adopted a bland expression as she said, "Fine. Sorry you missed it."

"Me, too. But I'm glad you got to go, Jack."

"Me, too," he echoed. "Very glad."

That was all Joe needed to hear. He chuckled all the way back to his apartment.

Emma grimaced at his back, then shut the door and looked at Jack, "Did you have to be so obvious?" she complained. "I love Joe dearly, but sometimes he has a very wicked sense of humor."

"Sorry," Jack said unrepentantly. "I guess I wanted to show off a little."

"Show off?" Emma was puzzled.

Jack took her in his arms and smiled down into her face. "When a guy wins a princess, he's proud."

Emma laughed. "Some princess," she scoffed. "I have to wear my clown outfit tomorrow because it's little Susan's birthday. We'll see how much you think I resemble a princess then."

Jack looked thoughtful. "I've never made love to a clown," he mused. "It might be interesting."

"Well, you won't be making love to this one," Emma said firmly. "Not unless you want to end up with half my makeup smeared on your own face, that is." And then she paused, and her eyes lit with mischief. "Although, that might be interesting, too," she added. "I have an instamatic camera, and I could take a picture of you. There's something to be said for having an ace in the hole."

"Leave the blackmail to Tony Caro," Jack suggested dryly.

"Darn," Emma sighed. "Don't you cops have any sense of humor?"

"Sometimes." Jack grinned wickedly. "For instance, if you're willing to take something besides money, which I haven't got much of, as payment for your blackmail, maybe I could be persuaded to go along with you."

"Something that you wouldn't mind paying, you mean?" Emma raised an eyebrow.

"Exactly."

Emma smiled and shook her head. "I have a feeling you're going to insist I take off the makeup rather than risk blackmail at all. It really is greasy and unattractive."

"I can't imagine you looking unattractive," Jack said and pulled her closer. Leaning down, he kissed her, gently at first, and then with more insistence. But Emma didn't kiss him back with her usual responsiveness, and he finally drew back and looked at her questioningly. "What have you got on your mind?" he asked. "It obviously isn't me at the moment."

She gave him an apologetic look. "I'm sorry. I was thinking about Joe," she explained.

Jack raised his eyebrows. "Should I be jealous?" he asked.

"No, of course not," Emma smiled. Then she sobered again. "Jack, it was wrong of me to involve him in all this, wasn't it," she said, her voice tinged with worry. "I didn't realize it fully until tonight, but it's possible I've put him in danger?" She looked questioningly at him, hoping for reassurance.

Jack hesitated. Then, considering it was better for her to be on guard, he opted for bluntness. "From my perspective, it was wrong of you to involve yourself in this. I feel the same way about you as you're feeling about Joe right now—only much stronger."

"I don't regret getting involved myself," she said. "I want to get Tony Caro. But I volunteered, Joe didn't."

"It's too late to do anything about it now, Emma," he said matter-of-factly. "But if it helps, I meant what I said about getting protection for you and Joe if it becomes necessary." And as she opened her mouth to protest again, he put a finger across her lips and shook his head. His eyes were steady and very firm. "You dealt yourself in, but I'm calling the shots, remember? And one of the shots I'm calling concerns your safety and Joe's. Don't fight me on this, Emma. You'll lose."

Considering the expression on Jack's face and the tone of his voice, she decided it would be pointless to argue with him. Instead she kissed his fingers and her eyes smiled at him.

Jack sighed. "Women," he said, shaking his head as he took her in his arms again. "You never fight fair."

"GET YOURSELF HERE to the office about eight o'clock tonight," Tony ordered over the phone the next afternoon.

Jack frowned. "Why?"

"Never mind why, just do it." Tony slammed down the phone.

Puzzled, Jack sat back in his chair and stared at nothing, wondering what the hell Tony had in mind.

EMMA WAS A LITTLE LATE getting home the next day because she'd had to talk to a parent about a child's medication. Then she stopped by Joe's apartment.

"You got the call you've been waiting for," Joe said rather grimly after they'd exchanged greetings. "And I don't like the sound of this guy at all."

Emma didn't like the sound of Tony Caro, either, but she was eager to listen to his message.

"Ms. Truman," Tony's gravelly voice addressed her, "I would like you to come to my office tonight at eight-thirty to discuss the investment I told you about. I hope you don't have nuthin' else planned 'cause I got some pictures I wanta' show you...of your Valentine party."

That was the extent of the message, and it alarmed Emma.

"Jack isn't going to like this," she said gloomily.

"I don't like it, either," Joe said, his expression grave. "Does he really have pictures?"

Emma shook her head. "No, he couldn't have. He's just hoping I'll believe he has and using that as a threat to make sure I show up."

"Let's see if Jack's home," Joe suggested.

Jack wasn't home yet, so Joe went back to his place and Emma left a note on Jack's door then went to her apartment to shower and change. She had just stepped out of the shower when Jack knocked on her door. She answered his knock in her robe, and with her hair wet.

"Charming." Jack smiled as he stepped in and shut the door behind him. "I bet you'd look good in a potato sack."

"Thanks," Emma said and reached up to peck him on the lips briefly. "I'm glad you're here. Tony called."

"He called me, too," Jack said as he took off his coat. "What did he say to you?"

"He wants me to come to his office at eight-thirty tonight," she said, and almost flinched at the look her statement brought to Jack's eyes.

"No way," he said with cold firmness.

Emma hadn't made up her mind whether to keep the appointment with Tony. But if she decided to do it, she didn't intend to take Jack's refusal as his final word. She didn't say so yet, however. Instead she asked, "What did he want when he called you?"

"He wants me at his office, too," Jack said dryly, "only my date with him is for eight o'clock. Let's go listen to the tape. I want to hear his message to you myself."

Emma hesitated. "You go," she said. "While you're listening, I'll dry my hair and get dressed."

"All right," he said.

Jack left and Emma headed for her bathroom. Her hair style was the sort she only had to dry and fluff, and she put on the bare minimum of makeup. Within twenty minutes, she was dressed in slacks and a sweater and heading for Joe's apartment.

"I don't like this," Joe said bluntly after Jack had listened to Tony's message. "Why'd you ever let Emma get mixed up with a character like Caro?"

Jack's expression was grim. "I didn't let her, remember?" he said shortly. "I told you, she went around me."

"Yeah, you're right. Emma's got a lot of good qualities, but she's also got a stubborn streak a mile wide. In some ways, I don't envy the man she marries. He'll have his hands full."

Jack had heard Joe, but his mind wasn't on marriage at the moment. *What the hell has Tony got in mind?* he wondered. *Am I supposed to be there just to add emphasis to Tony's threat of blackmail? And what will he do next if I keep Emma from meeting him?*

As much as Jack's personal inclinations were to keep Emma as far away from Tony as possible, the professional side of him knew that she wasn't likely to be in any danger from him at this point. The danger would come later when Tony found out she was going to testify against him. But Jack wasn't sure Emma was capable of putting on the kind of act she'd have to in a face-to-face meeting with Tony. And he didn't know if he could, either—not when it was Emma who would be his acting partner rather than a policewoman.

By the time Emma arrived at Joe's apartment, she had made up her mind that as scary as the proposition was, she was going to keep the appointment with Tony. Otherwise everything she'd set out to do might be jeopardized. But she wasn't sure how she was going to convince Jack to go along with her intention. She didn't think he would actually physically prevent her if it came down to it. But going against his wishes was certain to put a strain on their relationship.

She had to remind herself very strongly that she wanted Jack to know exactly what he was getting into if their relationship became serious. And she reminded herself that the coming confrontation with him would tell her some things that she needed to know as well.

When Joe let her into his apartment, Jack was sitting on the couch, staring into space. Emma wasn't sure he was even aware she was there.

"Jack?" she said as she sat down beside him.

"Hmm?" He sounded very distant.

"I want to meet with Tony," she said with quiet firmness. "Otherwise the whole case against him may fall through."

At that, Jack came out of his thoughts and turned his head to look at her. He didn't immediately answer, but continued to stare at her hard. It was Joe who spoke up.

"Emma, you can't be serious!" he said, dismayed.

"I am very serious," she responded without looking at Joe. She wasn't going to break away from Jack's stare. She wanted him to see how strongly she felt about her position.

Joe opened his mouth to protest, but then became aware of the silent battle going on between Jack and Emma and said nothing.

Finally Jack said, "Okay. But we'll have to stop by the station first. I want us both wired."

Emma was startled. She couldn't believe he had given in so easily. "Do you mean it?" she asked, hesitantly.

"Sure," he said, crisply. "Come on, let's go get your coat."

"Hey, Jack, wait a minute—" Joe started to protest.

Jack cut him off. "Leave it alone," he said, his voice now hard. "It's settled."

Joe looked at Jack with annoyed surprise.

Emma, glancing uneasily at Jack, didn't say anything further, either. She had an idea that underneath his impassive expression, he was very angry. But what had she expected? She'd known how he felt, but had elected to ignore his wishes. She wondered rather unhappily if catching Tony Caro was going to be worth it to her on a personal level. But the stubborn streak Joe had commented to Jack about rose inside her, and she didn't seriously contemplate backing off. Jack Spencer could take her as she was, or he wouldn't be taking her at all.

He didn't say a word to Emma until they were in the parking lot.

"You'll have to take your car and follow me," he said, without warmth. "I have to meet Tony half an hour before you do, remember?"

Emma studied his impassive expression, her gaze warmly regretful, but firm. "All right," she said quietly. But as he started to turn away, she put her hand on his arm. Jack paused and looked at her, but his expression made the words she'd been about to say die in her throat. "I'll follow you," she said, dropping her hand. And she turned on her heel to go to her own car.

Emma was right that Jack was angry. But she was wrong in thinking that he was solely angry at her for disregarding his wishes. Sure, he was angry that she had dismissed his view on the matter as though it didn't count. But he was also angry at himself, because by letting Emma go through with this meeting, he was essentially putting his job first and her safety second. Would a man who really loved a woman do that? He didn't think so, even though he'd previously been sure he was on his way to loving Emma more than he'd ever loved anyone.

Maybe Janice is right, Jack thought soberly. *Maybe I'm never going to be able to love any woman more than I do my job.*

EMMA FROWNED AS SHE LOOKED down at herself. "Don't you think it shows through this sweater I'm wearing?" she asked the police technician who had attached the wire to her body.

"Yeah, it does a little," he said. "Let me see if I can find you something else to wear."

When the technician had left the room, Emma looked at Jack, who was already wired, with a cold expression. By now she was thoroughly angry with him because of the way he was acting. What she was about to do was one of the hardest things she'd ever done, and the closer the time came to meet with Tony Caro, the more scared she felt. She could have used a little support from Jack. No, she could have used a *lot* of support! Instead he was behaving as though they were strangers.

"I guess I'm supposed to act outraged and angry with Tony at first, and then cave in?" she asked crisply.

Jack nodded, his gaze almost blank. "And if it turns out he wants me there to remind you of what you and I supposedly did, you're to act angry with me as well."

"That won't be hard," Emma grated, her gaze eloquent of her feelings.

Jack opened his mouth to respond, then closed it again. He ached to take her into his arms and make peace between them. But his doubts about his own feelings constrained him. Besides, he thought glumly, her present attitude toward him was better for Emma's safety. It would help convince Tony that they were essentially strangers except for the one night Tony thought they'd spent together.

When Jack didn't answer, Emma turned away to hide the hurt his attitude had caused. She found it hard to believe that he could be chauvinistic enough to act like this toward her simply because she had decided to act independently of his wishes. But what other explanation could there be for his behavior?

An aching, stinging sensation of loss filled Emma's heart, making her aware that things had gone too far between her and Jack for her to be able to lose him without experiencing a great deal of pain.

Fortunately the technician returned just then, bringing with him a loose black sweatshirt. "This belongs to one of the smaller guys," he said as he handed it to Emma. "I think it'll do."

"Thank you," she said. And then she turned to Jack, staring through him rather than at him. "Would you mind giving me some privacy while I put this on?" she asked.

The technician looked surprised. Emma Springer hadn't protested Jack's being there before when she'd had to take her sweater off in order to have the wire taped to her chest.

"Sure," Jack said, and though it cost him, he managed to say it with no expression in his voice. "Come on, Baker," he said to the technician. "Let's step outside."

The technician hesitated. He wanted to check to see if the sweatshirt hid the wire adequately. But he could do that when Emma was dressed, so he shrugged and accompanied Jack out of the room.

"How come she got so shy all of a sudden?" he asked Jack once the door was closed behind the two of them.

Jack shrugged. "Who knows with women?" he answered, his tone bleak.

Jack's tone made the technician glance at him sharply. Then he looked away. "Sure," he said. "They'll fool you every time."

Jack's mouth twitched into an unamused smile. "Maybe we all fool ourselves, Baker," he said wearily. "And that's how we end up fooling others."

Puzzled, the technician merely shrugged.

Chapter Nine

Emma glanced at her watch yet again, then rubbed her hands together. Despite the chill in the car, her palms were sweating.

"Ten more minutes, Emma," Eddie said soothingly. "Take it easy. The waiting's the hardest part. Once you get in there, you'll do fine."

Emma glanced over at the huge black detective behind the wheel of her car and though, at first meeting him, his size and the fierce roughness of his features had at first startled her, she was now very glad Jack had insisted Eddie drive her to Suave's office because it was located in a rough area of town and Jack hadn't wanted Emma driving there alone.

"Do policewomen get this nervous on their cases?" she asked.

"Depends on the policewoman." Eddie shrugged his monstrous shoulders.

Emma wondered where Eddie found clothes that would fit him. But his size no longer intimidated her. She suspected that Eddie was probably every bit as rough as he looked in his dealings with the criminal element of society, but with her, he had been a calming influence with his gentle, encouraging attitude.

"I wonder what Tony's saying to Jack," she said.

Eddie smiled a wide white smile tinged with grim satisfaction. "We'll know soon enough," he answered. "The boys in the van are picking up every word."

"BUT WHY DO YOU WANT to see Josephine Truman?" Jack, faking nervous puzzlement, was saying at that very moment. "And why do you want her to see me? If you've got something in mind that can get me in serious trouble, I'd just as soon be counted out. I didn't plan on doing anything I could go to jail for when I signed up with you."

Tony shrugged and looked at Jack with contempt. "You could already go to jail for takin' money from the Truman dame for services rendered," he pointed out. "But if you keep your head, you ain't got nuthin' to worry about. All you gotta do is look at her and say hello in a way that reminds her of what the two of you done together. Then you scram. You don't need to know what else me and her talk about. But it ain't gonna do me no good if you stand there lookin' like you wanta crawl on your mama's lap and cry for your bottle. Get yourself together, man. You wanta work for me, you gotta have a little backbone."

Jack's scowl wasn't faked. He was in a foul mood. Despite his earlier doubts about his feelings for Emma, he hated this case now because she was involved in it. And as he stared at Tony Caro, he felt a strong desire to beat the man to a pulp.

Tony looked at the expensive watch on his wrist. "She'll be here pretty soon," he grunted. Heaving his bulk up from his chair, he walked over to a floor safe in the corner of the room.

Though he would very much have liked to, Jack couldn't see around Tony's bulky frame in order to see the lock combination he used.

After he opened the safe door, Tony picked up a ledger that was on a shelf inside, then shut the safe door, spun the tumbler and came back to his desk.

Jack eyed the ledger, but knew better than to ask what it was. Since Tony seemed to have gotten it out in anticipation of Emma's visit, Jack figured it had to do with the phony stock scheme, and he took careful note of the color and appearance of the ledger in order to be able to recognize it again.

Jack wished Tony wasn't quite as cagey as he was. It would have been great if Tony had spelled out to Jack what he had in mind where Emma was concerned, then they'd have it on tape twice. He also wished he could stay in the room during Emma's interview with Tony in order to give her silent support. But maybe it was better this way, he thought wryly. He wasn't sure if his protective instincts were up to seeing Emma intimidated by Tony.

EMMA PAUSED AT THE DOOR to the Suave office and took a deep breath.

Just pretend this is a play, she told herself shakily. *You haven't been given a word-for-word script, but you know how the scene is supposed to go, and you can do it!*

The room she stepped into was obviously a reception area. There was a desk and a telephone and not much else. And no one was sitting at the desk. But she had heard a buzzing noise as she opened the door, so she assumed Tony Caro, or whoever was behind the door to the right of the desk, was aware that she had arrived.

She stood looking around her nervously, waiting for what was to come.

"THAT'S HER. GET THE DOOR," Tony instructed.

Jack got up from the chair in front of Tony's desk where he'd been sitting, walked to the door and opened it. And at his first glance at Emma, standing in the middle of the small reception area, her hazel eyes wide and fearful, he cursed himself again for ever mentioning the Suave case to her. He wanted to take her in his arms and protect her from ever being afraid again.

Emma, seeing the look on Jack's face, was grateful he had his back to Tony. Otherwise, the game would have been blown at that moment. She strengthened her backbone and said loudly enough that Tony could hear, "What are *you* doing here?"

Jack admired her courage. And though he would have preferred to turn around, cuff Tony and take him straight to jail, he pulled himself together in order to play the game that might result in getting Tony incarcerated for a lot longer than would stand up in court for the moment.

"Hello there," he said in the sort of suggestive tone his role called for. "You look great, baby. I've been hoping you'd call and ask to see me again, since we hit it off together so well the first time."

He managed to sound so oily and insinuating, he wasn't surprised when Emma glared at him.

"I don't think I'll be using Suave's services again," she said haughtily. "I don't appreciate being called down here to this hole in the wall at night like this."

For a man of his bulk, Tony could move quietly when he chose to, and Jack was a little startled to hear his voice directly behind him.

"Come in, Ms. Truman," he said with heavy cheerfulness. "Jack's gotta leave."

Jack nodded and walked into the reception area, keeping his eyes on Emma's face. He knew she was nervous, but he admired the way she was controlling herself.

"Good night, baby," he said. "See you again soon," he added in order to give her moral support by reminding her that in a short while, all this would be over.

Emma didn't respond verbally. She merely gave Jack an angry, dismissive look before she switched her gaze to Tony.

Perfect, Jack thought with wry appreciation. *At least our earlier fight is serving some purpose.*

Even though Emma was doing a reasonably good job of acting her part, walking past her and out the door of the Suave office was one of the hardest things Jack had ever done. Outside he hesitated. Though it was the wrong thing to do, he wanted to linger as close as possible to Emma in case she needed him. But then Eddie opened the door of the police van parked down the street and Jack hurried over so that he could hear what Emma and Tony were saying.

ONCE EMMA HAD SEEN TONY, her nervousness decreased. She despised him on sight, and her desire to see him caught and punished overrode her fear.

Seated across from him, she stared at the man with angry contempt. "What do you mean calling me down here like this?'' she demanded. ''And where are these pictures you claim to have?''

Tony settled back in his chair with his hands clasped over his prominent belly and stared back at her with cold amusement.

''I ain't got no pictures,'' he said.

Emma immediately faked a fleeting expression of relief, then carefully wiped the expression from her face. She knew Tony had seen it, which was what she'd intended.

''But I got Jack,'' Tony added amiably, ''and he's better'n pictures, ain't he?''

''I have no idea what you mean,'' Emma responded coldly. But she dropped her eyes in a guilty manner rather than continuing to hold Tony's gaze.

''Sure you do,'' he said. ''Otherwise you wouldna come down here when I told you to.''

At that, Emma raised her head. ''So what?'' She faked defiance. ''It would be my word against his, and who's going to believe a sleazy male escort instead of a respectable businesswoman?''

''What kinda business you in, Ms. Truman?'' Tony asked.

''That's none of your concern,'' she answered stonily.

''It don't matter nohow,'' he said calmly. ''I bet whatever it is, you ain't anxious to have people know what you done with Jack.''

Emma stiffened and gazed at Tony angrily. ''If you think you can blackmail me, Mr. Caro, you're wrong,'' she stated contemptuously.

''Nah,'' he grunted. ''This ain't blackmail. I'm just lettin' you in on a good investment.''

"I'm sure," Emma spoke with scathing contempt as she got up. "Well, I wouldn't invest in anything you proposed. So as far as I'm concerned, this meeting is ov—"

"Sit down!" Tony said. His mildy amused manner dropped away completely, and his expression was hard and cold and determined.

As Emma slowly settled back onto her chair, she didn't have to fake her sudden attack of cautious alarm. As much contempt as she felt for the man, she could see that he wasn't a person to be treated lightly.

"Did you read that information I sent you?" he demanded.

Emma nodded. Then remembering who was listening to these proceedings, she said aloud, "Yes, I read it."

"You see anything wrong with it?"

"Not on the surface," she finally replied.

"That's 'cause there ain't nuthin' wrong with it," Tony said. "It's a good deal, and you oughta be grateful I'm lettin' you in on it."

Emma clenched her jaw. "I'm not in the market for any investments right now," she said firmly.

"Sure you are," he responded. "Everybody wants to make money, right?"

"Of course, but . . ."

Emma's voice trailed off as Tony leaned forward in his chair and held her gaze. And despite her negative feelings about the man, she had to give him high marks for his intimidation skills. She couldn't look away from that cold black gaze.

"You can start out slow," he said. "Five thousand will get ya in. I'll take your check right now. Later if you wanta get in for more, we'll see."

Emma stirred uneasily in her chair. "And if I refuse?"

Tony smiled coldly. "I don't think you will," he said with a satisfied nod.

"But if I do?" she persisted, wanting to get a firm blackmail threat from him on tape.

Tony shook his head. "Then you're gonna be seein' a lot of Jack," he said sharply. "In places where you don't wanta see him, around people you don't want to know about Jack. If that's okay with you, fine. Go on home. But if it's not, let's see your checkbook."

Emma gave a convincing impression of a woman struggling between a rock and a hard place for a few moments, and then sighed as though defeated.

Tony smiled with satisfaction.

"All right, I'll invest in your company," she said angrily. "But I don't trust you enough to give you a personal check."

Tony frowned threateningly.

Emma withdrew five thousand dollars in cash from her purse and extended it toward him. The police department had provided the money, and the numbers of the bills had been carefully recorded. "Take it or leave it," she said. "I don't want anything in my financial records that says I've ever dealt with you. I never expect to see any return on this money anyway despite your pretense that it isn't blackmail. And there's too much chance that someone braver than I am will explode your little blackmail scheme in your face someday. If that happens, I don't want to be called on to testify against you. I can't afford the publicity." That part was Jack's contribution as an added safeguard for Emma.

"You're a smart woman, ain't ya, Ms. Truman," he said. "You figured out why I wanted to see you before you ever got here, didn't ya?"

"I had a pretty good idea of your intentions," she said stonily. "But don't count on getting any more money from me. This is all the blackmail I'm willing to pay."

Tony eyed her thoughtfully. "Maybe," he said, his tone amiable again. "And maybe not."

Emma glared at him. "May I go now?" she asked, her voice frigid.

"After I give you a receipt, sure," Tony said blandly. He wrote out the receipt and handed it to Emma, who took it and immediately got up to head for the door. But when she reached it, Tony spoke, making her pause.

"If you like, to show good faith, I'll send Jack over to see you for a freebie." His voice was contemptuously amused.

"Don't bother!" Emma grated. "I've seen all of him I want to see!" And then she jerked the door open, slammed it behind her and left the office, shuddering with emotional reaction.

Outside she headed for her car in case Tony had someone watching her. Out of the corner of her eye, she saw the police van still parked by the curb. A few minutes later she was driving toward the police station, and the van was following close behind.

"YOU DID GREAT," Eddie praised her as he and Jack walked Emma toward the room where the technician would remove the wires she and Jack wore. "A trained policewoman couldn't have done it better."

Emma was only vaguely pleased by Eddie's praise. She was too emotionally drained to feel much of anything. But she did notice that Jack didn't have any words of praise for her performance, which made her mood slide farther downhill.

"Thank you, Eddie," she said, giving him a wan smile. "But I'm just glad it's over."

"Sure," he said. "It takes a lot out of you."

Emma glanced at Jack then. "Did we get enough to convict Tony?" she asked him, her tone reserved.

"We got enough to serve a search warrant," he said quietly. "We'll know more about where we stand when we get a look at his books."

Disappointed, Emma looked away. She had hoped everything would be open-and-shut now.

Half an hour later, she and Jack walked to her car.

"Go on home," Jack said after opening Emma's car door for her.

Emma frowned. "Aren't you coming?" she asked.

"No, I want to go over the tapes and get the process for obtaining a search warrant started," Jack said.

Emma hesitated, wanting to ask when she would see him again. They needed to talk.

"Will you keep me posted?" she asked. It was as close as she could come to asking what she really wanted to know.

"Yes. I don't know when . . . it depends on how fast things move now. But I'll be in touch."

She looked directly into Jack's eyes for a long moment, but she couldn't tell what he was thinking . . . or more importantly, what he was feeling.

"Thanks for your help," he said in a level tone. "See you later."

Will you? Emma thought bleakly. *I wonder.*

"Good night, Jack," she said aloud as she moved to get into the driver's seat of her car.

"Good night," Jack said as he shut the door for her.

As she drove away, Emma glanced in her rearview mirror. The ache in her heart eased slightly when she saw that he was still standing where he'd been, watching her drive away.

"Good, you're home," Joe said over the phone a few minutes after Emma arrived at her apartment. "I'll be right there."

"Joe, I . . ." Emma wanted to beg off bringing Joe up-to-date that night. She was tired and she was feeling blue over how things were developing between her and Jack. But he hung up before she could discourage him from coming over.

Emma had a pot of coffee started by the time Joe knocked on her door, and she led him to the kitchen rather than the living room.

"So how did it go?" Joe asked impatiently as Emma began to get cups down from the cupboard.

"All right, I guess."

Joe gritted his teeth with frustration. "Okay," he said with exaggerated patience, "start from the beginning and tell me everything."

So they sat at the kitchen table and drank coffee while Emma brought Joe up-to-date.

When she was finished, he frowned at her. "What's wrong with you, Emma?" he asked. "You seem down about something."

"I'm just tired. Fear," she added wryly, "tends to sap one's strength. It makes me wonder how law-enforcement people ever have any energy since they do this sort of thing all the time."

But Joe wasn't put off by Emma's explanation. "You're sure you're not feeling down because of that little battle I witnessed between you and Jack before he agreed to let you see Tony Caro?"

"Battle?" Emma managed to sound surprised. "Jack and I didn't fight."

"Not verbally or physically," Joe agreed, "but there's such a thing as a silent battle of wills, isn't there? And I'm pretty sure that's what you and he had."

Emma didn't feel like fencing with Joe right then. "I thought he ought to know what I'm like in case things get serious between us," she said quietly.

Joe raised an eyebrow. "That's not how it usually operates between men and women," he said dryly. "Normally neither really gets to know the other until after the vows are spoken."

Emma smiled faintly. "My mother would agree with you. She always said you never know anyone until you live with them."

"But are things getting that serious between you and Jack?" Joe asked gently. "The two of you haven't known each other long."

"True," Emma agreed, unaware that her expression was sad. "But I thought things could get serious between us—before tonight, that is."

"You think he's going to back off from you because you tend to go your own way?"

"Maybe. But I'm not going to change, Joe. So it was only fair, don't you think, to let him see me as I am?"

Joe hesitated. "Well, my mother had a few comments to say about the way things operate between the sexes, too," he said.

"What?" Emma eyed him curiously.

"She said if everyone knew about all the warts their intended spouse has before the wedding, no one would ever get married at all."

"You mean the rose-colored glasses we all put on in the beginning of a new relationship serve the purpose of getting us to the altar, and it's up to us to deal the best way we can with what comes after?"

Joe nodded.

"Maybe so," Emma said. "But I have too many children attending my nursery school whose parents are divorced not to want to do the best I can to enter marriage with my eyes open—and I think any potential husband I may have deserves the same consideration."

Joe reached over and put his hand on Emma's. When she looked up at him, he nodded encouragingly at her. "Independent or not, you're going to make a great wife for some lucky man, Emma," he said seriously. "And I hope Jack's the man for you. But if he isn't, the right one will come along eventually. I'm sure of that."

"I am, too," Emma said confidently. Inwardly, however, she was thinking, *But if Jack's not the right one, you could have fooled me. And if he isn't the right one, I'm in for a rough time for a while until I get over him. Right or wrong, I'm afraid I love him.*

THE SMALL BLUE EYES of the weak-chinned young man seated at the desk in Suave's reception area opened to their widest as Jack, Eddie and two uniformed policemen came in the door the next morning, and he jumped to his feet, hovering nervously as though he couldn't make up his mind whether to run or stay put.

"Tony in?" Jack asked casually, but he didn't wait for an answer. He continued walking toward Tony's office door.

"Hey...you can't...!" The young man's nervous sputter died away as Jack thrust open the door.

Tony was seated at his desk, and he looked up, scowling, as Jack entered his office. "What the hell you doin' here?" he demanded. "I didn't call..." But as Eddie and the two uniformed policemen followed Jack into the office, Tony took one look and immediately understood what was going on.

Uttering a resigned curse, Tony shook his head. "I shoulda known," he grunted disgustedly, eyeing Jack with hostile acceptance.

"Yeah, you should have—" Jack smiled "—but since you didn't, you have the right to remain silent..."

Jack went on reading Tony his rights, though Tony obviously wasn't listening. He looked first at his desk to ascertain what was there that might be used against him, then slid a nervous glance in the direction of his safe.

Jack finished reading Tony his rights as he walked to the safe and stood beside it. Then, without a pause, he said, "You want to give me the combination to this safe, or would you rather we use our own methods to get the door open."

"I wanta talk to my lawyer, that's what I wanta do," Tony growled.

"Fine," Jack said, "now what about the combination?"

Tony merely gave Jack a contemptuous look and turned away. Eddie stepped forward, hauled Tony out of his chair and cuffed him, and after a short search, the combination to the safe was found in Tony's desk.

After the safe was opened, Jack leafed quickly through the ledger he recognized as the one Tony had gotten out in preparation for Emma's visit the night before, and his eyes settled with satisfaction on the last entry. Sure enough, Tony had Emma down for an investment—only the investment she supposedly had made was in the amount of fifty thousand dollars, not five thousand.

Lifting his head, Jack winked at Tony. "I don't think your lawyer is going to do you much good this time," he said amiably.

"I ain't worried!" Tony shot back.

"Then you're not as smart as I thought you were," Jack responded in a friendly tone. Turning to Eddie and the two uniformed cops, he said, "Let's clean out the rest of what's in this safe, then head downtown."

EMMA OPENED HER DOOR, then stood looking at Jack for a long moment, taking in his appearance, which reminded her of the first time she'd met him. He was red eyed, morose and unkempt.

"I can only stay a minute," he said after crossing the threshold without kissing her. "I've been up all night and day and I need some sleep."

Emma stared at his back for a moment before she shut the door and followed him into the living room where Jack immediately collapsed into a chair, tilted his head back, closed his eyes and stretched out his legs.

Emma sat across from him. Instead of being annoyed over his manner, she felt tenderly concerned about his fatigue. She wanted to lead him to bed and tuck him in like one of her nursery-school children.

"We got a search warrant, arrested Tony and took his records into custody this morning," Jack said, speaking as though he were making a report to his lieutenant instead of discussing things with a woman he cared about. "He's out on bail now, and after we check his records thoroughly, we'll know how good a case we've got against him. I think we're on solid ground for his trial . . . if he doesn't fly the coop, that is."

"Do you think he will?" Emma asked quietly.

"Maybe, but I doubt it. Kansas City's Tony's base . . . his hometown. He won't leave here unless he absolutely has to. This is not the first time he's been arrested, but he's always been able to beat the rap before. So he'll probably stick around. He can afford good lawyers, and sometimes they can pull things out of the hat you wouldn't believe."

"In any case, it will be a while before you know if you need me to testify," Emma said.

"That's right."

Jack then opened his eyes and sat upright. For a long moment, he looked searchingly at Emma, wanting more than anything else to hold and kiss her. But he knew they had to talk first, and he didn't feel up to it at the moment. He was too tired to make much sense. Besides, he had some things to sort out in his own mind before he and Emma had the talk that would probably decide where they were headed in their relationship.

"I'd better get home," he said as he got to his feet.

Even though she could see that Jack was in no shape for anything but sleep, a shaft of disappointment coursed through Emma. But an instant later, she decided he was right to go home. There were some things that needed to be settled between them before they could get back to the way their relationship had been.

"Yes, you look as though you could use some sleep," she agreed as she got up and walked him to the door.

At the door, Jack hesitated. He wanted to kiss the remote expression from Emma's face and replace it with the warm, accepting one she'd worn for him before they'd gotten off track with each other.

And then Emma surprised him. Stepping close to him, she slipped her hand around the back of his neck, pulled his head down and kissed him without passion, but with gentle acceptance. When the kiss was over, she said in a quiet voice, "Good night, Jack. Have a good rest," and she stepped away from him.

He studied her calm expression for a long moment, unaware of how weary his own face looked. Then he nodded. "We'll talk soon, Emma," he said equally quietly. "Good night." Then he turned and walked away.

Chapter Ten

At hearing little Carrie Johnson burst into howling screams, Emma looked up from one of the mugs into which she was pouring milk. The little girl was trying frantically to snatch her small radio away from Johnny Brubaker and screeching her lungs out at the same time.

Emma was tired. She hadn't been sleeping well for the past few days because Jack hadn't contacted her for the talk they were supposed to have—and she had a headache. The fact that Johnny's behavior at the moment was far outside the boundaries of anything he'd done before—he'd never intimidated any of the girls in class the way he had the boys in the past—both puzzled her and snapped her already frazzled patience.

Setting the carton of milk down on the table, she strode to where the children were tussling over the radio. Taking an arm of each, she pulled them apart. Carrie was sobbing and accusing Johnny at the top of her lungs.

Emma let go of Johnny and soothed Carrie for a while until the child was able to speak coherently.

"Now tell me what happened," she said to the little girl.

Carrie pointed at Johnny. "He took my radio!" she blubbered.

Johnny, who had adopted his usual stance in these situations, arms crossed over his chest and scowling, defended himself.

"I didn't take it," he asserted. "I traded for it."

Carrie shook her head, her lower lip protruding in a trembling pout. "That's not so! I wouldn't trade for his rotten old teddy bear, and he just threw it at me and took my radio!"

The teddy bear, which looked as though it had been through the wars several times, was lying on the floor where Carrie had thrown it. Emma recognized it as one that had originally belonged to Freddie Mena. She was glad Freddie wasn't here today, or she would probably have had three unhappy children to deal with.

She looked hard at Johnny. "Is that what you did?" she asked.

There must have been something in Emma's voice or expression that alerted Johnny to the fact that she was in an exceptionally bad mood. He looked away and shrugged instead of concocting one of his usual facile excuses.

"Give the radio back to Carrie," Emma instructed.

Johnny quickly turned his head to look at Emma, a protest dawning on his childish face. But then he handed the radio to Carrie, who snatched it and hugged it to her small chest, then glared belligerently at Johnny.

"Ah, I didn't really want it anyway," he scowled. "I was just havin' some fun."

Emma decided that if Johnny's behavior had deteriorated to this extent, the time had come to deal with him more forcefully. She gathered all the children in front of her and addressed them firmly.

"We have a new rule here at school," she said. "I'm not going to allow any of you children to trade your toys back and forth."

Johnny's mouth fell open in dismay.

Emma fixed him with a meaningful look for a second, then looked at the other children.

"If any of you bring something from home to play with here, you will take your toy home with you every day," she added. "And no matter what anybody offers you to trade it, it is now against the rules to do that."

Most of the children looked pleased by the new arrangement. A few looked as though they weren't sure how they felt about it—Johnny wasn't the only child who liked to trade his or her possessions.

"That's not fair!" Johnny protested.

"Yes, it is," Emma said firmly.

"My dad says it's okay to trade!" he blurted out.

"Then trade at home," Emma said flatly, "not here."

When he opened his mouth to protest further, Emma ignored him and spoke first. "It's lunchtime," she told the children. "Everyone go get your lunch boxes and sit down in your seats." Then she turned away to go get the milk.

A few minutes later when she set Johnny's milk in front of him, he said fiercely, "I'm going to tell my dad on you!"

"Fine," Emma replied calmly. "You do that."

"He's gonna be mad!" he threatened.

Emma fixed Johnny with a look that made him subside. And then she said, "I can get mad, too."

She was gratified when her statement brought a look almost of shock to his face. It was obvious it had never occurred to Johnny that anyone, especially his normally mild-mannered nursery school teacher, would stand up to his dad.

WHEN DINNER CAME AND PASSED once again with no visit from Jack, Emma's already bad mood deteriorated further. It wasn't that she disputed Jack's right to end things between them if that was what he had in mind. It was the way he was doing it that infuriated her. Surely a final discussion of their differences was in order, and he had promised her they would talk.

After thinking it over for a while, she dialed his number. There was no answer. Far from being displeased, Emma was glad.

Hanging up the phone, she got the key Brad and Nancy Spencer had given her long ago. Then she went to the hamster cage, pulled the rubber band off it and reached in for Oscar.

Shortly thereafter, Oscar was hunkering down in the middle of the Spencer living room, gazing up at Emma with the same sort of shocked look Johnny had given her earlier that day.

"Don't look a gift horse in the mouth," she said irritably. "And don't get the idea I'm going to make a habit of this, either. This is a onetime thing. So start doing whatever it is you do whenever you come over here and enjoy yourself while you've got the chance!"

Five minutes later, she was back in her own apartment stirring up a batch of chocolate chip cookies. She would take most of them to school the next day, but some of them were going into her own stomach to soothe her mangled feelings.

AFTER UNLOCKING his apartment door, Jack paused a second, glancing down the hall at Emma's apartment. Damn, he wanted to see her! But the long hours he'd been working this past week had him feeling dead tired and short-tempered. Better wait, he decided, until he was rested and in a good mood.

In his apartment, Jack wolfed down a sandwich and a beer, then headed for his bed, which he never made. Donning the pair of sweatpants he slept in during the winter and keeping on the white T-shirt he'd worn under his clothes that day, Jack climbed into bed. But this time, when he shoved his feet under the covers, they came in contact with something furry, warm and alive!

Cursing, he bounded out of bed, then stood at the side of it staring down in astonishment. The covers were moving. And though Brad and Nancy hadn't mentioned having mice in their apartment, that was the first thing Jack thought of.

Reaching down, Jack flipped back the covers. He just had time to see Oscar cower in surprise for a moment, before the hamster leaped off the bed and headed at top speed for the living room sofa.

Cursing steadily, Jack went after Oscar and spent the next ten minutes lying flat on his stomach in front of the sofa, reaching for a slippery bundle of fur that was as fast as greased lightning. Every time Jack had it cornered, it somehow slipped out of his grasp.

By the time Jack had the creature in his hands, he wanted to strangle the little rodent. Instead he got to his feet and headed for Emma's apartment. He wasn't sleepy anymore, but he was more tired than he'd been earlier, and his mood was more than a little surly.

Emma was munching one of the cookies she'd baked when she opened the door to Jack. He held Oscar out toward her with both hands, and the glare in his bloodshot eyes wasn't quite what she'd expected when she'd planted the hamster in his apartment.

"Oh," she said. "I see Oscar got out again. Sorry."

Being face-to-face with Emma for the first time in days, Jack's longing for her rapidly sapped his anger. She looked great in tight jeans, and the blue cashmere sweater she was wearing molded her breasts lovingly. Her hair was tousled just the way he liked to see it, and there were chocolate chip cookie crumbs on her delectable mouth.

Emma popped the rest of the cookie into her mouth and reached for Oscar. "One of these days," she said with her mouth full, "I'll have to get around to buying that new cage."

With Oscar wriggling in her arms, she looked at Jack with curiosity. "Is that what you wear around the house when you're relaxing?" she asked.

"No," he said, making no move to leave, though he'd planned to a moment earlier. "This is what I wear to bed. But when I climbed in tonight, I found somebody already there."

Totally without shame, Emma grimaced at Oscar and chided him accusingly. "Haven't you gotten the hint yet that you're not welcome next door?"

Jack shrugged, and a slight smile began to form on his lips. "He's okay," he said. "I just don't want to sleep with him."

Emma returned her gaze to Jack. "Been working hard?" she asked with studied mildness.

Jack nodded. Then he lifted his head and sniffed. "Have you been baking?"

"Chocolate chip cookies for the kids," she said.

"Just the kids?" Jack focused his eyes on the crumbs at the corners of her mouth.

"Why should they have all the good stuff? Want a cookie?"

"Don't mind if I do." Jack quickly crossed the threshold and closed the door behind him.

"The cookies are on the coffee table," Emma said, as she walked toward the hamster cage. "And there's coffee in the kitchen if you want it."

"You got any milk instead?" Jack asked as he bent to pick up a cookie. "I've had enough coffee in the past few days to last me for a while."

"The milk's in the refrigerator," she replied.

While Emma deposited Oscar back in his cage and refastened the door with a new rubber band, Jack poured himself a glass of milk, then returned to the living room to sit on the couch near the cookies. Emma joined him and sat down, leaving about two feet of space between them.

"These are good," he mumbled around his latest bite. "Better than my mother makes."

Emma smiled, rather distantly it seemed to Jack. Eyeing her cautiously, he decided it might be time to make a few explanations about why he hadn't been in touch for a while.

"I've been really busy these past few days," he said. "Besides my usual duties, I've been trying to keep an eye on Tony."

"He didn't skip town?" Emma said in a deceptively mild tone.

"No. But he's keeping a low profile."

"Was he very upset when he found out you're a cop?"

"I'll say," Jack answered with grim satisfaction. "You should have heard his language when..." He paused, glanced at Emma, then shook his head. "No, come to think of it, it's a good thing you didn't."

"Does he know about me yet?"

"We've been careful about that, but knowing Tony, he may have figured out you were working with me. I'm just glad he doesn't know your real name or address."

Emma changed the subject. Eyes containing nothing more than a mild expression of curiosity, tone amiably concerned, she said, "The police department has phones, doesn't it, Jack?"

Jack immediately felt cautious again. "Yeah," he said.

"I see." Emma smiled sweetly. "You just haven't yet learned to operate a telephone, is that it?"

Jack sighed. "You're mad because I haven't called you."

"Mad?" Emma repeated thoughtfully. "No, I wouldn't put it that way. Disappointed or baffled or concerned would describe my feelings more accurately, I believe."

He shook his head. "You're mad."

Emma's gaze lost its mildness. "Okay, so I'm mad," she grated. "Wouldn't you be?"

"You didn't call me, either," Jack pointed out.

"Yes, I did," she said flatly. "You were always out."

"Oh."

Emma held on to her temper. "Listen," she said in a crisply matter-of-fact tone, "if you don't want to see me anymore, that's your privilege."

At that, Jack looked up, startled.

"But it seems to me," she went on, "that it's my right to hear you tell me face-to-face that you want to end things between us, as well as the reasons for your decision." She paused for half a second, then added, "And it would certainly be common courtesy to keep me posted on what's happening with Tony Caro in any case."

Jack shook his head. "What the hell makes you think I don't want to see you anymore?" he asked.

Emma gave him a look filled with incredulity.

"Hey," he declared lamely. "Just because I don't call or come by doesn't mean anything. I've been working my butt off."

But the look on his face and the self-defensive note in his voice told Emma that Jack knew very well she had a right to be angry. She clenched her jaw, by no means certain at this point whether *she* wanted to see any more of him.

"A telephone call to explain that would be courteous," she said stiffly.

Jack hesitated. Then he capitulated. "All right, Emma," he said quietly. "Though it's true I've been exceptionally busy, I know I should have called. The truth is, I figured you'd give me a hard time," he admitted, "and I wasn't in the mood for an argument with you."

Emma frowned, puzzled. "A hard time?" she repeated.

Jack nodded. "All the other women I've been involved with hated it when I called them to tell them I was held up at work, and they despised it even more when they had something to discuss with me I didn't want to talk about. I know I said you and I needed to talk, but I'm not ready for that yet. I need to get some things sorted out in my own mind before we have our discussion, and I haven't had time to do that yet.''

Emma felt as frustrated with Jack at that moment as she often felt with Johnny Brubaker.

"Do me a favor," she said, her tone cold. "Don't compare me with other women you've been involved with."

Jack merely looked cautious again.

His look made Emma sigh with frustration. She gathered her patience and said, "I understand your being held up at work. I can even understand your not being ready to have a serious discussion with me yet about what's wrong between us. What I don't understand is being left hanging when one simple telephone call would explain the situation."

Jack didn't believe her, and at seeing his disbelief in his expression, Emma abruptly lost her patience again.

"Would you like to know what I thought was really going on?" she asked heatedly. And without waiting for his reply, she continued, "I knew you didn't like it when I called Suave against your wishes. And then you really got upset when I insisted on going to see Tony personally. So when you didn't contact me, I decided you didn't want a woman who would act independently of your advice. Was I right?"

Jack frowned. He would have preferred this discussion to take place when he was rested and ready for it. But it was clear that if he cut off the conversation now, Emma might not ever want to reopen it.

"It's true I didn't like the way you discounted my wishes and contacted Suave," he confirmed. "And it's even more true that I resented the way you insisted on seeing Tony personally regardless of my advice."

Emma's angry expression softened. On one level, she was relieved to finally have this discussion with Jack. But she didn't have much hope that the talk would end favorably for her and Jack's relationship, and that made her feel empty inside.

"But that's not really what bothers me the most," he went on, surprising Emma. "That's not why I didn't call you."

"Oh?" She sounded as confused as she felt.

Because he wanted so much to look away as he made his admission, Jack looked straight into Emma's eyes instead.

"What really bothers me the most," he said, "is that I let you go on with the case against Tony the way I did. I could have stopped you if I really wanted to. But I wanted to get him more than I wanted to protect you, apparently. And that made me wonder if my job is more important to me than you are—than any woman ever can be."

For a moment Emma felt as though Jack had struck her physically. But then she had a thought that made her smile bleakly.

"And what do you think the fact that I went ahead against your wishes means?" she asked, her voice quiet.

Enlightenment started to dawn in his eyes.

Emma nodded. "That's right. Obviously, retaining my right to act independently meant more to me than what you thought of me. In fact," she added with a shrug, "that's part of the reason I first called Suave and why I fought for my own way so strongly about going to see Tony Caro. I wanted you to know that that's the way I am. I'm not the submissive type at all.

And I thought if that's the kind of woman you like, you ought to know what I'm really like before..."

Emma paused and then looked away from Jack's intent expression. "Well, anyway, when you didn't show up or call these past few days, I thought you'd decided I was too independent for your taste and you were just going to disappear from my life without a goodbye. But I wasn't going to let you do it that way. I wanted to hear you say it. I don't like things to taper. I like definite beginnings and..." She hesitated and returned her gaze to Jack's face. Then with soft regret, she added, "...endings."

For a long moment, they stared at each other. Then Jack leaned back and propped his head on the rear of the couch while he stared at the ceiling.

"So where does that leave us?" he finally said.

Emma frowned uncertainly; his question took her by surprise.

Jack turned his head to look at her. His eyes contained a drowsy, questioning look. "Your independence doesn't bother me as much as you think it does," he said softly. "I never intended to stop seeing you. I still want to be with you. I just don't know where it is we're heading. I'm confused about my feelings. I thought I was falling in love with you, but love doesn't square with putting you in danger, does it?"

Emma had been so certain that he wanted their relationship to end that it was an adjustment to revise her thinking.

"I don't want to stop seeing you, either," she finally said, slowly. "But I don't know where we're heading any more than you do." She glanced at him, trying not to give in to her desire to touch him. "But are you sure you don't mind what I've done about this Suave case?''

Jack shrugged. "I'm not saying I like what you did. I like to have my advice taken seriously. But I told you what I really minded. And what about you? Are you saying you don't mind the fact that my job comes first?''

"Of course, I mind it," Emma said. It was the simple truth.

Jack nodded. "I don't blame you," he said. "I would, too.''

"Do you think you'll always feel that way?''

"I don't know.''

Emma sighed. "I don't know what's best to do," she confessed. "My feelings for you are very strong. But if we continue to see each other, and I never come to feel that I mean more to you than your job, I'm not sure I can live with that. It isn't that I want to interfere with your work in any way. I would never ask you to resign from your job for my sake. But I do need to know that if you ever had to make the choice, I would win.''

Jack shook his head. "And what if you always value your independence more than me? I'm no dictator, but I want to come first with the woman I marry just the way you want to come first.''

Emma nodded. "I don't blame you.''

They were silent for a few moments, thinking things over.

But Jack eventually found he'd stopped thinking about the future and was focused on the present. Just looking at Emma was arousing him more and more. He had been too long without her. He reached over and took her hand in his, and ran his thumb over her palm.

Emma reacted predictably to his touch. But she said, "That isn't going to solve our problems."

Jack moved closer. "There are long-term problems, and then there are short-term ones," he said softly before leaning down to kiss the soft skin behind her ear. "And right now, it's the easy problem that's bothering me most."

Jack kissed her throat, then made his way downward to her shoulder. Emma's skin tingled where his lips were lightly grazing.

"This isn't fair of you," she murmured, weakening.

"Sure it is." Sensing that she was responding, Jack slid his free hand over her stomach, rubbed lightly for a moment, then moved his hand to her waist and turned her toward him.

Emma looked into his eyes for a long moment, and the warmth in Jack's returning gaze drained away what little resistance she had.

"I've missed you," she whispered.

"I've missed you, too," Jack whispered back. Leaning forward, he took her mouth in a long kiss.

When he stopped kissing her, Emma sighed, looked deeply into his eyes, and nodded.

"Does that mean we can stop talking and make love now?" he smiled.

Emma nodded again. "But I do have a headache," she said truthfully.

Jack winced and then smiled. "I've got a surefire cure," he assured her.

"Surefire?"

"Well...almost."

"That's good enough," Emma said as she slipped her arms around him.

Jack picked her up and headed for the bedroom, glancing at Oscar's cage as they passed it to make sure they weren't going to have any unwelcome company.

"Does he climb in bed with you when he gets out?" he asked, nodding at the cage.

"He never has," Emma said, smiling. "Maybe you're more his type."

Jack grimaced. "He's got a mate."

"But he strays from home often."

In the bedroom, Jack set Emma on her feet beside the bed and helped her remove her sweater.

"Personally," he said, his eyes moving hungrily over her smooth skin, "I think Oscar's got a screw loose."

Emma helped Jack remove his T-shirt, then shook her head. "No, he doesn't," she said softly as she ran her fingers through the hair on Jack's chest. "If you ask me, he has excellent taste."

Jack smiled as he pulled Emma close and tilted her head so that he could kiss her. And when his mouth closed over hers, he wondered how he'd ever made it so long without the taste of her in his mouth and the feel of her against his body. It didn't occur to him to wonder at all, however, why he no longer felt the least bit tired.

Chapter Eleven

Emma had never met Johnny Brubaker's father in person. His wife had made all the arrangements to enter her son in school and she was the only one who'd ever shown up at any of the open houses. But when Emma saw a strange man pacing impatiently in front of the entrance to the school the next morning, she knew immediately who he was.

"Good morning, Mr. Brubaker," she said lightly as she approached him.

Mr. Brubaker—a tall, slender man whom Emma suspected of being hyperactive from the way he'd been pacing when she'd driven up—frowned. She noted that the strongest resemblance between him and Johnny was their blue eyes.

"You Ms. Springer?" he asked.

Emma nodded as she inserted her key in the lock of the door.

"Have we met before?" Mr. Brubaker asked.

"No." Emma opened the door. "Come in," she said as she crossed the threshold, unbuttoning her coat.

"Then how'd you know who I was?" Mr. Brubaker asked as he came in behind her.

"I guessed," Emma said as she shut the door behind him, then headed for the coffee machine, slipping out of her coat as she went.

"Well, I wondered," Mr. Brubaker said. "Me and Johnny don't look that much alike. So you figured I'd be coming to see you, huh?"

"I figured," Emma acknowledged as she began to make coffee.

"Say, do you mind holding off on that?" Mr. Brubaker said impatiently. "I haven't got all day, and I want to talk to you."

Emma glanced at him, her gaze calm, but she didn't stop what she was doing. "We can talk while I do this," she said mildly. "I have a schedule to keep."

Mr. Brubaker's scowl was another thing he and Johnny had in common. "Yeah, I got one, too," he said sarcastically. "That's what I meant."

"Then you should have called and made an appointment with me," she pointed out. "We could have set a time to meet that was most convenient for both of us."

To her surprise, Mr. Brubaker's scowl faded and the look in his eyes began to reflect a slight degree of admiration.

"You're a cool cookie, aren't you?" he said.

"I try to be civil at all times," Emma commented. She had the coffee started now and turned to him, a polite expression on her face. "Would you like to sit down?" she asked.

"Nah, I'll stand," he said. "Johnny says you're picking on him."

Emma's surprise was genuine. "Picking on him?" she repeated.

"Yeah," Mr. Brubaker replied belligerently. "He says your new rule about trading was because of him."

"Yes, it was." Her gaze and voice were calm. "His habit of forcing the other children to trade away their toys while he didn't give them equal value in return was causing trouble. So I banned such trading entirely here at school."

Mr. Brubaker gave her a disgusted look. "What for?" he demanded. "Just because Johnny's better at it than the other kids?"

"Not entirely." Emma shook her head. "If it was only a matter of Johnny's skill at trading, I'd have left it alone in the interest of teaching the other children something. But he was using intimidation to make the other kids trade when they didn't want to. And yesterday he simply took something from one of the little girls."

"No, he didn't." Mr. Brubaker scowled. "He said he gave the kid a teddy bear in exchange. And anyway, you made him give her back the radio, didn't you?"

"Yes."

"Then what's the problem? Why stop the kid from trading entirely? I'm trying to bring him up to follow me in my business."

"Then I'm afraid you'll have to train him on your own," Emma said firmly. "Here at school, it's different, and I'm under no obligation to help you train Johnny your way."

At that, Mr. Brubaker straightened and glared at her. "Ah, come on!" he said angrily. "This place is a business for you. Don't you know how the world operates?"

"I am a businesswoman, yes," Emma said, holding Mr. Brubaker's hostile blue gaze without giving an inch. "I have to make a living just like you do. But I deal with children, not adults, Mr. Brubaker, and there's a big difference. In any case," she added, "even if I did deal with adults, I think my business ethics might differ from yours."

"Sure," Mr. Brubaker snorted contemptuously. "And you'd go broke within a month! The competition in the car business weeds out the do-gooders from the smart guys."

"I don't think so," Emma disagreed. "In my hometown there are three car dealerships. Do you know which one is the most successful?"

"The one with the smartest owner," Mr. Brubaker snorted. "Or else the one that sells the Japanese cars," he added, his scowl deepening.

"No," Emma said. "The most successful car dealer in my hometown sells American cars. What makes him a success is that everyone in town respects his integrity. They know he never misrepresents what he's selling, and if it turns out you get a lemon, he'll do his best to fix it, and if he can't, he'll go to bat for you with the auto company."

"I'll bet the company loves him," Mr. Brubaker snapped. "I'm surprised they haven't dumped him."

"Maybe they would if his sales weren't so outstanding."

That remark seemed to make Mr. Brubaker even angrier. "Hey, we're not here to talk about your hometown," he said. "We're talking about Johnny and how you're picking on him."

"I'm not picking on him," Emma said firmly. "I'm very fond of your son."

"It sure looks like it!"

Emma ignored that. "But I have an obligation to the other children, too," she went on. And then she added, very quietly, "And though I'm sure you'll probably disagree with me, I don't think it's good for Johnny to be allowed to get away with the kind of sharp dealing and intimidation he practices."

"What are you talking about?" Mr. Brubaker demanded. "I taught him everything he knows!"

"And as a result, Johnny has no close friends," Emma said gently. "In fact, I think he's very lonely. He started out trading like you taught him because he trusts that you know best. You're his father, after all, and he wants to please you. But as a result of trying to please you, none of the other children care for Johnny very much now. And I suspect that he's getting more hostile in his trading because he's angry about being rejected . . . and it's the only way he can get any attention from the other children."

For a moment, something in Mr. Brubaker's eyes made Emma think she'd gotten through to him, but then it was gone.

"Ah, you can't pay attention to people getting mad at you," he scoffed. "It happens all the time. You got to look out for yourself."

Emma sighed inwardly. "But Johnny's not an adult like you, Mr. Brubaker," she said quietly. "He's a little boy. He not only wants friends, but needs them. He has to learn how to make friends and keep them. If he doesn't, he's going to have a very lonely life."

"He'll have his family," Mr. Brubaker said stubbornly. "Just like I got mine."

"And is that enough?" Emma asked curiously.

"Sure it is!" But Mr. Brubaker looked away as he said it.

"Mr. Brubaker," she said quietly, "just as you make the rules at your place of business, I make the rules at mine. If you don't agree with the way I do things, you have the option of finding another school for Johnny, you know."

He turned his head sharply. "And don't think I wouldn't, if it wasn't for Johnny's mother!" he said. "But she's hung up on your place…says it has the best reputation."

"I'm glad to hear that," Emma said simply. "As I told you before, I'm fond of Johnny and I'd like him to continue to come here. But if he does, he'll be doing things my way."

For a moment, Emma saw angry frustration in Mr. Brubaker's eyes. She assumed he wasn't used to being thwarted.

"You haven't got the right to teach Johnny different than I want!" he blustered.

Emma shook her head. "No, you're wrong. What I haven't got the right to do is to tell him straight out that I disagree with his father on a number of things. And I don't do that. But I do have the right to try to show him another way of behaving. And I also have the obligation to protect the other children who come here."

"Who are you to judge me!"

"I don't judge you. I disagree with you."

Mr. Brubaker and Emma stared at each other for a long moment, neither giving an inch. Finally Mr. Brubaker shrugged. "If it was up to me, I'd have Johnny out of here and in another school today!" he said forcefully. "But since he's only got another three months to go, I'm going to let his mother have her way.

But if I ever hear of you running me down to him, you're in big trouble, lady!''

"You won't hear of that," Emma said quietly, "because I won't do that. It's important for little boys to admire their fathers. When they grow up, they can make their own judgments."

Glaring, Mr. Brubaker turned on his heel and headed for the door. But after putting his hand on the knob, he paused and looked back at Emma.

"You don't have a wife and kids to support. If you did, maybe you wouldn't be so high-and-mighty!"

"I'm not trying to be high-and-mighty, Mr. Brubaker," she replied soberly. "I just happen to believe that the lessons we teach our children by example are more important than whether we have steak on the table and expensive clothes to put on their backs."

"Sure. That's what all you do-gooders say," Mr. Brubaker snorted, and then he angrily turned the knob and let himself out, slamming the door behind him.

Emma sighed and went to pour herself a cup of coffee. And as she drank it, she made a mental note to talk to Johnny and find out if the boy really did think she was picking on him...or whether he'd gotten that idea—along with a lot of other ones Emma didn't agree with—from his father.

"THE DOCUMENTARY EVIDENCE against you is impressive," Tony Caro's lawyer said. "We can muddy the water of Jack Spencer's testimony by claiming entrapment. But if the police can come up with someone else willing to testify that your escort business actually participated in male prostitution, we may be in trouble."

Tony merely shrugged, and his attorney went on.

"If they can't prove the male prostitution charge, then there's no basis, of course, to assume you had anything with which to blackmail your female clients into buying stock. But I wish they didn't have your ledger. Now they can question the women listed in the hope that one or more will cooperate."

"Don't worry about it." Tony smiled thinly. "None of those women will testify. I chose who to put the arm on very carefully."

The attorney frowned. "I'm not sure you should be so confident. The prosecutors are as aware as I am how important even one woman's testimony can be at your trial, and they must be feeling confident, or they wouldn't be pressing forward like this."

"This won't come to trial," Tony assured his attorney. "I'll make sure of that myself."

"What do you mean?"

"Never you mind," Tony grunted as he got up to leave his lawyer's office. "What you don't know can't hurt you."

"So I AM GOING TO have to testify?" Emma asked Jack.

For once they were having supper at Jack's place. He'd bought Chinese take-out and invited her over.

"That's what the prosecutor says." Jack nodded. "He's afraid Tony's attorney will be able to convince the jury it was entrapment if my testimony isn't supported by someone else's." Then he looked at her searchingly. "Having any second thoughts?" he asked.

"About testifying?"

Jack nodded.

Emma shook her head. "No, I'm ready to do it. How long do you think it will be before the trial?"

"Several months, probably. It depends on how many delays Tony's lawyers can throw in the way."

Emma grimaced. "And meanwhile he's free to do what he pleases."

"That's the way the system works," Jack told her, then decided it was time to change the subject. "How was your day?" he asked.

Emma smiled ruefully and told him about her visit from Johnny's father.

"The guy comes on pretty strong, doesn't he?" Jack commented with a frown.

"Yes. He would have bullied me if I'd been the type to let him," Emma agreed. "I wonder how he handles his employees," she added with a dry smile. "Or how he gets anyone to work for him in the first place."

"I imagine no one works for him for very long if they don't produce," Jack said. "He's got his eye on the bottom line to the exclusion of anything else, if you ask me."

Emma nodded. "I'm glad he didn't take Johnny out of school," she said. "I still hope to change the boy's mind about a few things."

Jack sat back in his chair and wiped his mouth with a napkin, his expression thoughtful. "Maybe I can come up with something to help," he said.

Emma looked up at him hopefully. "What do you have in mind?"

Jack just shook his head. "I'm not sure if I can put it all together, but I'll see what I can do."

They were clearing the table when Joe knocked on the door. They brought him up-to-date on the Suave case as they loaded the dishwasher.

"Well, it'll be nice to have a breather from all this," Joe commented, smiling. "If the trial's down the road, maybe we can talk about something else for a change."

Emma noticed something unusual in Joe's attitude and said, "Is something on your mind?"

"Maybe."

Emma grinned. "Do you want me to drag it out of you, or will you spill it of your own free will?"

"I guess I'll spill it. I've met a woman."

Emma beamed at him. "Where?"

"At work. We hired a new financial planner who just finished getting her master's degree, and I've been assigned to train her."

"Sounds like you're looking forward to it," Jack said with a smile.

"Well, after one look at her, I didn't complain, I'll admit." Joe smiled back rather sheepishly. And then he sobered. "But I want you to meet her, Emma," he said. "You've got a good track record predicting how things will go with me and the woman I date, so if you and Jack will join me and Nicole for dinner Saturday night, I'd appreciate it."

Emma frowned. "Joe, I never make judgments about the women you date. What are you talking about?"

"You don't have to say anything," Joe said. "I can tell how you feel about someone just by watching how you react to them. I called it right about Jack, didn't I?"

Emma made a face at him, while Jack looked curious. "What are you talking about?" he asked

Joe grinned. "I knew Emma was keen on you before she did."

"You did not," Emma said, scowling at him.

"Hold it," Jack drawled, but his eyes were on Emma, sparkling with warmth and humor.

"Well, anyway, I don't want to take responsibility for who you date and who you drop, Joe," Emma complained. "That's up to you."

"Sure, ultimately," Joe agreed. "But since I'm going to have to work with Nicole, I don't want to plunge either of us into a sticky situation we might both regret later. When I invited her over, I didn't make out like it was a date. It was just a friendly invite, colleague to colleague."

"But if I don't like her, I'm not going to tell you," Emma said, frowning.

"I said you won't have to because I'll be able to tell."

"And you'll stop seeing her just because I don't take to her?" Emma asked, dismayed.

"Not necessarily." He smiled. "But I'll sure as hell take things a lot slower than I normally would."

Jack looked at Joe thoughtfully. In some ways Joe knew Emma better than he did.

"Well, I gotta go," Joe said. "I've got a whole briefcase full of mail to catch up on that came in to the office while I was away this week. See you two later."

After Joe had left, Jack and Emma went to the living room and sat down on the couch.

"I wish Joe hadn't told me he depends on my opinion so much," Emma said quietly. "I can be as wrong as the next person, and it's his life."

"He must have good reasons to depend on you," Jack said as he twisted around to put his head in Emma's lap.

"I can't think of any," she said as she stroked Jack's thick hair. "I wasn't even aware he was watching to see how I reacted to his girlfriends."

Jack merely grunted. He still hadn't caught up on his sleep from the hectic previous week and Emma's caressing was making him tired.

"Are you going to sleep?" she asked.

"Nah." His voice was drowsy.

"Liar. Come on, Jack, get up and go to bed. I'll go home and let you rest." She stopped stroking his hair and shoved his shoulder gently, trying to make him sit up.

Jack opened one eye and peered up at Emma's smiling face. "It's more comfortable here," he said, refusing to budge.

"For you, maybe," Emma laughed. "Not for me."

The next thing she knew, Jack's hand was on the back of her neck and he was pulling her face down to his. But she could only bend so far. Still laughing, she shook her head. "This isn't going to work."

Jack obligingly shifted and came up on one elbow, meeting Emma halfway. Then he kissed her.

"I thought you were sleepy," Emma murmured a moment later.

"I am." Jack kissed her again.

"That wasn't a sleepy kiss," she pointed out breathlessly when she could speak.

"How about this one?"

After a few seconds, Emma was even more breathless. "No," she said shakily, "that kiss wasn't a sleepy one, either."

"Well, hell, then," Jack said, faking resignation as he sat up, then got to his feet and reached to pull her up as well. "If I'm not sleepy, then why go to bed alone?"

"Joe Truman."

Joe answered his phone absently. He was concentrating on the document he was reading.

There was a slight pause on the other side of the phone line. Then a rough voice said, "*Joe* Truman?" with the emphasis on the first name.

"Yes, who is it?"

But all Joe got for an answer was a click as the man on the other end of the phone hung up.

Joe, looking puzzled, put the receiver back on the cradle. And after a moment, he went back to his work.

"I think it was a setup," Tony reiterated to the man in the passenger seat beside him. "I don't think there is any Josephine Truman."

"You could be right." His companion shrugged. "But what if you're wrong? And either way, what you're planning could cause a big stink and an even bigger investigation. You know the old man wouldn't like that."

"Look," Tony said harshly, "there was only one dame that undercover cop went out with. I sent him out twice, but the second time he said the woman chickened out and took off before he ever got to the meeting place. I thought Ms. Truman was a smart lady because she had the whole deal figured out before she came to meet with me. But now I think she probably knew the score because the cop was using her. I'd lay odds she shows up at my trial to testify, and you know I don't bet on nuthin' but sure things."

His companion shrugged again. "Supposin' you're right," he said. "How you figure on finding her?"

"She's gotta know the guy who just answered the phone," Tony grunted. "So we stake out that place and watch for her to show up."

"And if it's a waste of time?"

"You're gittin' paid," Tony pointed out. "What do you care if you just sit in a car doin' nuthin' for a few days?"

"I don't care," the man growled. "But the old man might. I work for him, not you, remember?"

"I'll clear it with the old man. I think he understands the problem here anyway better than you seem to, else why would he have you even meet me to talk about it. He's got somethin' to lose, too, if that dame testifies about the stock deal, because she's gonna be tellin' them she gave me five thousand bucks and the receipt I gave her as well as my ledger says fifty thousand. That'll give the cops a lead, and it's mostly the old man's money I been launderin', so all this could backfire in his face."

"That's between him and you," the man said as he reached for the doorknob. "You fix it with the old man, he'll give me the word and I'll get on it. Otherwise forget it." With no farewell, he got out of the car and walked to his own.

Tony started his car and drove to the nearest pay phone to call the old man. When he came out of the booth, his expression was satisfied.

Chapter Twelve

As she got out of the car, her arms laden with groceries, Emma was annoyed with herself for buying so much that she was going to have to make two trips from her car to her apartment. Usually she managed her purchasing better. But then she hadn't had to buy so much before Jack started eating dinner with her regularly.

The man in the car recognized Emma from the description Tony had given him, but he didn't move to intercept her because another car was just pulling into the lot at that moment. There would be a better time.

His patience was rewarded a few minutes later as Emma reappeared and headed for her car. Starting his engine, the man backed out and timed his progress in order to reach Emma's car at the same time she did.

Emma glanced up as the car stopped behind her own and a man opened the driver's door and got out without killing the engine.

"Good evening, ma'am," he said in a friendly manner as he came around his car. "I wonder if you could help me with some directions."

"I'll be glad to if I can," Emma agreed, but she wondered why the man couldn't just speak to her over the hood of his car instead of coming all the way to where she was standing.

"I'm looking for a guy named Joe Truman," the fellow said as he approached Emma.

"Joe?" Emma said, relaxing. "He lives in this building." She pointed back over her shoulder.

The man stopped directly in front of Emma and kept one hand in his pocket. "And what about Josephine Truman?" he asked pleasantly, watching Emma's face. "Does she live here, too?"

At that, Emma knew she was in trouble, but it was too late. As she opened her mouth to scream for help, the man grabbed her arm with his free hand and shoved the hand in his pocket, which held a gun, against her waist. "I wouldn't do that if I were you," he said with soft menace. "Not unless you want to die right here and now."

Emma looked directly into the man's eyes. What she saw there made her close her mouth.

"Get in the car," the man said as he exerted pressure on Emma's arm and dragged her to his car.

Never in her life had she been in such a situation, and she didn't know what to do. Her inclination was to fight and scream. But she'd seen her abductor's nature in his eyes, and she didn't have a doubt in the world that he was capable of killing her if she fought him.

She looked frantically around as the man shoved her into the passenger seat of his car, but there was no one visible to call to for help. And once the man slammed the car door shut on her and started walking around to get in the driver's seat, Emma couldn't get the door open again, though she tried. The lock had been broken off.

She squeezed herself as far into the corner away from her abductor as possible after he'd climbed in, staring at him in terror as he put the car in motion.

"Where are you taking me?" she asked, her voice shaking.

"Relax. Somebody just wants to talk to you."

"Who?"

"Shut up and keep still," the man said as he pulled onto the street fronting Emma's apartment house.

Emma had a good idea who it was that wanted to talk to her. Her only hope was that Tony would only try to browbeat her into agreeing not to testify against him. She quickly decided to pretend ignorance of the setup against Tony as long as it seemed wise to. Maybe she could get away with it. And if she couldn't, she would agree to anything he wanted in order to get free of him.

JACK PULLED into his parking space. He was a little late, but Emma had said she was going to buy groceries before coming home, so he knew he wouldn't be spoiling dinner. In fact, he could help her fix it.

When Jack reached his apartment, he looked down the hall and saw that Emma's door was open. He shrugged, thinking she might be at Joe's. Entering his own apartment, he hung up his coat and then checked his mail before starting for Emma's place.

But she wasn't in her apartment, and there were groceries still in their sacks on the kitchen table.

Maybe she intends to have Joe over for supper with us, Jack thought as he turned around to head for Joe's apartment.

But when Joe opened his door, he said, "She's not here. I haven't seen her this evening."

Jack frowned. "Her door's open and there are groceries waiting to be put away," he said.

"Maybe she's in the laundry room," Joe suggested.

"I'll check," he said. "But if she's not there, is there another tenant around here she visits sometimes?"

Joe shook his head. "I only know the tenants on the other floors by sight," he explained. "I'm not aware of it if Emma has other friends here in the building. Is her car in the lot?"

Jack nodded. "I saw it as I came in, but she wasn't around."

Joe frowned. "Let me know if you can't locate her," he said.

Fifteen minutes later, Jack was back at Joe's apartment, and he was puzzled and growing alarmed.

"I can't find her anywhere," he said. "Can you think of anyplace else she might have gone?"

Joe was becoming alarmed, too. He shook his head, beginning to look as worried as Jack did.

"I'm going out to check her car," Jack said. "Meanwhile you start checking with the other tenants."

The two bags of groceries in the back seat of Emma's car didn't alleviate Jack's misgivings in the slightest. She wouldn't leave food on the table and in her car for this long. He slammed the flat of his hand on the roof of Emma's car and looked around. There was no one in sight to question.

Half an hour later, Jack and Joe had been to every apartment in the building, but no one had seen Emma that evening except one man who remembered seeing a woman fitting her description entering the building with her arms full of groceries earlier.

"Did you see anybody suspicious in the parking lot?" Jack asked grimly.

"Suspicious?" the man repeated.

"An unfamiliar car...someone who didn't seem to belong," Jack prodded, doing his best to keep his tone from showing his impatience and anger.

"Well...there was a strange car in the Miller's space. They're away for a few days. But sometimes people here let friends use their parking spaces when they're going to be away, so I didn't think much of it."

"Do you remember what make it was? What color?"

The man shrugged. "It was maybe black or burgundy. It was too dark to tell. And it looked fairly new...maybe it was a Chevy, but I can't be certain."

"Who was in it?"

"Just one man."

"Can you give me a description of him?"

The man shook his head. "All I could see was a hat."

"Mind if I use your phone?" And without waiting for agreement, Jack shoved past the man, went to the telephone and dialed the station. He gave the cop on duty a description of the car and of Emma and asked that they be put on the radio. Then he called Eddie and asked him to meet him at the Suave office as fast as he could get there.

EMMA WAS SITTING on the floor of a vacant, unheated, unlit house in a section of Kansas City she was completely unfamiliar with. She wasn't even sure she could find her way back here if she had to—or if she ever got the chance. Her abductor was standing at a front window of the room smoking one cigarette after another. He threw the butts down on the floor and stepped on them.

He made a sound but she wasn't able to distinguish it. A moment later, she heard a car door slam, and realized someone else was coming. She got to her feet.

A man with a flashlight stepped into the house a moment later and after shutting the door behind him, played the light over Emma. She raised a hand to shield her eyes.

"You Josephine Truman?" the new man asked.

It wasn't Tony Caro, but Emma didn't know whether that was a good or a bad sign. "N-no," she stuttered. Her teeth were chattering from both cold and fear.

"What's your real name then?"

Emma hesitated. "June Blake."

"You're lying."

Emma shrugged, then wrapped her arms around herself. Her whole body was shaking.

"It don't matter anyway," the man said. "We know where you live, and we can always find out your real name."

"What do you want with me?" Emma demanded.

"Nuthin' much. Just wanted to give you a friendly warning."

"About what?"

"Don't play dumb. You know what."

"No, I don't." Emma made her tone as firm as possible.

"Sure you do. You're figurin' on testifying against Tony Caro, ain't you?"

"I don't know what you're talking about. I don't know any Tony Caro."

"Come off it," the man said in disgust. But then he added, "Never mind, though. This is just a friendly warnin', like I said. You keep your mouth shut, and you ain't got nuthin' to worry about. You talk, and there's no place you can go we can't find you. Remember that. No place.''

He gestured with his flashlight toward the man who had abducted Emma. "Let's go," he said.

A moment later, Emma was alone in the vacant house.

JACK AND EDDIE STOOD in front of Tony Caro's desk. Tony was leaning back in his chair with his hands clasped over his belly, looking at the two of them with contemptuous hostility.

"I told you," he said, "I been here all evening. I even had my dinner sent in from the restaurant down the street. You can check with them if you don't believe me."

Jack was on the edge of losing control, and Eddie knew it. Eddie therefore reached over and took hold of Jack's arm just above the elbow.

"We'll check," he said. "Let's go, Jack."

"Not yet," Jack said, his voice as hard as granite. "Who'd you send after her, Tony?" he grated. "You'd better tell me where she is, or..."

"Let's *go*, Jack," Eddie interrupted. And using his tremendous strength, he dragged Jack out of Tony's office.

Outside on the street, Jack shook Eddie off. "What the hell?" he demanded through gritted teeth.

"You know he's not going to tell you anything, Jack," Eddie said patiently, "and if you lost your temper in there, you could blow your case."

Jack stared at Eddie, his gaze unrelenting.

"Also, if he didn't know before, you just told him in so many words that you and Emma are connected," Eddie pointed out.

"He knows already. He sent someone after Emma," Jack bit out. "And if I have two minutes alone with the bastard, I'll get out of him where she was taken."

"No," Eddie shook his head. "Not Tony. The guy's got nerve. And he's smart. You lay a finger on him, and you'll be the one in jail before the night's over."

"I don't give a damn!" Jack said. "If anything's happened to Emma, I don't give a damn about anything!"

He hadn't known himself until he'd said the words that they were true. But at that moment Jack realized he'd been wrong before in thinking his job was more important to him than Emma. Somehow, without his even realizing it, she'd moved into first place. But it wasn't going to matter if he couldn't find her.

"Jack, get hold of yourself, man," Eddie said. "You land in jail, then you ain't never gonna find Emma. Let's check in with the station and see if she's been spotted."

Jack went to the car with Eddie to radio the station, but he had no intention of taking Eddie's advice about leaving Tony alone if it turned out Emma hadn't been located yet.

"Yeah," the cop at the station said a moment later. "She called in a little while ago. Sounded pretty shaken, but she's okay. She said she was going home."

Jack headed for his car at a dead run.

Grinning, Eddie called after him. "Now ain't you glad you're not in jail?"

Jack didn't bother answering. He would thank Eddie another time for restraining him. First things first.

EMMA WAS SITTING in Joe's apartment holding a steaming cup of tea in her hands, and shaking uncontrollably.

"Relax, Emma," Joe said soothingly. "It's over now."

"Jack's still out there," Emma said through chattering teeth. She was still cold, and afraid. But most of her fear at the moment was for Jack. She could imagine what he might be doing to Tony Caro in order to try to find her. That was why she'd called the station at the first public phone booth she'd come to after walking away from the house where she'd been held. Then she'd caught a taxi home.

"Jack will check in at the station," Joe said, speaking quietly in order to try to calm Emma down. "They'll tell him you called."

"I hope so," she breathed. "And I hope he calls before he does something foolish."

"Like what?"

"Like killing Tony Caro."

Joe grimaced. "I wouldn't mind having a shot at Caro myself," he said grimly.

Emma smiled faintly, then managed to hold her tea cup steady enough so that she could sip the hot brew.

Both she and Joe looked up, startled, when a pounding started on Joe's door, and Jack's muffled voice yelled, "Joe! Is Emma in there? Let me in!"

Joe hastened to open the door while Emma set the tea down on a nearby table and shakily got to her feet. But Jack crossed the room so fast after Joe had let him in that she didn't have time to move toward him. Then she was clasped in his arms being alternately smothered and frozen by the cold wool of his coat.

"Emma!" Jack said her name from deep in his throat. "God! I was afraid—" He broke off what he'd been about to say and tightened his embrace.

A violent shudder went through Emma's body in reaction to the cold of Jack's coat and her emotional response to his manner. Feeling the shudder, he held her even tighter than before.

Finally Jack loosened his hold on Emma and backed off enough to look her over. "Did they hurt you?" he asked fiercely.

Emma shook her head. "No. They just scared me to death."

"They. There was more than one?"

"One abducted me and took me to a vacant house...another one came and threatened me about testifying against Tony."

Joe cleared his throat. "Can I offer you something to drink, Jack?" he asked.

Jack turned his head and looked at Joe. "No, thanks," he said huskily. "I want to be alone with Emma for a while."

"Be my guest," Joe said as he started to leave the room.

"Don't bother, Joe," Jack said. "We'll go to my place."

Emma kissed Joe's cheek as she and Jack were leaving. "Thanks for the tea," she said warmly. "And thanks for everything else, too."

"Everything else?" Joe questioned. "I didn't do anything else."

"You were here," Emma said soberly. "And you cared."

"Guilty," Joe admitted, smiling.

Just as Emma and Jack were about to enter his apartment, she remembered her groceries.

"Oh, Jack, I had ice cream in one of those sacks," she said, and she started to break away from him.

"If it's in one of those sacks on your kitchen table, it's already melted," Jack said firmly, pulling her back.

"But there's meat and milk, too," she argued. "Come on. Help me put everything away. Then we can talk."

"We'll talk *now*," Jack insisted, and a moment later, the door of his apartment was closed behind them.

He took Emma into his arms and kissed her for a long time, alternating between fierce possessiveness and eloquent tenderness, before he let her catch her breath. And when he did, she had stopped trembling. There had been something about the way Jack kissed her...

"Remember how I told you I was afraid my job was more important to me than you are?" Jack asked huskily, holding her gaze.

Emma nodded, her gaze locked in Jack's.

"I was wrong. I found that out tonight."

Emma went very still. "You did?"

He nodded soberly. "Yeah. When I thought I'd lost you..." He stopped speaking, took a deep breath, then folded her closer into his arms, holding on to her as though he never intended to let her go again.

Emma rested against him, smiling, feeling safe...and loved. Turning her head, she whispered in his ear. "Does that mean you love me, Jack?"

He moved his head and kissed Emma's neck. "Didn't I just say that?" he murmured, beginning to smile a little.

Emma's smile broadened. "Did you?"

Jack reluctantly lifted his head and searched her eyes. "I'm not much good with words, Emma," he murmured, low and sincere. "But if you need to hear it, then I'll say it. Yes, I love you . . . very much."

Emma's eyes softened. "I love you, too, Jack," she said quietly. Then she lifted her mouth to his to seal the truth with a kiss.

"WE CAN BRING TONY IN, Jack," the lieutenant said the next morning, "but his lawyer will have him out just about as fast as we can book him. What we need are the guys who took your girl and threatened her. Right now, all we've got is her word that they told her not to testify at Caro's trial. What we need is their confession that Tony hired them to do it."

"Her word's good enough for me," Jack said tightly.

"But not for the courts," the lieutenant shook his head. "Keep looking for the guys who took her," he added. "And meanwhile keep her safe."

"She's safe. She's living with me right now."

"But don't the two of you live right next door to each other?"

"Right. But she doesn't go into her own place alone. If I'm not there, a friend goes with her. And if he's not there, she doesn't go, period."

"What about work?" the lieutenant asked. "She owns a nursery school, doesn't she?"

"I drive and pick her up."

The lieutenant shrugged. "Okay. Just keep looking for the two thugs who got her before. Maybe if we have them, we'll have one more thing that'll stick to Tony."

"Yeah," Jack said grudingly. But he wasn't happy. He wouldn't be happy until Tony Caro was locked up for good.

Chapter Thirteen

Emma was determined that Joe wasn't going to be able to tell a thing, either positive or negative, about her reaction to Nicole Sanderson. But she couldn't help the widening of her eyes when she met Nicole. Emma had expected a buttoned-down modern MBA type, but Nicole turned out to be a voluptuous redhead whose slinky black dress could have used a few more buttons than it possessed.

From the expression on Jack's face as he eyed Nicole's bosom, Emma was positive he wouldn't be any more in favor of adding the needed extra buttons to Nicole's dress than Joe obviously was.

Men! Emma thought crossly as she pasted a polite smile onto her lips and shook Nicole's hand. *Why does it always turn out their brains are located somewhere below their belts?*

"I understand you own a nursery school," Nicole remarked over the broiled chicken breasts Joe had prepared.

"Yes, I do," Emma confirmed.

Nicole's face softened. "I love kids," she said.

Nicole's tone was so sincere, Emma believed her.

"How many children do you want to have?" Joe asked Nicole in a just-making-conversation tone.

Emma glanced at him and hid a smile. She didn't blame him for trying to find out a few pertinent details about a woman he was so obviously interested in. But if Joe thought he was carrying off his role of being politely interested, instead of avidly curious, he was fooling himself.

"Two," Nicole answered, smiling directly into Joe's eyes. "I have a brother, and we always got along fabulously. So two seems like a good number of children to me. But I'll take whatever I get, of course."

Joe smiled back at Nicole with such a fatuous expression on his face that Emma and Jack glanced at each other then quickly looked away in order to keep from laughing.

"Do you plan to work after you have your children?" Emma asked.

At that, Nicole's expression firmed. "If things work out the way I plan," she said, "I want to have my children two years apart, and I'm going to be a full-time mother until the youngest is three. Then I'm going to put him or her into a nursery school like yours, Emma, for part of the day while I get a financial consulting business started out of my home. I know many women have to work outside their homes while their children are small, but I really don't want to."

Joe's fatuous expression grew even more obvious. Nicole was winning Emma over as well.

"What about you, Emma?" Nicole asked. "Are you going to continue working when you get married and have children?"

Jack looked at Emma, mischief dancing in his eyes. "Yes, Emma," he said politely, "what *are* you going to do when you have children?"

Emma and Jack hadn't actually discussed marriage yet. But as Emma looked back at Jack, her expression deadpan, it wasn't at all hard to imagine being married to him, and she hoped with all her heart that that was where they were heading. But that hope didn't stop her from having some fun at his expense.

"Oh, you know what a liberated woman I am, Jack," she said in a deliberately mild tone. "So I'm going to have my husband quit his job and stay home with our children while I continue to operate my nursery school."

The look on Jack's face made Joe roar with laughter. Emma couldn't keep from joining in, which made Jack's expression turn to one of relief. But he still needed verbal assurance.

"You were kidding, right?" he asked when Emma and Joe had stopped laughing enough so that he could be heard.

Emma paused. Jack's question seemed to indicate he was thinking along the same lines she was concerning their future. Good! But her pause was making him look anxious again, so she put him out of his misery.

"Yes, I was kidding." She grinned. "I'm hoping to do exactly as Nicole plans to, only in my case, it will depend on finding someone I trust to run my nursery school while I'm staying home. Then I can take my children to nursery school with me when they get old enough."

Jack breathed a sigh of relief. "Sounds good to me."

That statement encouraged Emma's feeling that he was thinking of a future together for them as much as she was. But they had too much going on at the moment—such as the prospect of Tony Caro's trial. Besides, though Emma knew she loved Jack, she thought they needed time to get to know more about each other before making a firm commitment.

Nicole stayed behind when Jack and Emma left Joe's apartment to go home, and Joe stepped out into the hallway with them.

"Admit it," he whispered to Emma. "You like her."

Emma smiled. "Yes, I do. But the important thing is that you obviously do."

"I'll say." He beamed, then looked at Jack for his opinion of Nicole. But Jack didn't have to say anything. One look expressed his opinion clearly.

"Men!" Emma said, annoyed. "Beauty fades, you know. And marriage has a way of making looks less important than other things, anyway."

Joe and Jack exchanged identical male grins.

"Oh, for heaven's sake!" Emma exclaimed, pivoting on her heel. "Good night, Joe," she said over her shoulder. "Thanks for dinner. It was lovely."

Jack followed her, still grinning. "Yeah, thanks, Joe," he echoed. "And good luck with the rest of the evening," he added meaningfully.

That stopped Emma, and turning, she glared at both men before fixing her attention on Joe. But before she could say anything, he held up his hands and shook his head.

"It's up to her," he mouthed the words silently.

"And so it should be," Emma answered firmly, and then she pivoted sharply again and continued down the hall.

Inside Jack's apartment, he came up behind her and wrapped his arms around her. "Okay," he said with mock humility. "I confess. I was rude, crude and rottenly, superficially male to the core." He held out his wrists in front of her. "Cuff me, take me in the bedroom, lock the door and throw away the key."

"You wish," Emma snorted.

Jack smiled and kissed her behind the ear. "I adore you," he murmured contritely. "And I swear to you that not once this evening, not even when Nicole dropped her fork and leaned down to get it, did my mind turn from adoration of my true love."

"Jack Spencer, you're the biggest liar since Judas." She shook her head. "You all but leaped over the table to get a better look when Nicole dropped that fork."

"No, no," Jack protested. "I was merely preparing to assist in the retrieval of the fork like a true gentleman, had it been necessary. But she picked it up before I could help."

Emma sighed. "This might be a good time to inquire as to how you feel about fidelity in a relationship," she said dryly.

"I'm all for it," Jack swore.

"For both parties or merely the female?"

"Both." Jack put his hands on Emma's shoulders then and turned her around so that he could look into her eyes. His own contained laughter, but they also contained loving sincerity. "Trust me, Emma," he said in a much more sober tone of voice than he'd been using. "I don't deny that in my job there are plenty of opportunities to stray. I don't even deny that a lot of cops take advantage of those opportunities. But I give you my word that I won't."

Emma's expression softened. "I believe you," she said.

"You do?" He almost couldn't believe it was that simple to convince her of his intentions.

"I do."

"Even though I work around prostitutes?" Janice hadn't exactly been jealous of the prostitutes Jack dealt with, but she hadn't liked the idea much, either.

Emma tilted her head and studied Jack's face. "Have you ever been with a prostitute, Jack?" she asked curiously.

"No."

Emma shrugged. "Somehow, I didn't think you had. And if you haven't taken advantage of what they offer before now, why should you in the future?"

Jack smiled, his relief over Emma's attitude profound. "Exactly," he murmured. And then he kissed her, without heat or urgency. His more tender feelings for Emma were growing all the time.

THE RINGING OF THE TELEPHONE brought Jack and Emma awake. Jack reached over and picked up the receiver.

"Yeah," he said groggily. He listened for a couple of minutes, then said, "We'll be right down." He hung up, switched on the bedside light, then turned to Emma, who was blinking against the light.

"What is it?" she mumbled.

"They've picked up the guy you identified from the mug shots," Jack said, sitting up. "The one who abducted you."

Emma's eyes opened wider, and she began to struggle to sit up as well.

"They want to put him in a lineup," Jack added as he got up. "Come on. Get your clothes on. This could be what we've been waiting for—another way to nail Tony.''

An hour later, Emma was looking at several men in the lineup. She pointed without hesitation to the man who'd taken her from her apartment parking lot. "That's him," she said firmly.

"You're sure?" Jack asked with satisfaction.

"I'm sure," she replied.

"Good." Jack turned to one of the uniformed policemen in the rooms. "Take Emma somewhere where she can relax for a while. Give her some coffee. I'm going to question this guy."

An hour later, Jack and Eddie stood outside the interrogation room, looking and feeling frustrated.

"He isn't going to break, Jack," Eddie said wearily. "At least not this soon and not without some strong leverage."

"We'll see," Jack said, his tone grim. "I'm going back in there and try again. We've been too easy on him so far. You stay out here, and I'll—"

Eddie interrupted, shaking his head. "You're too close to this. I know how you feel, but it's not a good idea for you to be in the room alone with this guy." And as Jack's expression turned angry, he added, "Not for his sake... for yours. You're too good a cop to screw up your career for personal reasons."

Jack slowly relaxed. "Okay," he agreed grudgingly. "You can come in with me while we give it another try."

Eddie merely shrugged.

"We've got a positive identification on you, Frankie," Jack said grimly, hating the self-assured smugness of the thug on the other side of the table.

"People make mistakes all the time," he said in an unconcerned tone. "They change their minds, too."

At that, Jack frowned. "You think our witness is going to change her mind? Why would she do that?"

Frankie merely smiled.

Jack's anger began to slide toward rage. Eddie sensed it and got Jack's attention, shaking his head and frowning. Jack took a deep breath and got to his feet.

"Take him back to his cell," he grated contemptuously.

ON THE WAY BACK HOME, Jack told Emma her abductor wasn't going to admit anything and that they needed to take additional care for her safety now.

"Since you didn't hesitate to identify the guy who picked you up, Tony's going to know you weren't intimidated by his little plan. And that means he'll probably try again. Only this time, he may not stop at just trying to scare you."

Emma sat silent and thoughtful for a while. "Jack," she finally said, her voice quiet, "I hate uncertainty."

"So do I," he said. "But what can we do about it?"

"We could force their hand," Emma suggested in a neutral tone.

Jack's foot came off the gas pedal slightly and his glance at her was sharp. "What do you mean?" he asked.

Emma took a deep breath. "I mean that we could set a trap for Tony—with me as the bait."

"God, Emma, are you out of your mind?" He was furious at the very idea.

"Jack, I promise I wouldn't argue with you about any of the arrangements you wanted to make," she said soothingly. "I'd do just as you say. Only please at least consider the idea. I hate feeling as though I always have to look over my shoulder, and you said yourself it could be months before Tony's trial is held. I don't want to live like this for that long. I want this over with!''

Jack stayed grimly silent for the rest of the drive home. And he didn't speak until the door of his apartment had closed behind them.

"I'll consider the idea," he said as he tossed his coat on the couch. His expression and his tone were hostile. "But not using you as the target."

Puzzled, Emma frowned at him. "But I'm the only one they care about," she pointed out as she unbuttoned her coat.

Jack nodded. "But a policewoman who resembles you could take your place."

Emma's frown deepened. "And if anything happened to her, I'd feel guilty for the rest of my life."

Jack almost lost his temper. "And how am I supposed to feel if something happens to you?" he grated.

He had a point. Emma went to him and put her hands on his shoulders. Jack didn't soften, however. His hands stayed on his hips while his eyes held Emma's.

"Jack, we're on the same side, remember?" she said gently.

"Are we?"

"You know we are." Emma moved her hands to cup Jack's face and continued to look into his eyes, her own gaze soft.

He finally relented enough to put his hands on Emma's waist. "Your idea's a good one," he told her. "But you're not going to be a part of it, and that's final."

Emma studied Jack's expression and saw no give there. So she accepted that she had no choice.

"All right," she agreed. "Do it your way."

She could feel his tense body begin to relax, and she decided to help the process along by going up on tiptoe to kiss him. She kept kissing him until all his tension was gone.

"Let's go to bed," he finally murmured against her mouth. "We've still got a couple of hours to sleep before we have to get up."

A while later, Jack murmured something sleepily against Emma's ear.

"What?" she asked drowsily.

"I said, thanks," he repeated.

"For what?"

"For doing things my way."

Emma smiled. "This time," she said.

EMMA LIKED the policewoman who began sleeping in her apartment the next night. But aside from her height and weight, she didn't think Patti Franklin resembled her much.

"I don't have to be your identical twin," Patti assured her. "With the wig and makeup, we look enough alike from a distance to fool people. And if someone gets up close enough to recognize that I'm not you, it will be too late for him to do anything about it. We'll have him."

Jack continued to drive Emma to the nursery school and back, but one day something came up and he couldn't make it.

"That's all right," Emma assured him over the telephone. "Megan will give me a ride."

"I'd rather send someone to get you," Jack said.

"But that's completely unnecessary," Emma assured him. "No one's likely to come after me when Megan's there. Then they'd have two witnesses."

Or two dead women, Jack thought uneasily. But there was another flu epidemic going around, and the police were shorthanded. So he finally agreed.

"Have her drop you off right at the door of the apartment building," he instructed. "Then go straight to the apartment and lock the door behind you. Hopefully I'll be home around seven, but Patti should arrive by six-thirty anyway."

Emma agreed. And she did exactly as she was told.

"DON'T MAKE A SOUND!"

Emma froze as the rough-looking man stepped in front of her the moment she entered the hallway of her apartment building. He withdrew the gun in his pocket just enough so that she could be sure he had one. Then he slid the weapon back into his pocket as he quickly stepped forward and wrapped an arm in a viselike grip around her shoulders.

"I won't hesitate to shoot if you give me any trouble," he said harshly. "Start walking toward the laundry room."

No one was ever in the laundry room at this time of day, and Emma was sure this man had checked things out and knew it. She was also sure he didn't have orders just to give her a good scare this time.

For a minute, as the man dragged her along with him, Emma was too terrified to think. But she had to think before it was too late to do any good. An instant later, she remembered the toy water pistol she'd taken away from Johnny on the playground that day because he was shooting the other kids.

She had stuffed the realistic-looking black toy gun in her right coat pocket, then forgotten about it. But at the moment, she couldn't reach it. The man was holding her too tightly.

As she stumbled along, Emma forced her terror into the back of her mind and thought about the best way to make use of the only weapon she had. She could never fool her captor with it out here in the hallway. But the lighting in the laundry room was dim enough that it was possible the man would think the toy pistol was real. But in order to reach it, she had to get him to let go of her long enough for her to get it out of her pocket.

The door to the laundry room was at the end of a series of steps leading downward. The steps were too narrow for Emma and her captor to walk side by side, so he pushed her in front of him.

"If there's anybody in here," the man said in a soft, threatening voice, "you keep your cool...unless you want an innocent bystander to get hurt."

Emma nodded shakily. She was gathering all her strength for what would come next. She didn't really think she had much chance to make her hastily conceived plan work, but she had to try.

On the next-to-last step of the stairs, she abruptly pushed backward with all her strength, causing her captor to lose his balance and fall on the steps. She started making a break for the laundry room. Upon reaching the door, she slammed it open with both hands and slid around it as quickly as possible in order to shield her from the man. But she knew she couldn't hold it shut against his strength. Pulling the toy pistol out of her pocket, she ran to the end of the row of washers.

When the man pushed into the laundry room, twisting his head to look for her, Emma had just reached the last washer. She quickly took shelter behind it, stooping to keep the bulk of the washer between her and the man's weapon.

"That ain't gonna do you no good, lady," the man grunted, and he started to raise the pistol he now held in his hand.

Emma was faster. Raising the toy pistol in both hands, she pointed it at him. "Drop the gun!" she screamed at the top of her lungs.

The man froze.

"Drop it, I said!" Emma screamed again. The hysteria in her voice was doing as much to deter the man as the pistol in her hand was.

"Take it easy," he said, his eyes fastened on the toy pistol she held. "Don't do anything stu—"

"Do it!" Emma screeched.

She could scarcely believe it. The man let go of his gun and it clattered to the floor of the laundry room. Then he quickly raised his empty hands. Emma almost fainted with relief. She'd been terrified he would elect to shoot it out with her, in which case she would have been dead.

"Turn around!" she ordered, her voice shaking uncontrollably.

"Okay, okay..." the man said, eyeing Emma's gun. Slowly he began to turn around. "Take it easy, lady...don't let that thing go off!"

"Why shouldn't I?" she yelled at him. "You were going to kill me, weren't you?"

"Nah, I was just going to scare you," the man said, and now his voice was shaking slightly.

"The h-hell you were!" Emma sputtered.

"Let me go," the man began to plead. And he began to walk toward the door of the laundry room, moving very slowly. "Please. You don't wanta kill me."

Emma sensed that her anger was what the man feared most. "You're wrong! I'd love to kill you!" she said. "I've been carrying this gun ever since the last time Tony Caro sent one of you after me, and don't think I won't use it!"

At that, the man bolted for the door. He was through it in a flash and Emma could hear him scrambling up the steps at top speed. She was shaking like a leaf, and it took all her willpower to begin to follow him. She wasn't sure just what to do if she caught him, but letting him get away was out of the question!

Emma did take the time to pick up the thug's gun. Then, holding it gingerly away from her body, she started up the stairs.

There was a bend in the corridor just past the top of the stairs, and after arriving there, Emma peeked around it before turning the corner. The man was running down the corridor toward the entrance of the apartment building.

As she stood peeking around the corner, and just before the thug reached the apartment building entrance, the door opened and Jack and Patti came through it.

Emma shot around the corner and began screeching at the top of her lungs as she ran toward all of them. "Jack, stop him!"

Jack didn't have time to draw his own gun from his shoulder holster. So he made a flying leap at the man and crashed into him. His momentum carried both of them to the hallway floor.

While Jack and Emma's captor were struggling, Patti got her service revolver out of her purse. Then she stepped close enough to the two struggling men to point the pistol directly at the stranger's head.

"Freeze!" she yelled.

The man froze, but the fight was over too soon for Jack. He raised his fist and crashed it against the man's chin. But when he raised his fist again, Patti yelled his name in a warning tone, and Jack stopped. His face contorted with rage, he lifted the man by his coat lapels, then slammed him back to the floor before he finally climbed off him and stood. Then he looked up just as Emma came crashing into his arms.

She wrapped herself around Jack.

"Okay...it's okay," Jack said, trying to soothe Emma with his voice as he held her. He didn't take his eyes off the man on the floor, even though Patti was still standing there holding her gun. And then he saw the man looking at what Emma held in her hand. There was an incredulous expression on his face.

Frowning, Jack reached down and lifted Emma's hand to see what she held. When he saw the toy pistol, he was flabbergasted. "What the hell are you doing with this?" he demanded.

She lifted her head from Jack's shoulder. "I took it away from Johnny today," she said. "He was shooting the kids with it on the playground. And thank God I did." She nodded at the man on the floor. "He thought it was real, and it was all that kept him from killing me." Then she brought her other hand around from Jack's back and held out the real gun. "With this," she added.

Jack paled. He removed the gun from Emma's hand and looked at it. The safety was off, and it was cocked for firing. Jack took a deep, shuddering breath. "Good old Johnny," he said shakily. "Remind me to give him a medal."

From the expression on the face of the man on the floor, it was obvious he'd like to give Johnny something as well, but it clearly wasn't a medal he had in mind.

Chapter Fourteen

Jack followed Tony until they reached a deserted street, then gunned the car engine, whipped around Tony's vehicle and cut him off. Tony stopped his car with a screech of brakes.

Jack was out of his car in an instant, and when he appeared at Tony's window, the expression on his face was savage. Placing his hand on the butt of his service revolver under his sports coat, he ordered Tony to get out of the car.

Scowling, Tony opened the driver's door and heaved his bulk out of the seat. "You better have a warrant, Spencer," he snarled, "or I'm chargin' you with harassment!"

"You may not be in a position to charge anybody with anything much longer," Jack said, his voice deadly.

Tony narrowed his eyes. "What's eatin' you, Spencer?" he asked.

"I'll tell you what's eating me," Jack grated. "I don't like it when someone tries to kill the woman I love."

Tony scowled. "What are you talkin' about?" he demanded.

"I'm talking about Emma Springer—the woman you know as Josephine Truman."

Tony's black eyes shifted slightly. "So? What's she got to do with me?"

"I'm not in the mood to play games," Jack said. "So I'm just going to tell you how it's going to be from now on. You send anybody after her again, and I won't go after whoever it is you sent. I'll come after you... personally. And not as a cop."

Tony stirred restlessly. "You're crazy!" he snorted. "I ain't done nuthin' to nobody."

"I said no games," Jack repeated, his voice and his eyes flatly cold. "This is between you and me now. There's no microphone picking up what we're saying... there are no witnesses to say I was within a mile of you today. I'm warning you, Tony. You hurt Emma and I kill you. That's a promise."

Tony stared back at Jack for a long moment, then said, "You're bluffin'." But his voice betrayed his uncertainty.

"No, Tony," Jack said, his voice containing a deadly promise. "I'm not bluffing. She means that much to me. Maybe I can kill you without getting caught, and maybe I can't. But the thing for you to remember is, I won't give a damn about the consequences to myself. It'll be enough for me to get you."

Jack waited just long enough to be sure that Tony believed him. When he was sure, he turned his back on him, walked to his car and drove off.

EMMA AND PATTI were putting fresh food and water into the hamster cage when Jack arrived home. Jack kissed Emma warmly, then smiled at Patti, who was cooing at Oscar and Wilhemina.

"Aren't they darling?" Patti said, smiling back at him. "I think I'll get some hamsters when this assignment is over. Oscar and Wilhemina are good company without causing any problems."

At that, Jack gave Emma a meaningful look and she laughed. "Just be sure you get a cage with a good stout lock," she suggested to Patti, "and I'm sure your neighbors will enjoy your hamsters as much as you do."

"Huh?" Patti looked puzzled. "What have my neighbors got to do with it?"

"Never mind," Emma said, smiling up at Jack. He still had his arm around her and she sensed something in his manner that made her suggest the two of them leave Patti with the hamsters for the time being and go to his place.

"Have you got something on your mind?" she asked when he'd closed his apartment door behind them.

Jack pulled her close and kissed her lightly on the mouth. "I missed you today, that's all," he said, "and I want to be alone with you." He kissed her again.

Afterward, Emma smiled into his eyes. "I missed you, too, Jack," she said softly. "It's getting so that I miss you every time we're apart."

"Ah...I knew my incredible charm would get to you eventually," he responded teasingly, but his eyes were a great deal more serious than his tone. He kissed her again as he began backing her toward the bedroom.

It seemed to Emma that there was a different quality to his lovemaking this time. His tenderness was more pronounced than usual. But in between the periods of tenderness were short bursts of almost desperate possessiveness, as though he felt he might lose her.

Afterward, as she lay in his arms while they rested, she felt slightly bewildered. The lovemaking had been thrilling, but what was behind it? And then she thought she knew, and she unconsciously shook her head, smiling wryly.

"What is it?" Jack mumbled. His cheek was against Emma's hair, and his eyes were closed. "What are you thinking?"

"I was wondering why there was something different about the way you made love to me just now," she said.

"Different?" Now Jack smiled. "Well, I wasn't aware of doing anything different, but if I did, you seemed to like it, whatever it was."

"Yes, I liked it very much," Emma agreed.

There was something in her voice that made Jack open his eyes. "But?" he asked.

"But I think the difference was that you were feeling overly protective toward me because of what happened yesterday evening," she explained.

"Overly protective," Jack repeated in a dry tone.

"Yes." Emma nodded and shifted so that she could look at Jack's face. "Oh, I admit," she said, her tone serious, "that I've been shaken up all day because of what happened. It wasn't pleasant."

"No, almost being murdered doesn't usually feel very nice," Jack responded wryly.

Emma grimaced and went on. "But after feeling like that all day, I got tired of it. So I've decided something."

"What?"

"I've decided I simply will not let Tony Caro and his thugs determine how I feel. That gives him and his sort too much power over me. So I'm going to try to feel and behave as normally as possible. And you should too, Jack," she said soberly. "You can't do your job properly if you're always worrying about me. You must believe in the system you work for, and the system is set up so that Tony and his friends will eventually be brought to justice. Right?"

Jack kept his expression from revealing his reaction to Emma's naïveté. He merely said, "Right."

Emma nodded, her eyes lighting with relief over his agreement. "So will you try not to worry about me so much anymore?"

"Right." Jack's outward agreement was amiably convincing. Inside, however, he was grimly determined he would never again relax his vigilance the way he had the day before. The attack on Emma would never have taken place if he hadn't made the mistake of catering to her idea of taking proper precautions.

"And I'll try not to worry, too," she said with satisfaction. "You'll see, Jack. Tony's failed twice now in persuading me not to testify against him. Surely that will convince him that his gangster methods aren't going to work. And if it doesn't . . . well, we'll be careful, but we don't have to lead our lives in a constant state of paranoia, do we?"

"Right."

Emma was so caught up in her own version of positive thinking that she didn't hear the slight mockery in Jack's voice. She smiled at him then, her eyes sparkling and warm. "But," she added, "there were some things about the way you just made love to me I wouldn't mind seeing you repeat."

"Like what?"

"All of it."

AFTER MAKING SURE he wasn't being followed, Tony drove to a parking area situated on a high bluff overlooking the old airport that had served Kansas City before the new international airport had been built on the northern outskirts of the metropolitan area.

Parking his car, he waited for fifteen minutes before a luxurious automobile pulled up behind his. Then he got out and climbed in the back seat of the second car. The instant he closed the door, the driver had the vehicle in motion.

The small, elderly man bundled up in a thick winter coat seated beside Tony in the back seat offered no greeting. After waiting a polite interval, Tony voiced a respectful greeting of his own.

Instead of replying in kind, the elderly man, in a soft, dangerous voice, said, "I'm disappointed in you, Tony."

The car was overheated, but that wasn't the sole reason Tony was sweating. Withdrawing a handkerchief from his pocket, he nervously began to wipe his brow as he defended himself.

"How was I supposed to know the dame was Spencer's girlfriend? Who would have thought a cop would use somebody close to him for a job like this?"

The old man ignored Tony's defense. "Two of my best men have been arrested," he commented in his soft voice.

"You know Frankie and Vinnie won't talk," Tony quickly pointed out. "So there's no way they can implicate you . . . or me."

Slowly the old man turned his head toward Tony and nodded. "No, *they* won't talk," he agreed.

Tony went still.

"But then, they don't have the same kind of problem you do. They don't have your weakness."

"It won't come to that," Tony insisted. "Even if it comes to trial, I'll get off just like I always have."

The old man shrugged his small shoulders. "That's what worries me," he said quietly. "The way you plan to get yourself off the hook."

Tony swallowed. "I'd never bargain with 'em. You know that."

"Do I?"

Tony turned his head away to look out the tinted car window. They had been cruising along the downtown streets of Kansas City, which were almost deserted at this hour, and were now headed back toward the bluff where he'd parked his car, which meant the conversation was almost over.

"I give you my word," he said in a tight voice, in which there was now a tinge of desperation. "I'll keep my mouth shut."

"I believe you would," the old man said softly. "If you could. But we both know you might not be able to control yourself. So I think it would be best if you didn't stand trial this time."

Tony whipped his head back around, staring at his companion in consternation. "But—"

The old man ignored the interruption. "I think it would be best if you and Rosa took early retirement."

Tony's mouth hung open for a moment. Then he closed it and swallowed. "Rosa won't leave the kids and the grandkids."

"My niece will do as she's told." The soft voice was very firm. "Frequent family visits can be arranged wherever you go. But not here. Not for a long while, at any rate."

Tony shook his head angrily. "I was only helping you out, remember?" he pointed out. "The money laundering wasn't my idea."

The old man's voice was harder when he answered. "If you were not married to my niece, Tony, I would never have risked doing business with you at all, considering the unfortunate condition from which you suffer. But I have always been fond of Rosa, and if you recall, you and she were not doing very well financially until I stepped in to help. And now, if it were not for my niece, I would also not be offering you this opportunity to save yourself. You would be very wise to take the opportunity I am offering you. Otherwise..."

The last word was spoken with a finality Tony could not fail to understand.

"HE DID WHAT?" Jack gazed at Eddie in disbelief.

"Tony Caro skipped town," Eddie repeated. "The word came while you and Charlie were checking out that vacant house over on the east side the new gang from Los Angeles is supposed to be using to stash their drugs. It's like he dropped off the face of the earth. I checked one of my sources, and he said there's a rumor going around that the old man didn't want Tony going to trial. You can guess why."

Jack nodded, frowning. He didn't like all his work—and all Emma had done—wasted like this. They still had the man who'd abducted Emma and the man who'd tried to kill her, but neither of them was likely to break and implicate anybody else. Tony, with his claustrophobic fear of jail, had been the weak link in the chain and the only one in a position to implicate the old crime boss in money laundering. And he might have done just that in order to bargain himself out of a jail term. Jack told himself he should have foreseen that the old man wouldn't just sit back and wait when the stakes were so high.

"What about Tony's mother?" he asked. "And his wife?" If Tony had left them behind, they could be watched in case Tony tried to make contact with them.

"Tony just recently put his ma in a nursing home," Eddie said. "She's senile and can't tell anybody the time of day. He apparently took his wife with him. She's gone, too."

"She wouldn't have left the grandkids."

"She did."

Jack sat back in his chair, put his feet up on his desk and gazed up at the ceiling with a disgusted look on his face. "Did somebody check the airlines and trains?"

"Yeah, and came up empty. Looks like they drove— at least long enough to get away from here."

"Hell," Jack said, shaking his head. "So we've just lost the best chance we've ever had to put Tony away. Not to mention the old man, who would have been a bonus we didn't even think about at the beginning of all this."

"That's the breaks." Eddie shrugged. "It's my guess Tony and his missus are sitting on a sunny beach right about now. But remember the bright side of all this, Jack."

Jack gazed soberly at Eddie and nodded. "Yeah. I don't have to worry about Emma anymore."

"Sure. The two of you can lead a normal life again. And let's face it, Jack," he added. "If Tony had gone to trial and the old man had been worried enough, he might have gotten to Emma somehow, no matter what we did to protect her. That possibility has been eating you alive. I know it has. So as bad as it is to lose Tony, and especially the old man, if it was my woman's life on the line, I wouldn't brood over the way things have turned out as much as I would otherwise."

Jack and Eddie stared at each other in understanding for a long moment. Then something about Eddie's expression made Jack ask, "You got something else on your mind?"

"Yeah. But it ain't goin' nowhere farther than my mind."

"What is it?" Jack asked.

"My source told me another rumor," he said amiably. "Somethin' about a cop threatenin' Tony with his life."

Jack slowly nodded. "It would probably be best if you did keep that rumor to yourself."

"Uh-huh." Eddie smiled blandly. "That's what I figured."

Eddie had been sitting on the corner of Jack's desk. Now he stood up. It seemed to Jack the wood heaved a sigh of relief at being relieved of Eddie's bulk. He smiled at the thought.

"I got work to do," Eddie said. "See you later."

"Yeah, see you later. And thanks."

Eddie ignored the last two words and sauntered away.

Jack then got up and went over to Charlie Browne's desk. "Yeah, Jack," Charlie said absently. He was sorting through a pile of files. "What do you need?"

"You remember Petey the Pickpocket?"

"Sure. He was the best in the business before he went legit and became a magician."

"Doesn't he have a son?"

Charlie nodded. "Yeah...Pete, Jr. The kid ought to be about twelve now. Nice kid. Talented, too. He was gettin' as good at pickpocketing as his old man, and I was glad when Petey went straight for the kid's sake."

"Know where I can get in touch with Petey?"

Now Charlie was curious. "What you want with him?"

"Actually, it's his kid I want. I need a favor."

Charlie's bushy eyebrows went up. "Well, Petey advertises his magician show in the yellow pages," he said. "I think he does kid's birthday parties and stuff like that."

Jack nodded. "Thanks, Charlie," he said before turning to walk away.

"Hey...ain't you gonna' tell me what's going on?"

Jack paused and grinned at Charlie over his shoulder. "Not unless it works out."

Charlie grimaced at Jack disgustedly and waved him away.

EMMA COULDN'T STAND IT ANYMORE. It wasn't just that Johnny refused to talk to her, he refused to talk to anybody. And the sight of his lonely, belligerent little face hovering at the edge of things, never a part of them, was breaking her heart. If he'd been older, she would have told him how his toy gun had played a role in saving her life in order to make him feel good, but at his age, she was afraid the tale would make him anxious about his own safety.

"Megan," she called her assistant over.

"Yes?"

"Can you handle things on your own for a while? I want to take Johnny outside so I can have a talk with him."

"Sure," Megan agreed. "I hope you can do some good with him. Boy, is he stubborn."

Emma got up and went to the hooks on one wall where everyone hung their coats. She put her own on, then got Johnny's and walked over to him.

"Johnny?"

He stiffened, then looked up at her with a scowl on his face.

"Let's go outside."

"It ain't time."

"This is a special trip. Just you and me."

Johnny immediately looked suspicious. Emma ignored the look and held out his coat. He reluctantly put it on and stuffed his hands into his pockets as he trailed Emma to the door.

"Can we go?" Several of the children, noticing that Emma and Johnny had their coats on and were heading outside, wanted to go as well.

"Not right now." Emma smiled at them. "You can go out at your regular time."

"But how come Johnny gets to—"

Emma closed the door on the protest.

Outside she steered Johnny to a bench. He sat on the very edge of the seat and wouldn't look at Emma.

"Johnny, aren't you getting tired of being mad at me?" she asked.

"Nope."

"Are you going to stay mad at me for the rest of the time we have together? You won't be coming here anymore after May, you know."

"Yep."

Emma stifled a sigh. "I miss you," she said simply.

"I don't miss you."

"Sure you do. You've always liked me."

"I don't anymore."

"Just because I won't let you trade with the other children?"

"Yep." There was a slight pause, and then Johnny added, "And because you're picking on me."

"I told you I wasn't picking on you," Emma said gently.

"But you are."

Emma paused for a few moments. Then she surprised Johnny by saying, "Come to think of it, you're right. I *am* picking on you."

Johnny's head swung around and his blue eyes were wide with surprise.

Emma nodded. "I did make the rule about not trading because of you, Johnny," she admitted. "The other kids didn't need such a rule."

"I don't neither!"

"I think you do, but that's beside the point. The other kids need the rule so you won't take their best toys."

Johnny scowled and looked away. "My dad says it ain't your place to protect the other kids. He says they're gonna meet up with people like me all their lives and they need to learn to handle it."

"That's what I thought for a long time," she said mildly. "But that was before you started to get mean about what you were doing."

Johnny looked at her. She'd surprised him again.

"I ain't mean!" he said in a surly voice, giving Emma a mean look.

Emma smiled. "I wish I had a mirror and a tape recorder right now," she said.

Johnny looked puzzled. "Why?"

"Never mind. Listen, Johnny, remember that talk we had about why the other kids don't like you as much as you want them to?"

He looked down at his feet.

"I want the other kids to like you just as much as you want them to, Johnny."

"Ha!"

"And when I stopped the trading, if you had tried playing nicely with the other kids instead of being even meaner to them, I think they might have started liking you better."

"I didn't feel like playin' and bein' nice to 'em."

"I know. But are you starting to feel more like it now?"

Johnny didn't answer.

"Well," Emma said calmly, "I hope you are, because I'm about to make a new rule."

Johnny gave her a glance of alarm. "What kinda rule?"

"We're going to start having some group games."

Johnny shrugged. "We always have them," he said.

"Yes, but now I'm not going to let anyone sit out of them," Emma said.

Johnny sat still while that sank in. "I don't care," he finally said, belligerently.

"Good," Emma said calmly. Despite his attitude, she had an idea he was glad she was going to make him participate. She'd thought he might be getting tired of hanging around on the edges instead of joining in. And this way, since she was making it a rule, his pride was left intact as far as the other children were concerned.

"I'm cold," she said as she got to her feet. "Come on. Let's go back inside."

Johnny followed her. Later, when it was time for the regular play period outdoors, Emma announced beforehand that everyone had to play, then suggested that the children play Red Rover and Drop the Handkerchief, because there would be physical contact between Johnny and the other children. And she was gratified when he couldn't keep himself from yelling and screaming just like the other kids.

Back in the classroom, she had the children act out a story from a book she had read to them before and with which they were all familiar. And she made certain Johnny played a major role.

By the end of the day, Emma thought she'd made some progress. The boys especially—they seemed either to have shorter memories or less propensity to hold grudges than the girls—seemed to be accepting Johnny more, and he seemed to be responding to them better than previously. Things weren't perfect by any means, but she was grateful for even the slightest improvement.

At home over dinner, she told Jack about her day.

Jack smiled. "Good," he said. "You've made it easier for what I have in mind."

Emma looked up from her plate, her eyes wide. "What?" she asked.

He told her, and Emma blinked in surprise. "But the children are so young," she said. "I'm afraid telling them everything might make them scared."

"Then we won't tell them everything," Jack stated. "We'll water it down to something they can handle. It's worth a try, isn't it?"

Later, Emma intended to take a piece of cake over to Patti, but Jack stopped her, took the cake from her hands and set it aside.

"There's plenty left over, Jack," Emma said, surprised by his action, "and Patti and I have become good friends. She gets lonely all by herself in my apartment. I thought I'd chat with her awhile."

"Patti isn't there anymore," Jack admitted.

"What? But why?"

"Because Tony Caro has left town.'

Emma stared at Jack in shock. "You mean for good?"

"Who knows? I wouldn't bet on it, but I don't figure he plans to come back for a long time. And if he does come back sometime in the future, it will probably just be for fleeting visits with his kids and grandkids, and he'll keep pretty much out of sight."

"Tony Caro has children and grandchildren?" Emma simply hadn't thought of Tony as a family man.

"Sure," Jack shrugged. "Just because he's a crook doesn't mean he's not human."

Emma shook her head in mingled anger and bewilderment. "I don't know whether to be mad or glad," she declared. "After all the trouble he's caused me, I don't like the idea of his getting off scot-free, but now that I know he has a family..." She stopped, her expression reflecting her mixed feelings.

"Emma, most crooks have families," Jack said dryly. "That doesn't give them the right to be spared the consequences of their actions."

"No, of course not," Emma said, frowning. "Still..."

"Still...," Jack interrupted, cupping her face in his hands. "The farther away Tony stays, the safer you'll be, and that's the one good thing about this whole mess. And he isn't getting off scot-free. He's had to leave his home. I, for one,'' Jack added grimly, ''hope he hates wherever he's ended up.''

Emma couldn't help smiling at that. ''You're a hard man.''

''Sometimes,'' Jack agreed. ''When I have to be.'' And then he smiled. ''But on the other hand, sometimes I can be a real coward.''

Emma gazed at him in surprise. ''Like when?'' she asked.

Jack settled his hands on Emma's shoulders, then took a deep breath. ''Like when I want to ask the woman I love to marry me, but I'm not sure she'll say yes.''

Emma's eyes opened wider. Then, staring soberly into Jack's somewhat anxious gaze, she asked, ''What makes you think she won't say yes?''

''Well, there's all that independence of hers. She might not be sure she loves me enough to give some of it up. There's no such thing as complete independence in a marriage, you know.''

Emma slowly nodded. ''I know,'' she said quietly.

Jack's heart wouldn't settle down. Was she going to say yes or no? Despite his considerable powers of observation, he couldn't tell what was going on inside her head at this moment. Then she smiled at him in a way that made his heart lift.

''But then,'' she said softly, ''marriage has certain compensations.''

Jack let out his breath in a sigh of relief. ''Such as?'' he asked, slipping his hands to Emma's waist and pulling her closer to his body.

''Such as children, stability...''

Jack nodded. "So you're going to say yes?" he asked hopefully.

"Yes, Jack." Emma's eyes smiled happily into his. "I'm going to say yes."

"Thank God." Jack grinned. "You had me worried there for a while. I was afraid I'd bought this for nothing."

He stepped back, took a ring box from his jacket pocket, opened it and extracted an engagement ring set with a solitaire diamond.

"Oh, Jack," Emma murmured as he slipped it on her finger. "It's perfect." Then she locked her hands behind Jack's neck and shook her head. "I don't believe I had you worried," she chided him. "You know me well enough by now to have been pretty sure what my answer was going to be before you popped the question."

"Oh?" Jack raised an eyebrow.

"Yes," Emma said. "I know *you* well enough by now to be sure you wouldn't have asked if you hadn't been sure of the answer."

They grinned at each other, then drew closer together and kissed lingeringly to seal their engagement.

When Emma opened her eyes, Jack had a forceful look in his.

"What is it?" she inquired, smiling.

"I want a definite date set for our wedding."

"How about the first Saturday in August?"

"Why then?" Jack asked.

"Because Nancy and Brad will be back by then and can attend the wedding, and at least half my kids whose mothers don't work will have left nursery school for the summer. Megan can handle the other half without me so that I can have a honeymoon. Does that fit your schedule?''

Jack nodded. "I've got vacation due, and there shouldn't be any problem with my taking it then."

"Good. And now that that's settled..."

"...let's get back to sealing our engagement," Jack agreed, and he leaned down and kissed Emma as though she were made of precious glass and might break if he handled her without care.

Emma appreciated the sweetness of Jack's kiss. And when the sweet kiss ended and the next one was more passionate, she appreciated that kiss, as well.

Jack raised his head and looked down with loving warmth into the melting surrender in Emma's eyes.

"You know something?" he whispered.

"What?" Emma whispered back.

"You don't look very independent at the moment."

"That's because I don't feel very independent at the moment," Emma murmured sincerely. "In fact, I feel as though, if I didn't have you, my life wouldn't be nearly as worth living as it feels right now."

Jack, thinking about what he and Eddie had discussed earlier that day, nodded and wrapped Emma more tightly in his arms.

"I know what you mean," he said, his voice a low husk against Emma's ear. And silently he added, *A lot better than you do, my innocent Emma... better than I hope you'll ever know.*

Chapter Fifteen

Jack parked his car outside Emma's nursery school, then looked over at the boy in the passenger seat. Pete Jr. was twelve years old, but he was small for his age and looked more like seven. Jack figured that was all to the good.

"You ready?" he asked.

"Sure," Pete said, grinning.

Emma greeted them at the door and then Pete sat down at the back of the room. She took Jack to the front, where Megan and Mr. and Mrs. Brubaker were waiting. Jack looked around him curiously. This was the first time he'd ever seen Emma's nursery school, and he admired the cheerful atmosphere she'd created. There were colorful animal figures painted on the walls and lots of windows to let in light. There were small tables at which the children were sitting, staring at him, but there was also a lot of open room with toys and books.

A pretty little girl wearing pink overalls and with long, dark pigtails caught Jack's attention, and he winked at her and smiled. She ducked her head, giggling. Then Jack turned his attention to Johnny's father. The man looked irritable, uncomfortable and impatient. Jack knew Brubaker didn't even know why he was here. Emma had worked on Mrs. Brubaker to talk her husband into coming here today.

"Children," Emma addressed the class, "this is Detective Jack Spencer. He's a policeman."

There was a chorus of oohs and ahs from the kids as they stared at Jack wide-eyed. He smiled back at them.

"Detective Spencer is here today to award a medal," Emma went on. "Do all of you remember the other day when I took a water pistol from Johnny Brubaker out on the playground?"

Some of the children nodded and some didn't remember. But they all turned to look at Johnny. Jack had already picked out the boy from Emma's description of him. Until his name had been mentioned, Johnny had been sitting slumped in his chair with his legs straight out in front of him, his arms crossed over his chest and a scowl of gigantic proportions on his face. Now, however, he suddenly sat upright with an expression of nervous surprise on his face.

Jack then glanced at Mr. Brubaker. The man had a puzzled frown on his face. And he was tense.

"Well, if it hadn't been for Johnny's water pistol," Emma continued, "I would have been in big trouble the other day."

The children immediately switched their attention back to Emma. She already had all of Johnny's attention.

"When I got home that day, I still had Johnny's pistol in my coat pocket," Emma explained. "And when I came into the lobby of my apartment building, a man came up to me. And he was not a nice man, children. I think he meant to steal my purse."

"Ooooh," came from the children.

"So do you know what I did?" Emma asked. Twenty heads shook. "Why, I pulled Johnny's water pistol out of my pocket and made the man go away and leave me alone!"

"Yeah!" The children were all in favor of that.

"But!" Emma said, holding up a finger. "It wouldn't have worked if the lighting had been better and the man had had really good eyesight. Fortunately he didn't. He couldn't see clearly, so he didn't know Johnny's water pistol wasn't real. And it turned out he wasn't very brave, either. What do you think might have happened if he had known the water pistol was a toy and if he had been a brave man?"

"He might have hurt you!" a little girl spoke up.

"Yes, indeed, he might have." Emma nodded. "So none of you must ever try to do what I did, all right? Because you could get hurt."

All the children were in agreement again.

"When I told Detective Spencer what had happened," Emma went on, "he said Johnny deserved a medal because if it hadn't been for his water pistol, I might have been in so much trouble." She gestured at Johnny, smiling. "Will you come up here, Johnny?"

Johnny gulped, then grinned delightedly. He made it to the front of the room in two seconds flat.

Jack stepped forward. "Johnny Brubaker," he said. "I'd like to shake your hand."

Johnny's hand shot up. Grinning, Jack shook it, then reached into his pocket for a medal he'd bought at a pawnshop.

"I award you this medal, Johnny Brubaker," he said very seriously, "for being such a good citizen and helping the police catch a crook." He handed the medal to Johnny, knowing all the while that the boy would have liked it better if it had been one that could have been pinned to his shirt. But that wouldn't have fit in with the plan.

Johnny stood looking down at his medal in his hand, his expression dazed.

"Let's give Johnny a hand, class," Emma suggested, and she started clapping. The class joined in. Glancing at Mr. and Mrs. Brubaker, she saw that Johnny's mother had tears in her eyes, while Mr. Brubaker was grinning in a cocky manner.

When the applause died down, Jack added a short lecture to the one Emma had given, warning the children not to try what she had done. Then, after Johnny's mother had hugged her boy, and the children had all crowded around him to look at his medal, Jack went over and began talking to Mr. Brubaker, while Emma kept Mrs. Brubaker occupied. Megan, as instructed, managed to be quite a distance away from Johnny, too.

As the crowd of classmates around Johnny began to thin out, Pete Jr. made his move.

Swaggering up to Johnny, he said, "Hey, kid, let's see the medal."

Johnny looked at him in puzzlement as he closed his fingers possessively around the medal. "Who are you?" he asked.

"I'm with Detective Spencer," Pete said. Then he repeated, "Let's see the medal."

Johnny reluctantly opened his fingers. Pete's hand moved like lightning, and the medal disappeared from Johnny's hand.

"Hey!" Johnny yelled, grabbing at Pete's hand.

"Let's trade," Pete Jr. said in a mean voice. Both his hands moved like lightning now. The medal disappeared from one of them and with the other, Pete Jr.

shoved a dirty marble with a chip in it into Johnny's shirt pocket.

"I don't wanta trade!" Johnny yelled as he frantically fished the marble out of his pocket. He was looking Pete Jr. all over, trying to see where the medal had gone. "Give it back!" he said as he held the marble out to Pete.

Pete Jr. held up his now empty hands and started backing away. "Give what back?" he said innocently.

Johnny started howling at the top of his lungs.

"Hey, what's going on over there?" Mr. Brubaker looked away from Jack, trying to see what was happening.

"Why don't we see?" Jack said, sounding puzzled.

Emma and Mrs. Brubaker also went over to Johnny, who was tearful with impotent rage. Pete Jr. was standing nearby with his hands in his pockets looking as innocent as any angel straight from heaven.

"What on earth's the matter?" Emma asked.

"He's got my medal!" Johnny screeched, pointing at Pete Jr. "He took it away from me!"

Emma looked at Pete Jr. sternly, who took his hands out of his pockets and held them up in an innocent fashion.

"I didn't take it from him," he said blandly. "I traded him a marble for it. See, there it is." He pointed to the marble in Johnny's hand.

"I don't want your stupid old marble!" Johnny raged, and he threw the marble to the floor. "I want my medal!"

"Then you shouldn't have traded it away." Pete Jr. shrugged.

"I didn't! I didn't!" Johnny was screaming.

"Who is this?" Mr. Brubaker asked, scowling. "He doesn't belong here, does he?"

"I brought him," Jack said. "He's the son of—"

Mr. Brubaker cut him off. "I don't care who he is!" he said harshly. "You give that medal back to my son, boy!" he said to Pete Jr. "He doesn't want to trade it to you."

"It was a fair trade," Pete said. "So why should I give it back just 'cause your kid's a crybaby?"

Mr. Brubaker's face flushed bright red. "That marble wasn't a fair trade!" he stormed. "And my boy's not a crybaby! Now you give that medal back or I'll…" He took a threatening step toward Pete Jr., who backed up, his expression wary.

"That's enough," Jack said. He didn't raise his voice particularly, but there was something in his tone that made Mr. Brubaker pause.

Emma thought it was time she stepped in. "Mr. Brubaker," she said quietly, getting his attention. He whipped his head around, and now his eyes were blazing angrily at her.

"This is your school, isn't it?" he demanded. "And you made a rule against trading, didn't you? So why should some strange kid be allowed to come in here and take Johnny's medal?"

"Do you remember why I made that rule?" Emma said quietly, holding the man's gaze in a meaningful manner.

Mr. Brubaker opened his mouth to say something else, then closed it again. He looked decidedly frustrated, but light was dawning in his eyes.

"It isn't the same," he said stubbornly. "This kid has got to be at least seven years old! And he doesn't even go to this school!"

"And Johnny's older and bigger than more than half of the other children who come to my school," Emma pointed out. "Anyway, what difference does it make? Didn't you tell me—and haven't you told Johnny—that it's who is smarter and stronger and more skilled at trading that counts? Obviously Pete qualifies on all three counts."

Jack had been watching Johnny. And now he saw an expression come into the boy's eyes that was like a lightbulb coming on. However, an instant later, his face crumpled.

"I want my medal!" Johnny howled.

Mr. Brubaker glared at Emma. She gazed calmly back at him. Mrs. Brubaker looked heartbroken over her boy's anguish and Johnny was crying. The other children in the room were standing around staring at the adults, listening to everything.

Then Pete Jr. stepped forward. There was a flash of his hand, and suddenly the medal was resting on his palm. But when Johnny reached for it, Pete closed his fingers over the medal.

"Not so fast," Pete Jr. said, and his voice wasn't mean anymore. "I'll give it back, kid, but first I want you to admit something. I got this medal from you the same way you'd have gotten it from me or some other kid if you could have, right?"

Johnny, wiping tears from his eyes, just stared stubbornly at Pete.

"Right?" Pete repeated patiently.

Mr. Brubaker started to say something, but Jack put his hand on the man's arm.

"You want this medal, kid?" Pete said to Johnny in a mild tone. "If you do, you better tell the truth."

Johnny nodded. And finally, in a small voice, he said, "Right."

"Right, what?"

"I'd a got the medal from you like you got it from me."

Pete nodded. "Yeah, that's the way it works sometimes. Whoever's bigger or meaner or smarter takes all the medals. But no matter how big or mean or smart you think you are, there's always somebody who's gonna come along one day and turn the tables on you. Like I did today. If you got friends, Johnny, and you all stick together, you don't have to worry so much. But to have friends, you gotta treat 'em straight. You don't take stuff your friends like a whole lot away from them, no matter how bad you want it. And they don't take stuff from you. You understand?"

Johnny looked up at Pete, his blue eyes still wet with tears, and now clouded with his effort to absorb what Pete was trying to tell him.

"I never wanted nuthin' as bad as I want the medal," he finally said, his voice hesitant.

"But you took stuff somebody else wanted that bad, even though you didn't really want it yourself, didn't you?"

Johnny reluctantly nodded.

"Well, now you know how they felt," Pete said simply, and he reached down, lifted Johnny's hand and placed the medal in it.

Emma glanced at Mr. Brubaker. His face wasn't red with temper anymore. It was pink with embarrassment. And he wouldn't meet Emma's eyes.

"Fine, it's all settled," she said brightly. "Johnny, why don't you go play with the other children."

Johnny hesitated. He looked down at the medal in his hand. Then he looked up at Pete searchingly. Then he looked over at Emma in a shamefaced way, before quickly looking away again. Finally he closed his fingers over the medal and walked toward where the other children were clustered.

Jack then saw something he would never forget. The children moved and formed a protective circle around Johnny, and Johnny passed his medal around the circle so that everyone could get a good look at it.

Mr. Brubaker cleared his throat and looked at Jack. "I have to get back to work," he said gruffly. He hesitated, then added, "Thanks for giving my boy the medal."

Jack held out his hand to shake. Mr. Brubaker took it hesitantly.

"I was happy to do it," Jack said with an easy smile. "Johnny reminds me of myself when I was a boy."

Emma was surprised to hear that, and the look she gave Jack showed it. He grinned at her and winked.

"Thank you both for coming," Emma said to the Brubakers. "I'm sorry if you were in any way embarrassed, but these things happen with children."

Mr. Brubaker gave Emma a slightly disgruntled look. "Are you saying this wasn't all planned?" he asked in a skeptical tone.

Emma gave him a look of complete innocence. "I beg your pardon?" she said, as though she didn't understand the question.

Mr. Brubaker shook his head. "Never mind, Ms. Springer," he said dryly. "You got your point across."

"My point?"

Jack thought Emma was laying things on a little thick. "Pete, you ready to go?" he interrupted, speaking louder than was necessary.

"Sure," Pete said.

But Emma delayed the two of them until the Brubakers had left. Then she smiled at Pete Jr. warmly.

"Thank you," she said.

Pete shrugged and said, "When my dad was pickpocketing, he used to say there's a sucker born every minute. I don't think Johnny's ever going to be one of them, though. The kid's smart."

"What does your father say now that he's gone straight?" Jack asked.

Pete's face lit up with a grin. "He still says the same thing," he admitted. "And it's true, isn't it?"

Jack and Emma laughed. Then she turned to Jack. "Thank you, too," she said softly. "I think your plan really worked."

He gave her a sly grin. "You don't get something for nothing," he said suggestively.

"I've always believed in that philosophy myself," Emma said, laughing.

"Good. Then you won't mind paying my bill for Pete's services when I present it to you."

"Hey," Pete said, his tone surprised. "I'm not charging for this. I did it because it got me out of English and algebra today."

Emma smiled sweetly at Jack. "So I did get something for nothing, after all," she commented innocently.

Jack grimaced. "Just this once," he warned.

Emma's smile broadened. "It's the exception that proves the rule, isn't it, Jack?"

"You better believe it." He winked. "And you're about as exceptional as they come."

Emma beamed. "Just for that," she said lightly as she turned on her heel to go back to the children, "I may pay you for Pete's services anyway." An instant later, however, she paused and looked back over her shoulder at Jack, her expression a little worried. "Did you mean it when you said Johnny reminds you of yourself when you were a boy?"

Jack nodded, grinning.

"Oh, dear," she sighed. "Then I hope we have girls."

JUST BEFORE THE PARENTS came to pick up their children, Emma squatted beside Johnny's chair. "You still mad at me?" she asked.

"Yep."

Emma poked him gently in the ribs, making him squirm. But he began to smile as well. "No, you're not," she scoffed. She poked him again.

"Uh-huh!" Johnny insisted through his giggles.

"Uh-huh." Emma grinned. When the poking and giggling died down, she gave him a hug, despite his protests, then walked away.

There was a mirror on the back wall, and Emma glanced into it a moment later hoping to catch Johnny's expression, but she couldn't see it. Little Eric was standing in front of Johnny talking to him with animated friendliness, blocking her view.

Emma grinned, thinking Jack would be pleased when she paid her debt to him that night. He'd just earned double pay.

You'll flip . . . your pages won't!
Read paperbacks *hands-free* with

Book Mate · I

The perfect "mate" for all your romance paperbacks

**Traveling • Vacationing • At Work • In Bed • Studying
• Cooking • Eating**

Perfect size for all standard paperbacks, this wonderful invention makes reading a pure pleasure! Ingenious design holds paperback books OPEN and FLAT so even wind can't ruffle pages — leaves your hands free to do other things. Reinforced, wipe-clean vinyl-covered holder flexes to let you turn pages without undoing the strap . . . supports paperbacks so well, they have the strength of hardcovers!

Pages turn WITHOUT opening the strap

SEE-THROUGH STRAP

Reinforced back stays flat.

Built in bookmark

BOOK MARK

BACK COVER HOLDING STRIP

10" x 7¼", opened.
Snaps closed for easy carrying, too

INDULGE A LITTLE SWEEPSTAKES

OFFICIAL RULES

SWEEPSTAKES RULES AND REGULATIONS. NO PURCHASE NECESSARY.

1. NO PURCHASE NECESSARY. To enter complete the official entry form and return with the invoice in the envelope provided. Or you may enter by printing your name, complete address and your daytime phone number on a 3 x 5 piece of paper. Include with your entry the hand printed words "Indulge A Little Sweepstakes." Mail your entry to: Indulge A Little Sweepstakes, P.O. Box 1397, Buffalo, NY 14269-1397. No mechanically reproduced entries accepted. Not responsible for late, lost, misdirected mail, or printing errors.

2. Three winners, one per month (Sept. 30, 1989, October 31, 1989 and November 30, 1989), will be selected in random drawings. All entries received prior to the drawing date will be eligible for that month's prize. This sweepstakes is under the supervision of MARDEN-KANE, INC. an independent judging organization whose decisions are final and binding. Winners will be notified by telephone and may be required to execute an affidavit of eligibility and release which must be returned within 14 days, or an alternate winner will be selected.

3. Prizes: 1st Grand Prize (1) a trip for two to Disneyworld in Orlando, Florida. Trip includes round trip air transportation, hotel accommodations for seven days and six nights, plus up to $700 expense money (ARV $3,500). 2nd Grand Prize (1) a seven-night Chandris Caribbean Cruise for two includes transportation from nearest major airport, accommodations, meals plus up to $1,000 in expense money (ARV $4,300). 3rd Grand Prize (1) a ten-day Hawaiian holiday for two includes round trip air transportation for two, hotel accommodations, sightseeing, plus up to $1,200 in spending money (ARV $7,700). All trips subject to availability and must be taken as outlined on the entry form.

4. Sweepstakes open to residents of the U.S. and Canada 18 years or older except employees and the families of Torstar Corp., its affiliates, subsidiaries and Marden-Kane, Inc. and all other agencies and persons connected with conducting this sweepstakes. All Federal, State and local laws and regulations apply. Void wherever prohibited or restricted by law. Taxes, if any are the sole responsibility of the prize winners. Canadian winners will be required to answer a skill testing question. Winners consent to the use of their name, photograph and/or likeness for publicity purposes without additional compensation.

5. For a list of prize winners, send a stamped, self-addressed envelope to Indulge A Little Sweepstakes Winners, P.O. Box 701, Sayreville, NJ 08871.

© 1989 HARLEQUIN ENTERPRISES LTD.
DL-SWPS

INDULGE A LITTLE SWEEPSTAKES

OFFICIAL RULES

SWEEPSTAKES RULES AND REGULATIONS. NO PURCHASE NECESSARY.

1. NO PURCHASE NECESSARY. To enter complete the official entry form and return with the invoice in the envelope provided. Or you may enter by printing your name, complete address and your daytime phone number on a 3 x 5 piece of paper. Include with your entry the hand printed words "Indulge A Little Sweepstakes." Mail your entry to: Indulge A Little Sweepstakes, P.O. Box 1397, Buffalo, NY 14269-1397. No mechanically reproduced entries accepted. Not responsible for late, lost, misdirected mail, or printing errors.

2. Three winners, one per month (Sept. 30, 1989, October 31, 1989 and November 30, 1989), will be selected in random drawings. All entries received prior to the drawing date will be eligible for that month's prize. This sweepstakes is under the supervision of MARDEN-KANE, INC. an independent judging organization whose decisions are final and binding. Winners will be notified by telephone and may be required to execute an affidavit of eligibility and release which must be returned within 14 days, or an alternate winner will be selected.

3. Prizes: 1st Grand Prize (1) a trip for two to Disneyworld in Orlando, Florida. Trip includes round trip air transportation, hotel accommodations for seven days and six nights, plus up to $700 expense money (ARV $3,500). 2nd Grand Prize (1) a seven-night Chandris Caribbean Cruise for two includes transportation from nearest major airport, accommodations, meals plus up to $1,000 in expense money (ARV $4,300). 3rd Grand Prize (1) a ten-day Hawaiian holiday for two includes round trip air transportation for two, hotel accommodations, sightseeing, plus up to $1,200 in spending money (ARV $7,700). All trips subject to availability and must be taken as outlined on the entry form.

4. Sweepstakes open to residents of the U.S. and Canada 18 years or older except employees and the families of Torstar Corp., its affiliates, subsidiaries and Marden-Kane, Inc. and all other agencies and persons connected with conducting this sweepstakes. All Federal, State and local laws and regulations apply. Void wherever prohibited or restricted by law. Taxes, if any are the sole responsibility of the prize winners. Canadian winners will be required to answer a skill testing question. Winners consent to the use of their name, photograph and/or likeness for publicity purposes without additional compensation.

5. For a list of prize winners, send a stamped, self-addressed envelope to Indulge A Little Sweepstakes Winners, P.O. Box 701, Sayreville, NJ 08871.

© 1989 HARLEQUIN ENTERPRISES LTD.
DL-SWPS

INDULGE A LITTLE—WIN A LOT!

Summer of '89 Subscribers-Only Sweepstakes

OFFICIAL ENTRY FORM

This entry must be received by: Sept. 30, 1989
This month's winner will be notified by: October 7, 1989
Trip must be taken between: Nov. 7, 1989–Nov. 7, 1990

YES, I want to win the Walt Disney World® vacation for two! I understand the prize includes round-trip airfare, first-class hotel, and a daily allowance as revealed on the "Wallet" scratch-off card.

Name_____

Address_____

City_____ State/Prov._____ Zip/Postal Code_____

Daytime phone number _____
                          Area code

Return entries with invoice in envelope provided. Each book in this shipment has two entry coupons — and the more coupons you enter, the better your chances of winning!
© 1989 HARLEQUIN ENTERPRISES LTD.

DINDL-1

INDULGE A LITTLE—WIN A LOT!

Summer of '89 Subscribers-Only Sweepstakes

OFFICIAL ENTRY FORM

This entry must be received by: Sept. 30, 1989
This month's winner will be notified by: October 7, 1989
Trip must be taken between: Nov. 7, 1989–Nov. 7, 1990

YES, I want to win the Walt Disney World® vacation for two! I understand the prize includes round-trip airfare, first-class hotel, and a daily allowance as revealed on the "Wallet" scratch-off card.

Name_____

Address_____

City_____ State/Prov._____ Zip/Postal Code_____

Daytime phone number _____
                          Area code

Return entries with invoice in envelope provided. Each book in this shipment has two entry coupons — and the more coupons you enter, the better your chances of winning!
© 1989 HARLEQUIN ENTERPRISES LTD.

DINDL-1

How distant he seemed

He got that look in his eye when he had his mind on his work. But Emma could understand that. And she didn't really mind.

Jack at last came out of his thoughts and noticed how quietly Emma was sitting. "Sorry, I was thinking."

"I know," she said simply. "It's all right."

His expression softening, he began to stroke her cheek. "You're quite a lady, you know that?"

Emma smiled, and Jack slid her hand to the back of her neck, pulling her closer.

Emma didn't resist. The conventional part of her thought it was too soon for this. But as she studied the warm desire in Jack's eyes she wondered if it really mattered where feelings were concerned. And if she was waiting in order to protect herself from hurt she was fooling herself. Jack had already caught her heart.

ABOUT THE AUTHOR

In her twenties, Jacqueline Ashley was a working wife and mother. In her thirties, she found an engrossing hobby—writing. In her forties, to her surprise, her hobby turned into a fulfilling career. And in her fifties? "I'm leaving what happens then up to God," she says. "He's better at goal-setting than I am, not to mention wiser, more generous and tons more imaginative."

Books by Jacqueline Ashley

HARLEQUIN AMERICAN ROMANCE

20—LOVE'S REVENGE
40—HUNTING SEASON
78—THE OTHER HALF OF LOVE
136—IN THE NAME OF LOVE
157—SPRING'S AWAKENING
182—THE LONG JOURNEY HOME
208—A QUESTION OF HONOR
299—THE GIFT

HARLEQUIN INTRIGUE

4—SECRETS OF THE HEART

Don't miss any of our special offers. Write to us at the following address for information on our newest releases.

Harlequin Reader Service
901 Fuhrmann Blvd., P.O. Box 1397, Buffalo, NY 14240
Canadian address: P.O. Box 603,
Fort Erie, Ont. L2A 5X3